Realms of Fantastic Stories Vol. 2

by Solstice Shadows

Publisher's Note:

This is a work of fiction. All names, characters, places, and events are the work of the author's imagination.

Any resemblance to real persons, places, or events is coincidental.

Solstice Publishing - www.solsticepublishing.com

Table of Contents

Will a prophecy determine their fate?

Breandan Clooney lives the life of half leprechaun and half human. Whispers of the night he came into the world follow him wherever he might travel in beautiful Eire. After an incident where he is forced to kill or be killed and lose his pot of gold, he escapes the beautiful land he's always known for a penal colony far off in space.

Charani Borrell has always heard of the fate thrust upon her by an ancient legend. Daughter of Romany kings, she has been unwillingly betrothed to Gaeril Stefan, a man she despises with her whole heart. The day Gaeril kills an English lord seals her fate and she's taken away from her family, to serve out the punishment given a group of thievin' Romany that Gaeril leads on a planet far from where she's grown up.

Breandan falls for the breathtaking Charani and she can't stop thinking about him. Despite knowing their romance is doomed due to their circumstances, they can't stay away from each other. Will they escape the destiny thrust upon them? Can Breandan and Charani find true love in their desperate circumstances?

Aegeus depends on his honor in a life or death struggle.

Aegeus has spent the last four years of his life indentured to the cruel captain of the Agamemnon. The captain and his crew tempt the Gods by braving the Siren's call in search of the famed treasure that lies hidden on their island. They capture one of the beautiful creatures, but the temptress' revenge is swift. An act of kindness spares Aegeus from the wrath of the siren's, but he must further prove his worth in a series of tests that will pit him against the brutal man who owns him. Will his honor save him, or will it be his downfall?

 Long Course

Marcus accepts a difficult job.

Taking place one year prior to the events of First Wave, Marcus Aries finds himself in a sticky situation when he set out to rescue a trio of baby dolphins.

 Destination Bermuda

Only good ratings can save her father.

The last time the Bermuda Triangle claimed a ship was in the 1960s. Until Dax Porter's expedition vessel disappears.

Six months later, his daughter is in the most dangerous place on Earth. Alexandra refuses to leave until she finds him, even if it means the reality TV show she's hosting is cancelled.

Despite mysterious events, weird ships, and a crew that can't get along, Alexandra refuses to give up her mission.

Jane's Kingdom

For better or worse, Jane's incredible fantasy becomes her reality.

Jane excitedly anticipates her new role as princess. With great delight, she tours the kingdom and meets royal subjects. She quickly discovers her castle holds a myriad of secrets. She realizes enemies lurk in shadows. She's faced with serious challenges as mysterious foes threaten to seize her power. As she grasps the magnitude of her kingdom's daunting problems, Jane wonders if she's strong enough to fulfill her lifelong dream.

The Season of the Neuri Knight

Has she ever been told the truth… about anything?

Bridget Grace Stone, daughter of legend Luke Stone, carries his name, his blood, and his Neuri metaphysical gifts. In training as a Neuri Knight and Warrior, she prepares for the battle to come. But is this her fight? Or is she being used as a pawn in the decades- long crusade between her father and his nemesis, the black magician, Armand Jacobi?

Bagel on a Stick

A tale of great conscience and delicious treats.

Green-haired halfling Rufino Endicott has been a vampire for three years in a world that hates undead. He's adjusted, for the most part—he's learned how to dodge the undead-hunters and how to make a comfortable coffin out of an old merchant's trade cart. What he hasn't adjusted to is life without bagels. Sure, he can find stale leftovers just about anywhere, but his is a most unforgiving palette and stale leftovers fail to satisfy.

In the throes of withdrawal, intrepid Rufino overcomes the excessive security of an artisan bakery at midnight, intending to gorge himself during the next business day. What he doesn't realize is that he's going to find more than just pastry inside that bakery.

Cinniúint Fated

(Fated Destiny)

K.C. Sprayberry

In the year 2375, those in the land of Eire felt their luck had turned from bad to rotten. Gone were the days of freedom they so cherished, as the English had once again invaded their country and enslaved their people. Some of these hardy folks spoke of a legend bandied about by the little people, the leprechauns, of a woman from Eire fated to become a mother by one of their kind. Most ignored the rumors until near about Christmas time, when a gal of fair face and fiery hair fell for the charms of a roguish leprechaun by the name of Seamus McBlarney. The lad she produced was fine and strapping, with a set of lungs said to be heard halfway across the country—in Dublin Town, no less. His eyes were as green as the grass upon their wild land and his hair was a richer red than that of his mam. He had a smile that broke hearts wherever he went, and he grew tall, a mighty oak among the ash and thorn.

Whispers grew after that night of the babe's birth, of what had transpired as his mam brought him into the cold, cruel world. A wild storm had rocked the land. Some claimed the banshee herself refused to come out to call those to their death who dared to leave their homes in a desperate attempt to find better shelter than the crofter's cottages that had roofs consisting of not much more than thatched hay. Throughout this horrendous gale, the wail of a babe was heard upon the wind, causing most to fear the devil himself had snatched away a child to take him to the underworld.

The storm lasted for a week and then vanished as if it had never happened. Men and women alike whispered behind their hands about the strapping boy who grew into a man taller than most, with a heritage many thought of as unnatural. Breandan Clooney he was christened, and a cry he set up when the priest bathed his head with holy water from the baptismal font. As young Breandan matured into a man, the whispers grew louder when a Romany troupe assailed the countryside with evil on their minds.

All of Eire had the same question on their minds. Had the prophecy come true?

σ σ σ

"*T*is *lá mhór chun an Treasure sa talamh."*

Breandan Clooney spoke the chant in Gaelic: "Tis a grand day to place this treasure in the land" that would allow him to bury his pot o' gold, a task he had to accomplish at least once a month or the treasure he'd accumulated over his lifetime would vanish. Driving a golden shovel into the rich earth of Eire, he was rewarded with a rainbow landing on the position he'd selected.

Just as he was about to call the pot in which he stored his treasure, the sound of quiet footsteps alerted him that he was not alone. Breandan cursed under his breath. Rare was the occasion when he'd be interrupted, but it had happened and he was certain he knew who the rude fool was.

"Hello, me boy," Da said in Gaelic. "You doing as I taught ye?"

"Thieving jerk. *Folaigh sin ó radharc. Cosain dom fortune* (Hide this from view. Protect me fortune)," Breandan muttered under his breath before raising his voice. "Good morn to ye, Da. What brings you around this day?"

Removing his shovel from the dirt, Breandan watched the rainbow vanish quickly. If it had lingered, he would have been in trouble. This event meant he had at least a few more hours before losing his fortune, one that he'd earned from sweating hard day in and day out in the fields around the small croft where he lived with his mam.

"Burying your gold, are ye?" Da pranced up beside him.

Breandan glanced down. He was a tall man, especially given his heritage. Well over six feet, few had ever guessed his father was one of the "little people," although most spoke about the night he came into this world beneath their breath and wondered if he was the person fated to join with one not of Eire. He'd made certain that no one who didn't already know ever found out that his father was a purebred leprechaun. That would make for no end of trouble.

"What did ye want now, Da?" Breandan asked. "I don't have any extra coins for ye. My treasure be mine, as you taught me so well many years ago."

"Ungrateful brat," Da glared up at him. "I be in me cups and ye don't give me a bit to tide me over until I can find me pot o' gold."

"Just doin' as ye taught me, Da," Breandan said. "Never give up your gold, no matter who asks."

"Shouldn't have listened to me." Da tilted his head to one side. "Your mam tell ye about the prophecy yet? You're a big, strappin' lad now. She should have done so."

"What prophecy?" Breandan asked, feigning ignorance.

He'd heard the human side of this supposed prophecy, but had yet to hear from his father what the little people thought of it. Rumors he'd heard regarding the night of his birth indicated his father's race had come out to dance in the storm and curse humans for the trouble they foisted upon those who were Eire's original residents.

"Ye of half leprechaun and half human heritage shall wed a Romany lass," Da said. "It won't be in Eire, where you breathe the air of your ancestors, but in some far off place none from this land has ever visited."

"Sounds like one of your drunken dreams." Breandan shook his head. "Go find your friends, Da. Mayhaps they'll listen to ye."

He stared at his father, still hanging around, and wondered what it would take for Seamus McBlarney to leave him alone. Breandan couldn't think of a name more suited for his da, given the man could spin a tale with the best of them and have half the humans in a hundred mile radius handing over every penny they owned.

"Tis a fine thing, a son disrespectin' his da like you do me," Seamus said. "Be wary, Breandan. Ye mam might find it upon herself to tell you the full prophecy, or she might put it off as nothing but wild dreams of drunken men. There be a lot more to this tale."

"How much more?" Breandan groaned quietly, feeling as if he'd fallen into one of his da's traps.

"Ye will be on the run from the king's men," Seamus said. "For what I cannot tell yet, just that you'll have to abandon Eire and won't ever return."

"Why would I do that? I have no reason to leave my home." Breandan shook his head in disgust. "Be gone with ye, Da. I'm tired of hearing your drunken stories."

"You'll soon regret your hasty words." Seamus vanished from sight.

"About time."

Breandan abandoned the place where he'd been about to bury his pot o' gold. It would be just like his da to have set him up to be so frustrated from their conversation that he would put the treasure in the same spot he'd been opening up and walk away. Seamus would then reappear from wherever he'd vanished to, and claim the gold for his own.

"Stupid I'm not, Da," Breandan whispered into the gentle breeze. "You'll not trick me so easily."

The snap of a branch behind him put Breandan on guard. His senses buzzed with a warning that whoever was approaching him from the rear was definitely not his da, and appeared to have treachery on their mind.

σ σ σ

Charani Borrell slipped from house to house, from tree to tree, in what appeared to be a futile effort to avoid the man to whom she'd been betrothed when she was but a small child. She could still see the shadows of the men Gaeril had sent to follow her.

"Go away," she whispered, her back pressed flat against the trunk of a stunted tree that was still taller than she was. "Leave me alone."

The shadow moved, came closer, and a head appeared from around the corner of a house. The weasely mouth of her intended's second in command sneered, glanced in all directions, and then peered where she'd last been. Charani slid down the tree trunk, but kept a close eye on the man following her.

Gaeril. He'd been nothing but trouble since the day they were engaged. Charani shook her head vehemently. "Nay, since the day he forced my father to agree to this insane relationship."

A few minutes later, her fiancée's spy took off at a run in the direction of their caravan. Charani blew out a relieved breath and continued her journey toward the nearby town.

Despite her vehement efforts then and since, she would soon be forced to wed this individual whom she loathed so badly that she refused to speak his name.

Her duty this day was to find more cloth and bargain with the residents of this beautiful island, Eire, so the women of their clan could assemble a wardrobe suited to the future queen of the Gypsies. Yet, Charani would do anything she could to avoid this job at all costs. Oh, she'd get the fabric, if only to make herself some new clothing for every day. Charani had absolutely no desire to be the Queen of the Gypsies, nor did she want that mannerless oaf, Gaeril Stefan, putting his sweaty hands on any part of her body.

One other worry beset Charani—a tale told to her by their seer only months ago.

Informed that she was fated to love a man of Eire, a man who was part leprechaun, Charani had laughed long and hard with disbelief and astonishment. Everyone knew the leprechauns avoided contact with humans with a passion. They wouldn't be caught with a human female for fear she would steal their pot o' gold.

"Silly superstition," Charani whispered. "None of that fabled race would dare touch a human female. Why, that would cause no end of trouble."

She scampered across an open area, casting looks over her shoulders, and watching for trouble lurking in dark corners. Charani had avoided any contact with her betrothed for nearly a year now, and she wasn't about to let him find her now. Besides, Gaeril was probably getting into trouble with the group of men he'd surrounded himself with, in a desperate attempt to prove he was a true Romany.

"Little does that fool know that he's doing everything a true Romany would avoid." Charani stopped once she reached a treeline. "Still, I do need to take care that he doesn't catch me alone."

Shivers ran up and down her spine. She took off faster than a deer in flight, certain that Gaeril had finally located her.

σ σ σ

Gaeril Stefan gathered his group of followers close as they crept upon a lone traveler on the deserted road. Let it not be said that he'd actually attack one of the Romany he would one day command. This traveler was nothing more than an ordinary human, a citizen of Eire, but not one of those native to this country. From the individual's manner, he was looking for a nubile young woman to warm his bed and a few pints of ale to warm his head.

"He'll get neither tonight," Gaeril whispered, motioning his men forward. "Any man dressed as richly as this one is must have a nice, fat purse upon his person."

As always, he led his men in the charge to overtake the stranger—and therefore an invader—in order to relieve the gentleman of his purse and any other items of value he might be carrying. Gaeril had done this many times since their caravan had been deposited on this green, rainy shore. He was determined to prove the prophecy that his intended wife would wed another and leave him to be ridiculed by his own people was as false as the seer who'd delivered it to the Gypsies.

"What manner of men are ye?" the stranger cried out once he was surrounded. "Leave or I shall call the guard to take you away."

Laughing, Gaeril threw his massive fist into the man's face, pulverizing his nose.

"I be Lord Jonathon Calderone of Her Majesty Queen Elspeth's service," the man bellowed around the hands covering his nose. "You shall be whipped to within an inch of your life for assaulting me!"

A red rage took over Gaeril. Signaling his men to stand aside, he went to work with both hands, ignoring the pitiful mewling coming from Lord Calderone of the Queen's service. As far as Gaeril was concerned, this man was like too many others in this land, willing to steal from those who worked hard, only to turn them over to the guard if they complained. That he wasn't any better than the gentleman he was beating into a pulp made no difference to him. Gaeril had long taken the notion that he was far better than any other person on the planet.

"Stop."

A hand upon his shoulder brought Gaeril back to his senses. He stared at the bloodied body on the ground, still twitching, and delivered a kick with his boot to the lord's ribs. One pitiful squeak was all that was heard before the idiot went still.

"Check his pockets," Gaeril ordered. "Take whatever money he has, so we may drink and eat well tonight."

His men fell upon the lord, ripping away his clothing until they uncovered a money belt. They handed over what coins were found and Gaeril set about to checking the contents of the oversized purse.

"A veritable treasure," he said in an awed whisper. "We'll live like kings for quite a while."

Laughing and walking alongside him, his men made suggestions as to what to do with the stranger lying in a heap in the middle of the roadway.

"Leave him for the vultures," Gaeril announced. "He deserves no be—"

The rest of his words caught in his throat when a mounted legion halted their horses in front of him. Lances were pointed at his chest from all directions. The sound of more horses approaching from behind caused sweat to run down his face in copious amounts.

"Sir Martin, Lord Calderone has been beaten to death," a man yelled from the rear.

Lances held outward moved toward Gaeril. He gulped and tightened his grip on the purse he'd stolen.

"This man is covered in blood," a soldier on the far end of the column reported. "None of these other miscreants appear to have participated."

"Nay," the man at the front said. "It does appear one man caused this tragedy."

"Sir Martin." A rider rode over to the speaker. "What shall we do with Lord Calderone's body?"

"Take it to the nearest inn and request a doctor attend him," Sir Martin said. "Take these men into custody. We know who the murderer is, but I'm betting these others never raised a hand to stop him."

Gaeril fought hard, until a lance blow upside his head made his ears ring and everything around turn topsy turvy. The next thing he knew, his wrists were bound, and a rope around his waist tethered him to the other men in his group.

As they marched toward the nearest town, Gaeril caught sight of Charani, but the little bitch ran off before he could get her attention. Seconds later, the man he'd put on her trail noticed them and pointed toward the encampment before racing away.

σ σ σ

Breandan moved with great stealth, hoping to lose the man coming after him. He had a pretty good idea that it was his da, but had to be certain before he used his considerable strength to rid himself of an irritation. Once he was over a hill, Breandan hid behind a tall tree, trying to make himself as small as possible. That in and of itself was a near impossible task, given how tall and muscular he was.

As soon as he'd settled on a crouch near the ground, he heard footsteps approaching his location.

"Damn, he disappeared," a man said. "Where did that fool go?"

Breandan recognized the voice as belonging to Dylan Kelly, a man known for his light fingers and propensity to take what didn't belong to him. Fury rose within Breandan. He'd deliberately led the man on a useless chase but a few days earlier, in an attempt to lose him. It appeared that Dylan had somehow found where he'd gone.

"Breandan." Dylan stopped close to him. "Been wanting to ask you a favor."

"Leave now." Breandan curled his fists closed. "You and I, we have nothing to talk about."

"Oh." Dylan shifted his weight, leaning heavily on one leg. "I think we do."

Sighing, Breandan prepared himself for the inevitable. He'd been seeing this coming for a long time, after someone noticed him talking to his da a couple of years back. That was when the rumors began in full force. What had only been speculation bandied about by loose mouthed gossipers had become a tale told over many a pint of ale.

"I want your gold." Dylan's odd golden eyes darkened. "Bring it to me now. And no leprechaun tricks. I've watched long enough every month to know how you do it."

Truer fighting words had never been spoken. Breandan had no compulsion whatsoever to hand over what he'd worked hard to earn all his adult life. He shook his head and stepped back, hoping to avoid what he knew would be a fight once Dylan made a move. The only thing Breandan was careful to do was to keep his golden shovel firmly in his grip.

This tool had more than one use. The most important purpose was to allow him to bury his gold and know where to return for it. The second, however, was that the tool sensed when his stash was in danger of being taken. Once someone made an attempt to take the pot, the shovel reacted on its own, in a way that had only occurred once. Since that time, Breandan had made certain the shovel would never again feel him fearing for the safety of his gold.

"Stealing what I've earned would be a very bad idea," Breandan said. "Leave now. If you continue on this path, you are responsible for what happens."

He worked hard to keep his voice level, to keep the shovel from sensing his anxiety. Yet, despite his precautions, he couldn't contain the rage running through his body.

"That gold is mine." Dylan took a step.

The shovel flew from Breandan's tight grasp and swung itself against Dylan's head. A startled "Oomph!" was all Breandan heard as Dylan collapsed to the earth, blood spilling from a deep cut.

"Return," Breandan said in a calmer voice, grasping the shovel when it flew back to toward his hand

He took a step but stopped when his friend, Connor, stepped out from behind a tree.

"Dylan bragged to the Garda that you'd be penniless or he'd be dead by evening," Connor said. "The first person to see you will report your whereabouts to the Garda."

"What am I to do?" Breandan glanced at the rapidly cooling body. "I was defending my treasure."

"Leave." Connor pointed to the northeast. "There's a ship bound for the planet furthest from Pluto in a few days. Rumor has it the crew will be transporting prisoners. Stow away on board and get away before the Garda kill you."

With no other choice, Breandan held his shovel and muttered, *"Tóg laistigh tú an* Treasure *mé a fuarthas. Coinnigh go dtí go bhfuil muid i bhfad as an áit."*

The simple Gaelic words—"Take within you the treasure I've gained. Hold until we are far from this place"—flew from his mouth without thought. Breandan was never one to waste time nor his breath when there was danger afoot.

A pot o' gold flew through the air, settled beside the blade of the shovel, and seconds later, vanished from sight. Connor whistled and waved goodbye as Breandan strode down the road.

"Tell me mam the truth, Connor," Breandan said without looking back. "Let her know that I'll return someday."

"Aye, I will," Connor shouted back. "I'm sure she'll expect you if she sees you."

All that ran through Breandan's mind was that damned prophecy. Was this the beginning of the end of his life?

σ σ σ

Charani took her time in the shop she'd finally located. A young girl had already carried nearly half a dozen bolts of vividly colored fabrics to the counter. While that was more than enough, she wanted some white fabric for blouses and light wool for her undergarments. If she wasn't bothered over the next week or so, with the help of the women in her family, she would soon have a nice, respectable wardrobe. That would be in complete contrast to the clothing Gaeril had demanded she make for herself, where her charms would be on display for anyone happening to glance at her.

"Charani," a breathless voice called from the door. "The most awful thing has happened."

Drawing in a deep breath, Charani prepared herself to hear just about anything. Her parents might have been set upon by thieves. Her younger brothers and sisters might well be in trouble for stealing, as Gaeril had been enticing them into his idea of how the Gypsies should live for months now. As her siblings were at a very impressionable age, she was afraid he would divert them from their studies to stealing in order to force her into a confrontation. Mayhaps locals had decided the Romany no longer could keep their caravan in the small glade they'd been using, even though they'd careful about avoiding doing any damage to the earth or vegetation.

"What is it?" She faced the younger woman. "What has happened, Magda?"

Every fear Charani had had since arriving on Eire rose to the forefront. She couldn't imagine any scenario worse than her family was in dire danger.

"It's Gaeril," Magda said breathlessly. "He's been arrested for killing a lord. They'll be trying him in front of a magistrate tomorrow."

"Is that all?" Charani turned back to her purchases, now bound up neatly in brown paper and string. "How much will that be?" she asked.

"Fifty pence," the shopkeeper said in an apologetic voice. "I'm sorry if that seems too much, Miss, but you did order quite a bit of cloth."

"Tis far less than I expected." Charani counted out the coins and added a bit more for the excellent service. "Thank you."

"Thank you, Miss." The shopkeeper curtsied. "I do hope your Gaeril fares well before the magistrate. Lately, those committing murder, or assisting someone in that act, have been sent off planet."

This was a first Charani had never heard of in during their indoctrination into living on Eire. The English Lord who had spoken with them had only warned them that the consequences would be severe if they were found guilty of a crime. His final words returned to her now.

"All who disobey our laws will be sent far, far away. We have no place on this island for lawbreakers. Heed my words. Do not commit a crime."

She hadn't worried about herself or her family. Their parents had taught them well about obeying the law and not being like Gypsies of old, who were often accused of stealing whatever wasn't nailed down or taking children from their beds. Charani supposed she should be upset by the fact that Gaeril faced being sent to another planet, but all she could feel was great relief.

"Thank you for your kind words," she said to the shopkeeper. "I'm certain all will be well in the end."

Magda grabbed Charani's arm once they were on the road. Charani was attempting to keep her place slow, but her lifelong friend was practically dragging her toward where the caravan was parked.

"We have to hurry," Magda said. "Don't you understand, Charani? You must save your betrothed from a fate worse than death."

Never let it be said that Magda didn't lose any opportunity to be overly dramatic. Charani rolled her eyes and picked up the pace a bit. It didn't really matter to her if Gaeril was sent to some far off planet to pay for his crime. He'd gotten away with so many things for so long that she was surprised he hadn't been stopped before now.

"I'm not going to Dublin Town to appeal to the judge," Charani said. "Haven't I told you for years that I will not marry that man?"

"But you were betrothed to him!" Magda exclaimed. "You can't ignore his plight now."

"I was a baby," Charani said. "Nobody gave me a chance to say no, because I couldn't talk. And he was a monster even as a child. Don't you remember him dumping stinging ants down your back when you told him to leave you alone?"

"It was a boyish prank," Magda said primly. "My mother healed the stings and I was perfectly fine in a few days."

Charani rolled her eyes. She went along with Magda only because to argue was useless. Their journey back to the glade took much less time that Charani had spent getting to the store. The sight greeting her nearly made her run as fast as was possible in the opposite direction.

"What's going on?" Charani asked, grabbing a boy who was rushing past.

"We must save Gaeril," the lad said. "But there are some saying even if we do keep him from being sent away he will never become our king."

"Whyever not?" Magda asked.

"The Elders say he has embarrassed the Romany far too many times."

The boy ran off and was soon busy handing up items for a man to load into one of the round topped wagons they traveled in. Charani couldn't help smiling.

"He's right," she whispered.

"Who's right?" Magda demanded. "Aren't you upset that your betrothed won't be King one day?"

"No." Charani shook her head. "He would be the worst king the Romany have ever had."

Magda's snort caused her to smile. Charani hurried toward her family's wagon and discovered the same madness there as she seen throughout the glade, with a bit extra thrown in for good measure.

"Charani must go with Gaeril if he's sent off world," the seer was telling her mother. "It is written that she will find the prophecy wherever he's sent."

Charani's heart skipped many beats. This was even more reason to demand that her ties to Gaeril be severed.

σ σ σ

Breandan arrived in Dublin Town with nothing but his shovel and a sack that held his few possessions. As he stood in one of the town squares, he listened to the town criers. None mentioned his name or the Garda seeking a half leprechaun in the murder of a no-good fool from down country. Smiling, he made his way toward the spaceport he'd heard about on his journey here.

"I wonder if all those tales are true?"

Awe and amazement ran rampant through Breandan once he spotted the elliptical craft being prepared for a long journey. He wasn't sure how the thing would get off the ground let alone rise to the stars, but after thinking about his actions and what he'd done, he realized this was his only chance to save his hide.

Shouting from a nearby building, marked as Magistrate House, caught his attention. He gazed over there, surprised to see a caravan of brightly colored wagons placed haphazardly around the building. People clad in unusual clothing wept and wailed, some clinging to a medium-sized man who was shouting that he'd been falsely accused.

"Wonderful." Breandan took off for the spaceport, hoping he could climb aboard the craft he'd seen without anyone noticing him. "This unusual journey appears to be getting worse by the minute."

He slipped through a gate while the guard's attention was on the furor across the road. Breandan moved stealthily until he was near the boarding ramp. Once he was certain no one would notice him, he quickly entered the craft and searched the various compartments until he located one in the rear that would suit his purposes.

All he discovered was a single bed that took up most of the room. A lid hovering over the resting place gave him pause but after looking over the device, Breandan felt he could handle whatever occurred. The mattress looked to be comfortable, which was his most important consideration, especially since it would allow him to stretch out his long legs. Laying his golden shovel with his pot o' gold safely secured within on one side, he climbed in and reclined against the softness of the bedding.

"This might be nicer than I first imagined," he said. "Unless someone wants this bed."

An hour later, as he was fitfully dozing, he heard the sounds of others boarding. Some were quite loud with protests and complaints, while others were weeping. After a bit of arguing with men he assumed were the crew, silence reigned. Breandan closed his eyes, but opened them quickly when he heard the sound of a lid closing. To his horror, he couldn't move and the cover for this bed was sealing him in. A clank brought about a terror such as he'd never known and then a hiss sent him into a dreamless sleep.

σ σ σ

Charani stared at the magistrate in horror. She could not believe her ears. Despite her pleas, she'd just been sentenced to go to Planet Zeta with Gaeril and his troop of troublemakers. Her parents and siblings had turned away from her once they heard that it would be decades before she returned, if ever.

"Women, follow me," a male guard said. "We stop once, to retrieve your belongings. Take nothing more than you can carry yourself."

He escorted the half dozen women whose men had demanded their presence to the caravan. Charani hated the idea of being bound to Gaeril during this journey but she would not put her family in danger of the same fate she faced by arguing. She hurriedly packed the clothing she, her mother, and sisters had sewn during the month they'd been awaiting Gaeril's trial and sentencing. Once she had everything neatly packed, she rejoined the rest of the women and marched at the head of the line toward the most unusual craft she'd ever seen.

No one will know how scared I am of what is about to happen.

Her head held high, she followed the orders she was given: to secure her belongings and climb into the strange bed and lie still. The other women followed her. Her heart beat wildly as she heard Gaeril and his men escorted aboard. Fortunately, none of those cretins entered the room occupied by the women.

Maybe I'll be safe on this journey.

The lid of the bed lowered. She raised her hands to fight being closed in but was soon battling sleepiness when a hissing sound began.

σ σ σ

Gaeril walked proudly to the craft that would take him from his home and those he one day desired to rule. Any hopes of being the King of the Gypsies in Eire were long gone. He did have his men with him and plenty of women to meet his desires, until he could find more on this Planet Zeta. The only thing he wanted right now was a woman to warm his bed, and only one woman would do—Charani.

"In here." A guard pointed a pike at a room with a dozen bed-like compartments set against a wall. "Get in and don't argue. This pike will be most painful if I must use it on you criminals to keep the order."

The guard laughed at the men climbing into the small coffin-like beds. Gaeril got into his last, hoping that damn lid above him didn't lower. No one knew that he couldn't abide small spaces and he didn't want them to learn that fact by squalling like a newborn.

"Good night, murderer," the guard said, closing the door.

To Gaeril's horror, the lid lowered. Before he could scream out his terror, a hissing sound and the smell of gas soon had him asleep.

σ σ σ

A tinkling and then the blare of a siren jerked Breandan out of the retrospection he'd been in since awakening. He rose to his feet, remembering to duck his head to avoid a bulkhead. Hefting the shovel against one shoulder, he slung his duffel bag over the other and awaited the moment when he and those with him aboard this hunk of junk would land. Only then could he make his escape and hope that one day he could return to the green island on Earth that he'd abandoned.

"Tis a dreadful day when a man must run to avoid punishment for a deed that was naught but protecting what is his own."

The ship's speakers crackled and he tensed. This was the moment he had dreaded since stowing aboard. This was the moment when a head count would ensue, but not by the human crew. There were sensors that could pick up the heartbeat of a mouse stealing a piece of cheese.

"Good day, travellers," an electronic female voice said. "You have now arrived at Planet Zeta. Your punishment means you will be our guest in Gemma Town, where you must earn your keep and atone for your sins on Earth."

Breandan grimaced. The announcement was more than likely far from over and already, he was ready to run for his life. Somehow, the idea of being on the furthest planet from Pluto, in a place called Gemma Town sounded like a life sentence to the young half leprechaun-half human who had done nothing but protect his pot o' gold.

σ σ σ

Charani shook herself awake and donned a clean white blouse and a semi-wrinkled multi-colored skirt. Her belly ached with hunger, as did those of others who had not brought their own food. She'd only had stale water to drink since awakening.

Her parents had all but ordered her from their home to follow the man to whom she was betrothed, despite his being convicted of many crimes, including murder. She didn't understand the reason, but she knew she'd have to work even harder to avoid him.

A female voice that sounded more like a badly tuned lute spoke words that made her even more confused. Charani gathered the few belongings she'd been allowed to bring, mostly more clothing such as she now wore, and walked over to the sealed door in the miniscule room she'd been assigned when she reported to the docking on Earth.

"Once the local officials have declared you have atoned for your sins, you will await transportation to Earth," the voice said without any emotion. "Until such time, you are to dwell on what brought you to Planet Zeta, earning you a banishment from the great Kingdom of Earth, and hope that those allowed to remain behind don't forget you."

Shaking her head in disgust, Charani waited for the door to open. Her punishment had only just begun, and if she were lucky, she might survive the first week on this horrible planet.

How could a Romany end up like this?

σ σ σ

Gaeril, soon to be King of the Gypsies who'd followed him into exile, shook his head and grabbed a flask of water. He drank thirstily, aware of the female voice stirring his loins and telling him that he was doomed to live out his days on this planet.

"Twas the other man's fault," he muttered. "All them damned English gents know they pays their ransom on the spot and they can leave. But that one just had to fight us. How was I to know he was the damned King's cousin?"

He perked up when a woman started talking to him on the speaker above his door. Her voice was a bit flat, but she sure sounded pretty. Of course, to Gaeril, any woman able to walk and not in her grave sounded and looked pretty and available to him—even that bitch he'd been betrothed to for many long, miserable years.

"Ain't good enough for her that I toss her ass over my shoulder and take her whenever I want," he muttered darkly. "Nay, I must court the strumpet and await her consent to touch her."

The terms of the betrothal bothered Gaeril more than he'd ever told anyone. It was after the formal ceremony, when Charani Borrell was pledged to him, in an arrangement made between her family and his when both were naught but toddlers, that he learned she had the power to put off their wedding, and his coronation as King of the Gypsies, until she was satisfied he'd make a good husband.

He dressed and moved toward the locked hatch, as he'd been instructed the day they were dragged to this ship from the gaol in Eire. "If she hadn't avoided my man and run off instead of bedding with me, I wouldn't have had to take my revenge."

The memory of the night he'd turned his gypsies from simple scammers into a gang of thieves, kidnappers, and murderers brought a wry smile to his lips. How well he'd played all of them, and to a man, the others had vowed to follow him all over the galaxy—once they could find a way off Planet Zeta.

"We'll do it." Gaeril stared at the door, willing it to open so he could put his plan into motion. "I'll be damned if I'm living in the arsehole of the galaxy the rest of my life."

Inside his head, he quaked from fear—the fear of more rejection from the woman he was fated to wed, the fear of being stuck on this planet for the rest of his life, and worst of all, the fear of never being accepted as a Romany King.

σ σ σ

Breandan slithered and slid through a Jeffries tube until he reached a grate. After kicking with both feet a few times, he was able to get off the spaceship before the head count began. Once his feet hit the ground, a resonance rose from the soles of his boots traveled up into his head.

"Is it the prophecy?" he wondered.

He knew little of the prophecy his father had told him about during a fleeting visit, only hours before Breandan committed the crime that forced him to flee Earth. His only warning was that he would fall for a woman trothed to another, an impossible to change engagement, and if he pursued her, his future was uncertain.

"Well, I have no need to worry about that now." Breandan whistled a cheery tune and made his way over to a map tacked to a wooden board.

After ascertaining there would be three transports leaving in the next hour for Gemma Town, he paid his fare—outrageous in his opinion—and boarded the first.

"Let's see just what this Gemma Town is all about." He settled in the seat and stared out the grimy window. "It can't be as bad as having the King's men chasing me."

σ σ σ

Charani hurried ahead of the gypsies, ensuring she stayed as far from Gaeril as she could. Thankfully, one of the older women who had come along had ordered the men to ride in the last transport and the women would take the first and second.

"How more women than men came along I'll never figure out," Charani muttered under her breath.

Taking a chance that Gaeril couldn't see her, she darted aboard the second transport, flashing a marker she'd been given by her father before departing Earth. Once settled in her seat, she stared out a window with more grit than dirt on it and wondered if she would ever get away from Gaeril.

"Tis an impossible task," she whispered. "But I will do it. I swear on everything I hold dear that I will do it."

A tingling in her arms and legs warned her of the possibility that her ability to protect herself would soon be gone.

Is it the prophecy? she asked herself. *Have I finally been doomed to follow what the seer foretold?*

She worried that she would be the cause of an innocent man's death. Not once on Earth had she felt the warning signal that her true love was close. Charani had come to believe they were fated lovers, destined never to cross paths, but somehow they had.

"The only ones aboard our transport were gypsies," she muttered and watched the women boarding to ride with her. "How can I have avoided someone destined to make me fall in love with him, only to have one of us suffer a fate we would always regret, if it's that person who has been close to me all my life?"

Even worse, she wondered if Gaeril was the man she was fated to love. Perhaps leaving Earth was part of the prophecy and she was now beginning the fulfillment by walking into a trap set by the fates.

σ σ σ

Gaeril grumbled and stomped over to the third transport. No matter how hard he tried, he couldn't convince the man in charge of this benighted area to let him ride with the women.

"I have me orders," the man shouted around hands cupped around his mouth. "No men to ride with the women for you gypsies. Ye shouldn't have attempted to bed every woman in Ireland and England before you were convicted and sent here."

Kicking at a dog skulking around the transport, Gaeril climbed aboard. For once, he didn't consider revenge upon the personage of the individual insulting him. He had a bigger problem on his hands.

"What fool thought it was a good idea to question my ascension to the throne?"

He knew very well why the question had come up. It wasn't the first time. His father was full gypsy, but his mother was a Nordic noblewoman, one who came along willingly when Mastic, the former King, had invaded her town in an attempt to refill the gypsy coffers. When no riches were found, a ransom had been demanded—the lovely Ilsa's hand was to be given to Mastic, or all the buildings would be burned with the residents inside them. Ilsa had lived long enough to spawn one son—Gaeril—and then perished from the torture of having to abandon her homeland to live with a band of wandering tricksters.

σ σ σ

A month had passed and Breandan finally felt the pull he'd been waiting on. Without a second thought, he gathered his shovel and walked out of the inn where he shared space with a group of dirty, ill-mannered gypsies.

"Why in the world didn't I think to check out who was aboard before I joined this group? I'm doomed to putting up with their thieving ways until I can escape this planet."

His journey seemed difficult at first, but he let his mind wander back to Eire and was soon walking along with a smile on his face.

His thoughts centered around not only that damned prophecy his da had spoken about, but also how to stay out of trouble for however long it took to secure passage on an outbound ship. He figured the authorities would stop looking for him in three to four years. Then he could once again be in the land of his kind, able to play tricks upon the unsuspecting and hide his gold without worry.

"Ach, but it do be a rotten time I be having here." Breandan stopped at the top of a dusty hill, his heart yearning for the cool, rain soaked countryside of Eire. "I'll see me home again. Hopefully sooner than later. Nothing will keep from me beloved Eire."

Clad in a white shirt, Kelly green vest, black pants and boots, he glanced around the area in order to ascertain that he was alone. Once he was assured that no one would interrupt the ceremony, Breandan drove his gold shovel into the ground. A momentary flash of light became a rainbow starting in the pot o' gold now beside his foot and arcing across the sky.

"Only twenty minutes," he muttered beneath his breath. "I only have twenty minutes to bury this properly."

He'd learned his lesson very well back on Earth, when he took his time digging a deep hole. Fortunately, that misadventure had ended well, by buying the individual in question many pints of ale at the local pub, until he couldn't remember exactly where he'd been that day. The problem Breandan'd had with Dylan Kelly had come about without warning, and forced him to fall into survival mode to protect his treasure.

"Aye, Dylan Kelly learned his lesson well." Breandan drove the gold shovel into the ground. "He'll not tell a soul about where I planned to hide my gold that day, except in hell."

Putting his back into the job, Breandan dug and dug, all the while keeping an eye on the rainbow cresting far across the sky. He really had to hurry or he'd be doomed to losing his legacy and possibly killing another man.

σ σ σ

Charani peered out the window and stared at the only man in Gemma Town she hadn't known before being shoved aboard the outward bound spacecraft by her uncaring parents. Since feeling the prophecy activating, she had come as close to this man as she could, and had yet to feel the sensation a second time.

"I know he's the one."

She snuck around during the long journey to wherever he was going, always staying out of sight. From within her soul, she could feel the connection between them, but she was afraid to approach him. One thing said wrong, one action misunderstood, and she would be forever doomed to staying with Gaeril.

Once the object of her hunt stopped, she crouched behind a hillock and stared at the tall man digging a hole on the hill above her. Her eyes widened at the sight of a rainbow emanating from a pot o' gold and she knew that her mind hadn't been playing tricks on her.

"The stranger truly is the man the seer told me about," she whispered. "She always said I was destined to break free of what we were, to find a way to become a better woman than any other of the Gypsies."

A sense of relief filled her. This was what she had wanted for so long. Charani had fought against being betrothed to Gaeril for as long as she'd been able to speak. The man simply wasn't decent, and that wasn't just her opinion. Even though he would one day be King of the Gypsies sent to this planet, he had no honor, no ability to discern right from wrong—although since being disgraced because of his banishment, Gaeril would only be King of the Gypsies on Planet Zeta. Day in and day out, he'd attempted to bed her whenever he had her alone, not that she gave him much of a chance there. As far as Charani was concerned, he could fall off the face of this benighted planet and vanish forever, and she wouldn't shed a single tear.

"Killing's too good for that man." She shook her head and concentrated more on the person who had caught her attention earlier in the pub. "Now, that man up there is a fine specimen. I'd be more than willing to share a bed with him."

She fastened her gaze on the man more than the hole he was digging. Sweat beaded his forehead, plastering his curly fiery red shoulder-length hair against his tanned skin. Strong muscles rippled under his clothes. "An Irishman." She breathed in and out, quelling the momentary panic that rose within her. "I've been told those kind are dangerous as all get out, but he doesn't look at all dodgy."

Charani remained in place, her heart beating hard in her chest. For the first time in her ill-fated life, she had found someone she could give her heart to, but thanks to her foolish parents, it was no longer hers to give.

"What can I do to get out of the engagement to Gaeril?" she whispered. "How can I discover who this man is and why he's burying a pot o' gold on this horrible planet?"

With blood deeply Gypsy, she realized their love could never be, even if the man was interested in her. But her heart overruled her common sense.

"I'll find out who he is and where he's staying." She crept backward down the hill when he dropped the pot o' gold into a hole. "And then he'll explain if he's stuck on this planet forever like Gaeril or if he can get me back to Earth."

Soon, she was hurrying back to Gemma Town. Charani was free to move about the planet at will, but none of the others in the tribe with which she was associated had the same license. One and all, they'd been banished for crimes most foul—thieving, kidnapping, and murder. Gemma Town would be home for the rest of their lives.

σ σ σ

Gaeril leaned back in a rickety chair and threw his booted feet on the table before him. After a month here, he was ready for more action than he was getting. The woman thrust upon him many years ago had run out on his latest attempt to bed her and force her into marriage, so he could place the crown of King of the Gypsies upon his head. He was feeling more than ready to begin the same mayhem that had him banished to this planet in a back corner of the galaxy.

"More beer!" he shouted, smacking a serving girl on the ass and laughing when she yelped in pain. "Hurry, bitch. Bring me more beer."

His lustful eye took in her uncommon beauty, the white blouse, and multi-colored skirt marking her as one of his tribe, but he didn't recognize her face.

I'll bed this one if that strumpet, Charani, turns me down tonight.

A man of voracious appetites, he raised his voice again. "Bring me something from that place you call a kitchen, woman. Make sure it's edible."

The men at his table broke into uproarious laughter. One and all, they were as murderous as he was, as willing to steal a child from a rich family for the ransom that would be paid, or waylay a wandering person—be it man or woman—and relieve them of their riches.

"Did you figure out where that wench, Charani, ran off to, Gaeril?" his second in command, Johannes, asked. "I hear she went into the hills again."

"Nah." Gaeril snatched at another serving girl and laughed when she fought back. "Ain't going up in them hills. Didn't you hear that fool at the entry point? They're haunted by ghouls."

Every man at the table shuddered. While they would slit a throat without a second thought, the idea of dealing with a ghoul left them ready to cry for their mamas. Not a one would admit that, though. They'd just say that they weren't ready to tackle the hills a mere mile or two from where they sat day in and day out, drinking, eating, and chasing the serving girls.

"Here ye go, King Gaeril." The girl whose ass he'd slapped set down a pitcher of ale and a plate of steaming beef roast with what passed for potatoes and vegetables. "Did you be wanting anything else?"

"Bread." He yanked her onto his lap, to allow her to feel how much her pretty face had him hot for her. "Ye forgot the bread. Ye owe me a kiss."

Never one to take no for an answer, he forced his lips onto hers while allowing his hand to slide up under her skirt. She squirmed and squealed in fright.

"Let her be, Gaeril," a male voice said. "Me girl's naught but thirteen. I'll kill you if you touch her again."

A frisson of cold fear ran through Gaeril. He shoved the girl away. The only person in his pack of murderous thieves who could do that towered over him. Many said that Andre Mistly wasn't a true Gypsy, but the man was handy with a knife and had the strength of a hundred men.

"Beg your pardon, Andre," Gaeril said. "I haven't seen your daughter for quite a while. Didn't know she'd grown up so pretty."

"Now you do." Andre planted his backside on a chair that squeaked alarmingly under his weight. "And you'll naught touch her again. Take your own betrothed to bed. Force her to marry you. That way, we can truly be the most powerful band of Gypsies on this benighted planet.

"Sure, and how to you propose I do that?" Gaeril demanded. "The bitch drove a knee into me jewels the last time I tried."

"Then tie her down until she squeals with delight." Andre struck the table, causing a crack to run from one end to the other. "That'll bind her to you forever."

σ σ σ

Breandan made sure that no one could locate where he'd hidden his pot o' gold and began the trek back to Gemma Town. Once he'd snuck past the entry point, he'd hidden in a transport carrying a group of Gypsies to the most inhospitable place on Planet Zeta.

Guess I was testing me luck. He grinned and strode down the hill with long, ground eating strides. *Now, if luck is with me, I can find a decent meal and rest for the night.*

According to what little his irresponsible father had told him about protecting his riches, Breandan had to bury his pot o' gold in a new spot whenever there was a storm or right after the full moon. Neither piece of advice made a bit of sense on this planet. He couldn't figure out a storm pattern, since the ones they'd had were more of the type that dropped meteorites everywhere, but had plotted the moon's orbit and followed the rules faithfully.

He caught a glimpse of a comely young woman running along the road not far in front of him. Rich black hair streamed behind her and her brightly colored skirt fluttered in the wind. When she turned to look in his direction, he stared at how the white blouse she wore fitted her upper body in such a way as to make a man forget all sense he had.

A yearning rose within his heart, like nothing else he'd ever felt when looking upon a beautiful woman. In all his life, he'd only wanted to bed women and leave before they got ideas about settling down. Yet, one glimpse of the fear on her face, the distrust in her gorgeous black eyes, and he was ready to propose finding a decent home on this planet and starting a family.

"Who are you?" he whispered.

Her lips moved, white teeth flashed. For a moment, she shaded her eyes and mouthed words at him.

Breandan smiled. "Charani, such a lovely name for a gorgeous lass." He waved. "I'll see you soon, Charani," he shouted. "Where can I find ye?"

Instead of giving him a hint as to her whereabouts, she raced on ahead along the road. He took off after her, his long legs giving him an advantage over her much shorter ones. By his reckoning, she was a mere five-feet, five inches tall, to his six-feet, three inches. A smile made its way across his face as he imagined how well she'd fit into his arm, pulled up tight against his side, and how much he wanted to protect her.

σ σ σ

Charani pushed herself hard after mouthing her name at the gorgeous stranger. Any attempt to escape the torture arranged by her parents would spell doom but that man... oh, that man... he was breathtaking beyond belief.

"I have to forget him." She panted for breath. Just thinking about the man whose name she didn't know caused her to feel heat in places where she never had before. "It's too dangerous to let him invade my mind."

Despite her best efforts, he stayed foremost in her mind. Charani raced into the inn where the Gypsies had taken refuge and ran into her room. She splashed cold water all over her face and neck, straightened her hair, and changed her sweat-soaked blouse for another white one before heading over to the inn.

The only way they had to pay for their rooms, food, and other comforts was for the women to work as serving girls. One of the men with no talent for thieving, kidnapping, and murdering produced plain but filling food at the tavern's kitchen, while the rest spent their days getting drunk and bothering the servers.

Thankfully, she hadn't been put through that torture... yet. As soon as she forced Gaeril to understand that she wouldn't ever warm his bed, Charani knew her days of freedom from being pestered were numbered.

"Perhaps that man can assist me." She crept down the stairs, flattening against a wall when the man in question came through the entrance and headed up a second set of stairs, to the men's section of the inn. "Ohhhhhhh!"

Her moan of pleasure caught his attention. A quick turn of his head had his intense green eyes peering into hers. Charani gasped, backed further against the wall. She narrowed her eyes when his lips moved but no sound came out.

Breandan.

Her long-lost talent for reading minds burst forth. Not since her thirteenth naming day had she been able to delve into the thoughts of others. The seer had once said that when she finally found her true love, her talent would return with a force that could spell doom for the gypsies. It was also the seer's foretellings that had caused problems for the gypsies now banished to Planet Zeta.

What does this mean? The seer warned me that worrisome times would come with my foretelling. Does this mean that I'm not fated to be Gaeril's bride?

While that would be her fondest dream come true, Charani knew that spurning the man she'd avoided since their betrothal would become fodder for terrible events to those in Gemma Town. No woman would be safe from the marauding men seeking revenge when she embarrassed their uncrowned king.

σ σ σ

Gaeril swiped sweat from his brow and stumbled from the inn. He usually stayed until not long after closing, but the encounter with Andre had left Gaeril fearful for his safety. He wasn't a man who willingly looked Death in her mighty jaws, but he had today. How had he not missed the resemblance of the chit to her father?

I need to get away from that damned inn for a while. Maybe drag Charani up into the hills and force her to be mine. We can then come back as husband and wife. And I'll finally wear the crown lawfully.

It irked him beyond measure that his betrothed wouldn't stay in the same room as him, let alone her constant refusals to provide for his manly needs. Not only that, he was having to reprove his position as the uncrowned king daily. His father had wed one of the women he'd kidnapped when she was fourteen. The previous king, Mathias, had bragged that he'd taken his bride within days of "liberating" her from her home and brought forth a son who would lead the Gypsies to even more glory.

"Damn bitch was me mam." Gaeril shook his head in disgust. "Only thing the bitch gave me was her looks. She's been getting even with me dad since the day I was born. Only decent thing she ever did was die before spawning more brats."

Thankfully, his father hadn't ever taken another wife, but he had spawned a dozen or more illegitimate brats who could never threaten his ascension to the throne. But now, he faced other threats. Andre was a close cousin, close enough to make mating with his daughter dangerous, but Gaeril no longer cared. He had needs and the bitch, Charani, wasn't meeting them.

"What is that chit's name?"

Shaking his head at his inability to remember a simple name, Gaeril stumbled along the rutted road toward the inn. He came to a stop when he saw Charani coming toward him.

"Get over here and take care of me, woman!" he bellowed.

To his disgust and utter embarrassment, she ran around him as easily as a pickpocket scoring a heavy purse from a rich man.

σ σ σ

Breandan shook his head and turned around on the stairs. The vision of the woman was still in his head. No matter how much he tried, he couldn't rid himself of her beauty. Deciding that a glass of ale and a meal would help him sleep better, he headed for the inn. A man lurched toward him but Breandan avoided the drunk with ease.

"Damn women," the man muttered. "I'll bed that wench if it's the last thing I do."

A small smile brought some comfort to Breandan. He knew exactly how the man felt, but there was also unease being so close to this stranger, a sense of danger that he couldn't shake.

Never a man to ignore any kind of danger to his personal safety, Breandan leaned against the wall of a greengrocer's stall and watched the stranger with the scraggly blonde hair stumble along the rutted road. His thoughts turned to the pretty woman he'd seen and his less than pure thoughts about her. Still, he kept his focus on the man, who was now nuzzling the neck of a very frightened teenage girl.

"That one will be more trouble than I can handle."

Once the man had entered the inn with the girl, Breandan shook off any thoughts of coming to the girl's aid. She might look like a youngster, but he'd seen grown women of the same build far too many times to worry overly much about her getting into trouble.

"Or not." He stopped when a thin wail pierced the air.

"Aeryn!" A monster of a man burst out of the tavern and ran toward the inn. "Aeryn, what is it?"

"A small girl about this high?" Breandan held his hand waist high.

"Aye." The man nodded. "Did ye see where she went?"

"The inn." Breandan nodded in that direction. "A man was with her. About my height, maybe an inch or two higher. Thin, scraggly blonde hair."

"Gaeril," the stranger growled. "I warned him."

With that, he was off toward the inn. Breandan decided that was trouble he didn't need to witness. Still, he was hungry, and there was only one place to go. Chuckling, he headed toward where he could get a hot meal and a slightly cool ale.

σ σ σ

Charani jerked in surprise when Breandan came through the door. Sensations flooded her, the type of feelings she should only have for her husband-to-be. She smiled at him as he sat at a table near the bar and walked over, grabbing a tankard of ale on her way.

"Good even'," Charani said, bending low to give him a peek at what lay beneath her blouse and blushing a bit at her forward behavior. "May I interest you in some beef roast with roasted potatoes and vegetables?" She wiped the already clean table. "There's also some lighter than air bread I made myself this morn."

"Sure." He grinned. "I'm a starving man. Haven't had a bite since yesterday."

He laid several coins on the table. She picked them up one by one and then walked off, her hips swaying from side to side.

Her embarrassment grew even more acute when some of those in the bar began hooting and whistling. Never in her life had she acted in such a forward manner, but after being banned from Earth because she was Gaeril's intended and putting up with his attitude ever since, she was ready to see if a real man found her interesting.

"Need a platter of beef roast," she said upon entering the kitchen.

"Coming right up." Johan, their cook, began cutting thick slices from a beef roast turning on a spit. "Do up the rest of the plate, will ya? It'll save us both some time."

Without a word, Charani mounded roasted potatoes, corn, onions, and squashes beside the beef. She filled a small bowl with the drippings from the meat, sliced a small loaf of bread, and laid the meal out on a serving tray.

"I'm betting Gaeril will love that." Johan burst out laughing. "He's been wanting you to serve him all month."

She hefted the tray onto her shoulder, walked away, and paused at the open doorway. "'Tis not for Gaeril." Charani glanced over a shoulder. "I have no idea where he is—hell for all I care."

Her hips swaying even more, she walked back to Breandan's table and laid out his feast. The whole time, he stared at her with bright green eyes she felt herself falling into. The sensation she'd wanted to verify filled her whole body, leaving her nearly breathless at the intensity of emotion she felt around this man.

"Thank you," he said in a slightly breathless voice. "Who are you, Charani? Why do I feel as I've known you all my life?"

She opened her mouth to respond, to give this man her heart without reservation, but the door bursting open distracted her.

"Andre is killing Gaeril!" a woman shouted. "Gaeril attempted to bed Aeryn, and Andre has vowed to kill our future King!"

The tavern emptied of all Gypsies, except Johan and Charani. Breandan slowly and methodically began eating his meal, slicing meat, stabbing vegetables, and staring at the slowly swinging door as if mesmerized.

"Shouldn't you go to your betrothed, Charani?" Johan asked. "Gaeril will be needing a soft bosom and even softer words once Andre is done with him."

"He'll be needing the services of the undertaker if I go to him." Furious, Charani marched toward the kitchen, to get herself a glass of cold water. "That man doesn't know when to stop acting stupid."

It would take more than a glass of cold water to cool the fires burning in her body. She didn't understand how everyone failed to notice that she was acting worse than a strumpet around Breandan. And to have Johan remind her in the way that he had about her commitment to Gaeril was beyond infuriating.

"How dare he?"

She stormed out of the building, barely aware of the shouts and the sound of glass breaking from the direction of the inn. Charani turned in the opposite direction of the inn, running away from her troubles—from both of the men who vexed her so.

The sound of boots pounding the ground behind her granted speed to her feet. She was determined not to stop until she collapsed.

σ σ σ

Gaeril ducked as Andre's fist flew at his face. The soon-to-be King of the Gypsies wasn't fast enough, as was proven when the iron-hard knuckles made their imprint on his cheek. Reeling, he ducked another punch coming from the right. As the much larger man wobbled, Gaeril lifted a leg and kicked Andre in his well-padded arse, sending him flying face first into a muddy puddle of brackish water.

"Never, ever raise an angry fist against your King," Gaeril shouted, releasing his anger at both Andre and his tart of a daughter. "That little bitch was all sunshine and teasing, until I got her alone. That's when she squalled like a stuck pig."

The rest of his clan backed away. Some of the women, those he'd laid with, stared at Gaeril in astonishment.

"You lie." A woman's voice rang out above the angry mutterings. "You are not fit to be our King."

Anya, the oldest of the women, turned her back on him. She held out her left hand and turned a thumb down. One by one, the rest of the women followed suit. Several of the men shook their heads and did as their women had done. The "dethroning" continued until every gypsy had rejected Gaeril as their King.

"What good does it do you to reject me?" he shouted. "You're still stuck here. You're still considered thieves, kidnappers, and murderers back on Earth." He bellowed out a laugh. "None of you can ever leave Planet Zeta."

"Banishment," Anya said. "The betrothal promise to Charani no longer exists."

Again, the men and women he was to rule repeated the decree. Each time another individual spoke up, Gaeril shook as if he'd been again struck by Andre's fist. Rage began to overtake him.

"I will still rule you." He racked his brains, what little he still possessed after the beating he'd taken, for the one way he could retain his right to be King. "None of you can stop me."

Walking away from his unrepentant ex-followers, Gearil continued to think about what it would take to regain his position. He could think of only one thing.

"If Charani is with child—my child—then I will be King."

A wicked smile on his face, Gaeril went in search of his reluctant bride.

σ σ σ

Breandan finally located Charani. She had crossed the mountains separating Gemma Town from the rest of Planet Zeta. He looked around in amazement at the lush, green grass, the streams winding in and out of valleys as far as the eye could see, and the massive trees everywhere.

"This reminds me of Eire."

Breandan couldn't believe his eyes. He'd been so engrossed with his plight upon arrival that he'd failed to notice all of this on the journey to Gemma Town. Filled with joy, he sought the one he knew would be his. His gaze fell on Charani, on her tender stare in his direction.

"You followed me." Her voice didn't hold an accusation, as he thought he should expect.

Raising one hand, she waited for him to cross the short expanse between them. His long legs moved him to her side in just a few steps. They stood beneath a massive tree bearing fruit such as he'd never seen before in his life. Shaped like a pear, the fruit smelled like an apple, but had the coloration of an orange.

"What type of witchcraft is this?" he wondered.

"Not witchcraft." Charani plucked one of the fruits and handed it to him. "This is a *torgani*, native only to this planet. It will only grow when it senses love nearby." Her voice dropped to an almost soundless whisper. "The love of those fated to join."

His white teeth sank into the fruit and then he held the *torgani* out to her. Charani took a bite beside and overlapping where he had taken his.

His senses heightened. Breandan dropped the shovel that almost never left his side. He took Charani into his arms and captured her lips with his.

Nothing else existed except the two of them. His hands moved from her waist, to her shoulders. Beneath his fingers, her blouse fell aside, revealing bare, beautiful, unmarred skin. Sanity left him in that second, when she reached for the fastenings on his pants. In moments, they lay upon the ground, rolling, groaning, and joining in a love so great that the birds rose up in chorus.

σ σ σ

Charani felt it the moment his sperm discovered her eggs. She had always known that twins were in her future, and felt her soon-to-be babes in their creation. Visions raced past her eyes, of the children—a boy like his father and a girl like her mother—racing along the beauty of Eire.

"I love you," Breandan whispered in her ear as they continued to couple. "With all my heart and soul—I love you, Charani. You will be my wife."

The bonds that had been placed upon her when she was given over to Gaeril to be his Queen released. For the first time in many long years, Charani was free of the everlasting sadness attached to the promise made by her parents.

"I love you with all my heart and soul," she whispered. "You shall always be my husband. Nothing shall ever separate us."

Together, they rose and dressed. She drank in the perfection of his well-muscled body, the tenderness in his eyes, the way he helped her balance as she put on her skirt.

Hand in hand, they began the trek back to Gemma Town. Breandan held the shovel he was never without against one shoulder. She glanced at the tool several times, but its ordinary appearance never once changed from the golden tone she'd seen the day she first watched him covertly.

"Why is that shovel so special?" she asked.

"Tis the only thing me da ever gave me." His voice spoke volumes in what he didn't say—of a sadness that he had never known his father, of pride in that he carried a legacy. "He's full leprechaun, but I'm only half. Me mam fell in love with a man who could never fully give her his heart. But once I reached my majority, me da came back to teach me of his legacy, and a prophecy that I could never talk about, let alone share."

She listened avidly as he described the prophecy, much the same as the one the gypsy's seer had told to her. Charani believed once again that she could find true love— had found true love—as Breandan continuously glanced at her with love shining in his eyes.

"Now that you know about me," he said. "Tell me about you."

"There's not much to tell," she admitted. "I was bound to a betrothal I detested when I was naught but a babe. In all those years, I've never once accepted Gaeril as the man who would be my husband, because of the prophecy our seer told me about just recently." Charani smiled up at Breandan. "You are the man in my prophecy. She described you, right down to your boots."

"These old things." He laughed. "Surely, your seer was worried I might never be able to give you pots of gold. Wasn't she?"

"She promised that you would own pots of gold and that we would have a great love."

Charani left out the final part of the prophecy— what the seer reluctantly told her only moments before she boarded the spacecraft—that their love would be short-lived. She refused to believe that a love so powerful could ever break.

"I believe we need to gather our things and leave Gemma Town." Breandan paused on top of the hillock that lead into the town. "Don't you?"

"Where can we go?" she asked. "I'm sentenced to this place as long as Gaeril claims me."

"If you tell the authorities that you're no longer with Gaeril, won't they allow you to leave?"

"I think so." She took her eyes off the town to stare up at him. "I hope so."

"You need to know about the pot o' gold," Breandan said, staring off into the distance. "As long as this shovel is nearby—" he hefted it "—ye will never have to remember where you buried the pot. Ye must also bury the pot in a new spot every month, at the time of the full moon, or it vanishes forever."

"Why?" she asked.

"Ah, lass, tis the leprechaun's way." Breandan grinned.

He spun a tale so improbable that if she hadn't seen the pot appear last month, she wouldn't have believed him. Charani stood enraptured as she learned all about his leprechaun legacy, and how together, they would provide their children with a lifetime of laughter and love.

I can't believe that the seer was right. She leaned closer to her love. *Breandan and I are meant to be together.*

He lowered his head, capturing her lips again in a kiss that transported her away from the horrors that had been her life since Gaeril was sentenced. Only Breandan stiffening and falling away from her brought Charani back to her senses.

σ σ σ

Gaeril walked in a fury away from Gemma Town, determined to locate Charani. She was the only way he could regain the crown he'd so desperately sought all his life. He lost sight of her and that fool who had caused him so much trouble over the last month—a man whose name he had never bothered to learn. But he would find the both of them and teach them a lesson—her in cheating on him, and that man in taking another man's betrothed.

"Where are you, bitch?" Gaeril scanned the horizon, seeking his prey.

The sun was lowering on the horizon when he finally saw them. The matching footsteps, their hands clasped tightly, how they were always looking at each other reminded him of the way some couples he'd observed after they'd laid together.

"Slut," he growled. "You will pay for what you've done to me."

Her actions had probably broken their betrothal bonds, but Gaeril wasn't a man to let this woman go so lightly. She was his ticket to getting his crown back.

Charani came from a pure Romany clan—one never tainted by mixed blood.

A glance around the area provided him with a probable weapon. A large branch was nearly separated from the tree that had used it for many years. He was a strong man, despite the beating he'd taken at Andre's hands. Gaeril snatched up the branch and turned back toward the couple.

They were kissing—a passionate embrace that infuriated him even more. They were too engrossed in each other to notice him. He moved quickly in their direction, lifting the branch over his head, and bringing it down once he was close enough to teach the stranger a lesson.

To his satisfaction, the man who had seduced his wife-to-be collapsed, half his head caved in.

"I have bested you." Gaeril threw back his head and released a chilling laugh of victory. "Charani will always be mine."

σ σ σ

Breandan was aware of a terrible pain in his head. His numb fingers released the shovel as he fell. Then there was a darkness so deep he knew there was no coming back.

σ σ σ

Shocked to her core, Charani reacted quickly. She reached out and caught the shovel as it fell. Holding the handle in both hands, she swung, driving the tip of the shovel into Gaeril's throat.

The man who had tormented her for so long let out a bloody gasp and sank toward the earth. Charani leaned the blade of the shovel into the ground and released a torrent of tears. As the earth soaked away the blood on the shovel, a rainbow burst forth.

Startled, she glanced to her left. A pot o' gold sat on the ground. Remembering Breandan's earlier words, she dug quickly and silently, only checking occasionally for anyone who might see what she was doing.

Once the hole was deep enough, she used all of her remaining strength and pulled the man she loved into the earth and then set the gold atop his chest. Once again using the shovel, she covered up her lover, hoping the earth would reclaim his soul and allow his love for her to keep her going for their children.

σ σ σ

Nine months later, Charani birthed twins in the same inn where she had lived since coming to Gemma Town. The midwife, Anya, proclaimed both to be hale and hearty. From the sounds of their cries, Charani didn't disagree.

Although she'd been given the chance to return to Eire, Charani had chosen to remain close to where Breandan was buried, where she could go and speak to him as much as was possible. No longer did she yearn to return to the ways of the Romany. Her heart and soul was firmly attached to Planet Zeta and those who'd been forcibly emigrated here.

The sound of her children awakening brought a smile to her face. Charani lifted them one at a time and settled on her bed, holding them close.

"Ye shall always be safe here," she whispered. "No one will ever hurt you."

Thanks to Anya spreading the news of a prophecy fulfilled, of twins born to a Romany and a man with Irish and leprechaun blood, Charani and her children had no worries that anyone would harm them.

"Sleep, my babies," she whispered. "Your mama will make sure your daddy sees you from the great beyond."

She gazed at the children, at how much they represented both her and Breandan.

The boy, Aden, had her dark hair but his father's green eyes. Eileen, their daughter, had fiery red hair that matched her screaming temper, and her black eyes foretold of trouble later.

Holding her babes tight, Charani again whispered the story of the shovel in the corner, and the great love their father had for them, even as he was denied the right to be with them.

Aegeus' Honor

Noelle Myers

Aegeus' hands trembled as he wound another wax coated strip of fabric around his head to cover his ears. He wasn't fond of life on board the *Agamemnon*. The captain and crew were a rough, crude group. He did not fit that mold. Aegeus leaned more towards scholarly and gentlemanly pursuits. His father had been the town mapmaker before a fire had burned his shop to the ground, and Aegeus was forced to serve on board Cyrus' ship to reconcile his father's debts. He only had one year left of the five he had been indentured for.

It had been four years of hell. Every night, Aegeus prayed to Zeus to make a way out for him. He had even considered jumping into the depths of the sea, hoping Poseidon would accept his sacrifice. Cyrus had caught him perched on the rails and nearly beaten him to death. Aegeus wouldn't join in with the crew as they ravaged the women in the towns and ports where they stopped. He chose to stay on board the ship. His parents had instilled a high respect for human life and dignity. He would not lower himself to acting like his barbaric crewmates.

He tightened his grip on the wheel. His navigating skills had swiftly made him second only to Cyrus at the ship's helm. Since the captain would much rather be fighting, Aegeus was relegated to steering. That was just fine with him. The wind picked up, and the waves were pulling the ship towards shore. A mild feeling of drowsiness fell over him. He realized the sirens were singing. He wrapped two more strips around his ears and soon the drowsiness fell away.

"See, I knew this would work. The temptress' songs cannot hurt us now. That treasure will soon be ours, and the witches will be dead. Not even the gods can stop us now," Cyrus crowed.

Aegeus' heart stopped in his chest. "You should not tempt the Gods, Captain," he warned, shouting to be heard above the wind and through the wax.

"Bah. The Gods have lost their power. They cannot even protect their own creations, the sirens. We will show them." The captain's words were muffled.

Aegeus shook his head, but Cyrus just laughed and walked away, sword at the ready. Just as the boat hit the shallows near shore, the swarthy captain turned to him.

"Stay with the boat, Aegeus. You are not cut out for this."

With that curt order, the entire crew leapt over the side of the ship and into the shallow waters. Aegeus anchored the ship so it wouldn't beach on the sandy shores, and waited.

It was nearly dark when the men returned—most of them anyway. Bloodied and battered, they stumbled back onto the ship. They didn't come empty handed. Aegeus was horrified to see that four of the men carried a make shift cage. Inside the cage, a beautiful young woman cowered, bound and gagged. She appeared to be only a few years younger than he. The terrified look in her deep blue eyes tore at his heart.

"What have you done?" His words came out in a hoarse whisper.

Cyrus laughed as he pulled the wax dipped fabric from Aegeus' head.

"A captive—a hostage if you will. We found the treasure, and will spend the night loading it on board. She will ensure her kind do not attack us in the dead of night. She must be special. When we captured her, all the others took off into the underbrush."

He leaned close to the cage and shook it hard.

The poor girl shrank back in terror.

Aegeus stepped forward, his anger surging. "You shouldn't have done that," he ground out.

"They killed Dand and Ferris." The captain stepped close to the younger man, anger blazing in his eyes.

Aegeus' anger matched Cyrus', emboldening him. "They were only protecting their home," he said.

"And when they lured my brother and father to their deaths? Were they protecting their homes then?"

Even the wind stopped moving as the captain's words echoed through the night sky.

Aegeus was on treacherous ground and needed to be very careful about what he said next.

"They have been cursed. Perhaps they have no more choice in what they do than the men who hearken to their call." He opted for tact.

"Never question me again," Cyrus growled.

Aegeus could see he had made his point, and backed off, hands in the air. His gaze locked with the beautiful woman in the cage. He tried to communicate that she had nothing to fear from him. She held his gaze for a moment before the men picked the cage up and took her into the captain's cabin.

"You stay on the boat. Watch her. If she gets away, it is your head. And I mean that literally, I will separate your head from your neck if that girl gets away." Cyrus moved towards the gangplank, but turned before he reached it. "Don't take off the gag either, or she will enchant you." Cyrus glared at him.

Aegeus nodded and watched while the rest of the crew once again headed back onto the island.

Once everyone was out of sight, he turned on his sandaled heel and made a beeline for the captured siren. She shrank back into the far edge of the too small cage as he slowly approached.

"I am not going to hurt you. I promise. I am sorry about all of this. Cyrus is not someone I can cross. I wish I could get you out, but I cannot. It would mean my life, and the life of my family," he said softly.

He didn't even know if the woman could understand what he was saying.

Muffled sounds drew his attention back to the cage. The woman was talking, but because of the gag he could not understand her. Conflicting emotions warred with his conscience. He wanted to hear what she had to say, but Cyrus' warning rang true as well. The woman was trying to gesture with her hands. They were bound behind her. He realized she must be thirsty. His compassion won.

"Stop. Are you thirsty?" he asked.

She nodded, a single curl bouncing on top of her head.

"I am going get you some water, and remove the gag, but you must promise me, swear by Zeus, that you will not try and enchant me," Aegeus said earnestly. "Do you promise?"

A look Aegeus didn't recognize passed over the woman's face, but she nodded. He pulled some wax from the candle and set it nearby, just in case. Carefully he loosened the gag and lowered it down around her neck. A filthy rag had also been stuffed in her mouth. It must have nearly choked her. He gently pulled the dirty cloth from her mouth.

"I am sorry," he apologized again.

"Water, please."

Aegeus was surprised to understand the words that came out of her mouth.

"You speak the same language as me?" He helped her drink some water.

"I speak many languages. Poseidon has gifted us in this manner. We sing to you in whatever language is most appealing," she said quietly.

"If I hear the others coming back, I will have to replace the gag." Aegeus felt he needed to warn her.

"I understand. I appreciate your kindness." The woman's voice was sultry and appealing, but held no sway over him.

"What is your name?" He sat down on the floor next to the cage.

"I am called Iphigenia, by my sisters. You may call me Ginny." A sparkle came into her eyes, and she smiled— a beautiful smile. It took Aegeus' breath away.

"I am Aegeus," he said, somewhat clumsily.

"Protector," Ginny said with a wry look on her face.

"What?"

"That is what your name means. Protector. Are you going to be my protector?" she asked.

"I am not like the others," Aegeus blurted out.

"I can see that, but I am afraid that may not be enough to save you." Ginny's face was sad.

"I don't understand."

"My sisters will come for me. When they do, the crew of the *Agamemnon* will pay for kidnapping me. Even if you escape to the sea, my father will rescue me. I am the daughter of Poseidon."

Ginny's words struck fear into his heart. The daughter of Poseidon, niece of Zeus and Hades. What had Cyrus done?

"Why do you call to sailors, and destroy their ships?"

If he was going to die because of this vendetta of Cyrus', he wanted to know.

"We do not call to all sailors. Some are deemed worthy, and allowed to pass. Most are not. We merely sing of the treasure and wealth to be found here on the island. If greed overpowers the warning we also include in the song, their fate is sealed." Her voice cracked.

Aegeus helped her drink some more water.

"Poseidon tells us who to test. If you survive the song, and make it to shore of the island, there is yet another test you must overcome, but if you pass, you are free from the Siren Song forever, and never have to fear sailing near this island again, for you are blessed and protected by the Gods," Ginny explained.

"How many men have passed the test?" Aegeus had only heard tales of a few survivors.

"Jason, Odysseus, and many others. Not all men who are on the ships wish to follow the path of the captain. We are not merciless," Ginny's voice trembled.

He took a moment to look at her. She really was beautiful, shaped in every way like the women he was used to, but she was not a woman. Some tales had them swimming in the sea like mermaids, others had them flying over ships like birds.

"You do not look like a bird creature, or a mermaid, as I have heard tales of," he blurted.

"I see you seek knowledge. A good quality, and unusual in a sailor." Ginny's smile was kind, not mocking.

A noise on deck startled Aegeus. The men were returning.

"I must replace the gag. Cyrus is returning. I will do what I can to protect you, but for now I must replace this."

Aegeus spent precious seconds waiting for her to nod in assent. He did not replace the rag, but slid the binding up over her mouth and tightened it again. He stepped away just as the door to the cabin opened, and Cyrus strode through.

"What do you think you are doing?" Cyrus was as angry as Aegeus had ever seen him.

"Just checking on the prisoner, Captain." He stepped away from the cage.

Ginny gave a muffled yelp from behind the gag.

Cyrus grinned. "I knew you would eventually show your colors. Not so high and mighty after all, are ya?"

Aegeus felt sick at what Cyrus was implying, but managed a half-hearted grin back at the captain. The two men left the cabin and headed back up on deck.

Cyrus clapped him on the back as they made their way back to the helm.

"Treasure is almost loaded. After I have a go at the girl, I will give you a turn before we slit her throat," he whispered.

It took every bit of self-control that Aegeus possessed to keep from responding. His mind raced as he tried to think of a way to rescue Ginny before Cyrus got his hands on her again.

"Last chest loaded, Captain," one of the men shouted.

"Everyone on board?" Cyrus asked.

"Aye, Captain," came the response.

"Man the oars. I want to get as far away from here as possible before those creatures get brave and come back for their missing wench," Cyrus called out. "Aegeus, take us out to sea."

"Maybe we should leave her here, Captain." Aegeus suggested.

Cyrus laughed at him. "Getting cold feet?"

Aegeus gauged how far he could push the captain. He had to try. "Captain, I am not trying to question you, but this is a daughter of Poseidon, King of the Sea. Do you really want venture into his domain with his daughter as a prisoner?"

He kept his voice low, trying not to anger Cyrus.

"Don't push me, boy. I could leave you here too. How would you like that?"

"No, sir." Aegeus ducked his head and focused on steering the ship out of the small bay near the island.

Fortunately, the captain was soon distracted and moved away from the helm. Aegeus thought frantically for a way to help the siren locked below. He hit upon an idea.

It was dangerous, but it was his only chance. Waiting until everyone was distracted, he slipped down to the captain's cabin. Moving quickly, he pulled a knife from his waistband and knelt in front of the cage.

Ginny didn't shrink away from him. It was as if she knew she could trust him. With one swift slice, he cut through the bonds wrapped around her legs. He had just started to work on the rope wrapped around her wrists, when he was hauled to his feet by his hair.

"Wanting to get a head start were you, boy?" Cyrus' brown eyes were filled with rage, his lips curled into a sneer.

Aegeus never got a chance to say a word. Cyrus' fist slammed into his face, and his world went black.

When he awoke, he could see that Ginny was still in her cage, bound again. He was tied to the end of the table, and his back felt like it was on fire. He tried to move, but the pain was so severe he nearly passed out again.

"Did they hurt you?" he whispered hoarsely.

He sagged with relief when Ginny shook her head no. A terrible scream from above decks split the air. Aegeus realized the ship was rocking violently as though it were being tossed about in a terrible storm. More screams reached them as the door to the cabin was pulled off its hinges. Water began pouring in through the cabin.

"Sister."

"Ginny."

"Iphigenia."

A chorus of voices called above the screams and the wind.

Ginny tried to respond, but the gag muffled her shouts.

"She is in here," Aegeus shouted.

No matter what he did at this point, one side or the other would kill him. The least he could do was to ensure she was able to escape.

The ship lurched hard to the port side. Pain took his breath away. His vision began to cloud. Struggling to stay conscious, Aegeus realized the water was up to his knees. That would make it nearly up to Ginny's neck.

"Hurry." He used what strength he had to shout one last time.

The grayness was swiftly turning to black. He was able to make out three shadowy figures coming into the room. He hoped they were the sirens, not the *Agamemnon*'s men.

"No. Not him. We take him with us—him and one other."

Aegeus recognized Ginny's voice, but it was not the soft, sensual tone he had heard from her earlier. It was hard as iron. He let the blackness envelop him.

This time, when Aegeus awoke, he was in the cage. The pain in his back was much milder and he was able to sit up. He craned his neck to try to get an idea of the damage Cyrus had inflicted, but he couldn't see. Looking around, he saw Cyrus in a cage nearby. He looked as bad as Aegeus felt.

"Hello, protector." Ginny's voice was the seductive buttery timbre he remembered.

"Ginny." His voice was rusty from lack of use.

He had no idea how long he had been unconscious. He attempted to smile but he was slipping back into unconsciousness again.

"You never did answer my question," he said in an attempt to stay awake.

Ginny's head tilted, her blue eyes lit up with amusement. "You are a curious one."

Aegeus was vaguely aware that a lilting song was invading his mind.

"Sleep for now, protector. I will tell you the next time you awaken. Sleep now, and heal."

Ginny reached a delicate hand through the bars of the cage and stroked his face gently. With a sigh, Aegeus slipped back into a healing sleep.

σ σ σ

"Why do you insist on healing them?" One of Ginny's sisters peered into the cage that held Cyrus.

"They must be fully healed to go through the test," Ginny said.

"And why, my daughter, must you test them both?" a deep voice asked.

"Father!"

Several of the siren's rushed forward to greet the great Poseidon. Ginny held back until her sisters had all had a turn greeting their patriarch. She hugged him tightly. It was rare that Poseidon made a visit to their little island anymore. It wasn't that he didn't love them, but he had so many responsibilities.

"Why test them both?" Poseidon repeated his question.

"One I am testing, because I am certain he will pass. I owe him, for trying to save my life. The other, well, let's just say payback will be a pleasure." Ginny's voice was light, but her eyes were hard.

"You are certain he will pass?" A hushed whisper from her youngest sister made Ginny smile.

"Yes, little one. I am certain. Noble men are a rare breed, and birth doesn't necessarily make a man noble. Aegeus is noble of heart, soul, and mind," she said.

"He is still human," Poseidon mused.

"Ah, yes, but he has the best qualities of mankind," Ginny replied.

She couldn't quite tell whether her father approved or not. He seemed particularly interested in this set of trials.

"Do you care for him, sister?"

"Not in a romantic way, but I do care for him, as he cared about me, when he removed my gag and gave me water, and when he tried to set me free—in a friendship sort of way."

Ginny watched her father's face as she spoke. The furrow that was etched on his brow relaxed. His face softened. So that was why he was here. Ginny felt like laughing. Even the King of the Sea was worried about the mate his daughter chose.

Poseidon stayed for the rest of the afternoon. Ginny soaked up every minute of his visit. Most of the time, she and her sisters loved living on the island, singing their songs and playing in the meadows. Once in a while they got lonely. It was nice to have visitors.

σ σ σ

Aegeus' eyes fluttered open. He was no longer in the cage, but lying on a soft bed of feathers and furs. Cyrus was sitting nearby. He was awake and looking stronger than ever. Aegeus hoped the testing Ginny had talked about wasn't going to pit him against the physical prowess of the former captain.

"Protector, how are you feeling?" Ginny's voice brought him back to the present.

"Much better. Please convey my thanks to your healers."

Aegeus struggled to sit up. He was a little dizzy at first, so he waited to stand. Ginny surprised him, and sat on the bed next to him. A small girl, no older than seven, accompanied the beautiful siren. She had the same cheekbones and smile, but her eyes were a brilliant violet hue.

"Aegeus, this is my sister, Anthea. She has been fascinated with you and the captain over there. You are the first humans she has ever seen." Ginny ruffled her hair affectionately.

"Hello, Anthea. You remind me very much of my own little sister. She was your age when I left my home and went to sea. I haven't seen her in a very long time. I miss her very much." Aegeus tipped his head to look in the little girl's face.

She rewarded him with a timid smile, before Ginny shoed her off.

"You have a little sister?" she asked.

"Delphine, she would be about twelve now I suppose. She was such a pretty girl. I am afraid she may not even be alive now."

Aegeus put his head in his hands. He missed his family so much the feeling threatened to reduce him to tears.

"Why? Was she ill?" Ginny put her hand on his arm.

The concern on her face was not feigned. Aegeus found himself telling her his life story. His happy childhood, learning map making at his father's side, the day Delphine was born. All of it.

"Then the fire happened. I am certain that it was set deliberately. And I am almost positive that it was Cyrus' father who had it set. He was our landlord. He died at sea, shortly after the fire." Aegeus took a deep breath.

Running a hand through his thick dark hair, he continued, "Cyrus called in our debts, and forced me to work on his ship to pay it off. Father was too badly injured in the fire. Mother got out right away, but Delphine was trapped in the back of the house. Father went back inside to save her, and they were both badly burned. They lived, but at a cost." The guilt had only gotten stronger with his absence. "If I had been home, I may have been able to spare them both. I was looking at the stars with a girl that night."

"If you pass the tests, perhaps you will see them soon."

Ginny's gaze followed Anthea as she skipped through the meadow outside the tent. Aegeus understood the fierce protectiveness that passed across her face. He would do anything to see his sister again, and protect her again.

"I just wish I knew if they were alive." Aegeus could not stop the tears from rolling down his cheeks.

"Come with me."

Ginny took him by the hand and led him through the meadow, down to a turquoise pool at the base of a waterfall. A silver bowl sat beside the pool, along with a crystal pitcher. The beautiful siren filled the pitcher with water from the pool and poured it into the bowl. The water instantly became still as glass.

"Come, look into the reflection. What your heart desires most will be revealed there, but only for a moment" Ginny's words propelled him forward.

For one heart stopping moment, he didn't see anything. Then the water shimmered, as if someone was breathing on it, and figures appeared. Aegeus leaned closer to the water as the image cleared.

"Mother," he breathed.

She was older, her dark hair had streaks of silver, and there were more lines on her face, but she was as beautiful as he remembered her. He looked for something that would tell him where she was. There was the tapestry that had hung in their home, one side still charred from the fire. The image flickered as she moved closer to another figure in the room with the tapestry. It was Delphine, she was resting on pillows near the fire. She was so pale and thin, it wrung his heart, but she was alive.

"Eat, my daughter. You must eat." His father's voice drifted from the image.

Aegeus was stunned at his father's appearance. His hair was a stark white, and he had lost so much weight that he looked like a skeleton. Aegeus could have watched forever, soaking in this glimpse of his family, but the image shimmered, and they were gone. He sank to his knees, silently thanking Zeus that they were still alive. After composing himself, he stood and turned to Ginny. She was still standing beside the pitcher and bowl.

"Thank you. Thank you for that wonderful gift. Praise Zeus they are still alive," he said with a sad smile.

"Do you not wish to see more?" Ginny asked him.

"Of course, I do. I wish to look upon their faces and fall upon their necks, and never let go, but you have shown me more than I expected to see. You said you could show me for a moment, I have had my moment and I thank you for it." Aegeus said, his face a mask of pain and longing.

"Come, we must leave this place. You must eat."

The kindness that Aegeus saw in Ginny's eyes gave him the tiniest bit of hope that perhaps he would see his family again.

When they arrived back at the tent he had awakened in, he noticed that Cyrus was gone. A feast had been laid out just inside the tent. Ginny introduced two more of her sisters, and they, along with little Anthea joined him for the meal. Aegeus was a little uncomfortable with the beautiful company at his table, but soon began to relax. Ginny begged him to excuse her, as she had some things to attend to.

Anthea chattered away, while the other two girls ate silently. Aegeus enjoyed the different foods. Fresh fruits, some he didn't recognize, roasted vegetables, creamy milk, and some decadent bread littered the table. He helped Anthea pour another glass of milk, and when one of the other sisters had difficulty peeling one of the tough skinned fruits, he used his knife to remove the rind for her. He was rewarded with a brilliant smile of thanks.

He had just finished the last bite he could possibly fit into his stomach, when Anthea gave a little cry of distress. She had knocked the pitcher of milk over trying to reach something. One of the older girls began to chide her, and Aegeus stepped in.

"Don't cry little one. It is all right. It was just an accident." He righted the pitcher and scooped the sopping wet girl up onto his lap. "Please don't scold her. We will clean it up," he said to the older girls.

He used the hem of his robe to wipe Anthea's tears.

"There, see. You go find me some cloths to wipe this up and we will get it cleaned in no time," he instructed the little girl.

She raced off, and was back in minutes with several clean rags. He worked to clean up the mess. After a moment the two older girls pitched in as well. In no time, they had everything all cleaned.

"How was your meal?" Ginny had reappeared.

"It was delicious. Thank you. The company was wonderful as well." Aegeus smiled.

He was surprised when Anthea leaned close and kissed his cheek before dashing back out to play. The look on Ginny's face told him she was just as shocked as he was.

"Rest now. You will need your strength soon," she said.

He wondered why she kept saying that. If he only knew how he would be tested, he could prepare himself. He lay back on the soft bed and let his mind drift to home. He dreamed that he was walking in the door of his father's house, laden with gifts and treasures to make their lives bearable.

Movement at the edge of the bed awakened him. Dusk had fallen. In the growing shadows, he could see Ginny standing at the end of his bed. Nothing but a light silk robe covered her voluptuous curves. He could feel desire rising within him. She slid closer, allowing the robe to slip off her shoulders and puddle at her feet. Every inch of her was beautiful. Her skin was creamy and smooth.

Aegeus didn't know whether to stare or look away. Respect for women had been ingrained deep within him, but the desire burned hot.

"Don't you want me?" Ginny purred.

"No, Yes, Why?" Aegeus couldn't think straight.

A soft laugh escaped her lips. "It is the law. I must sleep with each man who is to complete the test."

A shadow of sadness touched her eyes.

"You don't want this."

It was a statement, not a question. When tears filled Ginny's eyes, Aegeus could sit still no longer. He closed the distance between them in two steps. Bending down, he picked up her robe from the floor and gently wrapped it around her shoulders.

"You have no reason to fear me," he said as he felt her tremble beneath his hands.

"Am I not desirable?"

"By Zeus, yes." Aegeus put a little distance between them, and sat on the edge of the bed.

Ginny slipped back into her robe, and sat next to him.

"Yet you will deny yourself, because I do not desire you in this way?"

Aegeus wasn't sure whether Ginny was asking him a question, or simply stating the truth. He decided to answer her.

"My mother was once forced to do this very thing, an indignity that has cost our family much. She and my father instilled in me a respect for others, especially women and children. My desires are not more important than yours, nor yours more important than mine. We should treat each other as equals."

Ginny sat back, a strange look on her face. "You treat all women this way? You are a rare man indeed."

"Not so rare, my father is a far better man than I am. I know of others, many others in my village who live this way. Life is honored above all."

"Yet you kill animals."

"Yes, we do, as sacrifices to the gods or to eat them, and to use their hides. But we only kill what we need, never to excess. Every part of the animal is used, none is left to waste. We do this to survive."

Aegeus rubbed the back of his neck. He was still stiff and sore from the days of healing.

Taking a deep breath, he continued. "Human life is important to us. Even the weak and poor are given equal value in my village. We have one man who has been crippled since birth. His parents fled to our village when the elders in theirs wanted to throw their son from the cliffs, saying he had been cursed by the Gods. He is one of our most respected elders now."

Ginny smiled, and stood. "Aegeus, my protector, your honor is great among men. Rest now. You will need all your strength for the final test tomorrow."

A lilting song rose from her throat. Aegeus found himself drifting off into a peaceful sleep once again.

σ σ σ

Blue and golden light filled the tent where Ginny stood watching Aegeus sleep. She turned to find both Poseidon and Zeus standing in the tent.

"Mighty Zeus." Ginny sank to the floor in a deep bow of respect.

"My favorite niece." The tall, handsome Zeus took her by the hand and helped her stand. "My brother informs me that you have a rare mortal here, I came to see for myself."

"How long have you been watching?"

"Since the first meeting with Anthea," Poseidon said as he hugged his daughter.

"Am I wrong, Uncle? Is he not a rare and honorable man?" Ginny gestured to the sleeping sailor.

"He is uncommon, although Hera tells me that his father is also honorable. This family has suffered much, and has remained faithful to us. Their faith has never wavered. *If* this man survives the test tomorrow, his reward will be more than he can imagine. Honor deserves honor," Zeus said.

Ginny was glad to hear her uncle approved of her choice. Aegeus was a human, and she had little love for humans, but if more were like him, perhaps she could learn to tolerate them. She was a little concerned about the test tomorrow. It would be a hard one—one that even the most honorable of men would have a hard time with. If Aegeus passed, it would restore her faith in humanity.

Zeus, Poseidon, and Ginny spent the evening in preparation for the events of the morrow. As the dawn crept across the sky, Zeus and Poseidon took their leave, riding a bolt of lightning back to Mount Olympus. Ginny sat and watched the sunrise in solitude, enjoying the peaceful moment.

σ σ σ

The sun was high in the sky when Aegeus found himself in the center of a field. He and Cyrus were standing in the middle of a barren dirt circle, surrounded by shoulder high grass. A tug on his sleeve caused him to glance down. Anthea was standing next to him.

"What are you doing here little one?" He squatted down to her level.

"I am here to help you," she said. "Diana will help the other man."

Aegeus looked across the packed earth to see Cyrus talking to his companion. He looked angry. His arms were waving in sharp motion; his face was like a thundercloud. Aegeus was too far away to stop what happened next.

Cyrus hauled back and slapped the young woman across the face. She fell to the ground. Aegeus moved.

"Stay here," he ordered Anthea, and raced across to the fallen girl. "Cyrus!" he shouted.

"Stay out of this, boy. She disrespected me. You of all people should know no one gets away with that." Cyrus pulled his leg back to give the girl a swift kick.

Aegeus used the opportunity to shove the bigger man off balance.

"Leave her alone. She is just a child," he growled.

Cyrus caught himself and laughed. "She isn't human. Remember? Tell you what, you are no competition for me, take her with you, you can have two helpers."

Aegeus didn't know what the rules of this test were, but he would lose before he would allow Cyrus to harm the girl further. She looked to be about ten years old; tears were flowing freely down her cheeks. He scooped her up into his strong arms and carried her over to where Anthea was waiting.

"Diana, are you all right?" Aegeus asked the trembling child.

She didn't speak, but nodded.

"Is she helping you too?" Anthea asked.

"If she wants to, she certainly can. If that is against the rules, then she can just stay here with us, and keep us company. I won't let her go back to Cyrus," he said the last part loud enough so anyone in the vicinity could hear him.

"Diana is free to help whom she chooses." A voice echoed through the sky. "For this test, you must leave the circle, and make your way to the west. The first to reach the river will receive an advantage."

The voice died away, and silence descended.

Cyrus immediately ran toward the long grass on the western edge of the circle. The grass locked into a solid wall and physically threw the big man back into the circle.

Even Aegeus' face flamed at the curses that Cyrus began to spew. He tried again with the same result.

Aegeus turned to his helpers. "How do I get past that?" he asked.

Diana's face was serious, but Anthea was grinning. "There are two ways to get past the grasses. You can either ask, or you can fly."

"Fly?" Cyrus had come closer to listen.

Diana and Anthea glanced at each other, and in response, the two little girls stepped away from the men.

"Allegi," they shouted.

As the echo of their voices died away, there was a flash of light, and a loud crack.

When Aegeus' eyes readjusted, the two little girls no longer looked like little girls. Their faces were the same, as beautiful as ever, and their bodies were similar, but now they both had a stunning pair of wings, their feathers different shades of the color of their eyes. Anthea had shades of violet and purple, while Diana's were many shades of green.

"Hey, I want my helper back." Cyrus moved towards the two sirens, his face a mask of anger.

Aegeus moved to block his former captain, but before he could take another step he found himself lifted up in the air. The two young sirens had a firm grip under his arms and were carrying him over the grass toward the river. Aegeus didn't know if he should be terrified, or revel in the incredible experience. If he fell, he would surely die, but the view was amazing, and the rush of wind in his face invigorating. The trio descended, and he was gently set down on the bank of the river. Ginny was waiting at the water's edge.

"As you can see, we can take on many forms. We prefer our natural visage, our wings are so glorious. To make you more comfortable, we put on the lower form of the humans. However, we can become anything, such as a bird."

Ginny gestured to Diana. With a flash, and a crack, the siren disappeared, and in her place flitted a small hummingbird. Aegeus was in awe.

"Or a cat."

Ginny grinned as Anthea changed into a sleek jaguar. Aegeus stumbled back in fear and nearly fell into the water.

"I like to be a cat."

Anthea's impish grin as she changed back, wiped away his fear. Human or siren, he liked both Anthea and Diana. A crashing in the brush drew their attention. Cyrus burst through the underbrush, out of breath.

Ginny spoke before Cyrus could open his mouth.

"Good. Both contenders are present. Aegeus, as you completed the challenge before Cyrus, you receive the advantage." She pressed a shining dagger into his hands. "Use it wisely."

"That is not fair. He didn't do anything! Those two witches completed it for him." Cyrus' face twisted into a sneer.

"Only two may cross the river. It is up to you to decide which two." In a flash, Ginny disappeared.

Aegeus stood in confusion for a moment.

"Come back to me, girl. You and I can go across. Stay with him and you will die. I will kill you myself," Cyrus said.

Diana shrank back behind Aegeus in fear. Anthea clung to him as well. This was an impossible choice. For a moment, he was angry at Ginny, for putting her sisters into this danger, but then Cyrus moved towards them and Aegeus had to act. He propelled the two sirens, now back in their birdlike form, behind him, holding the dagger between him and his former captain.

A healthy respect for the glistening blade slowed Cyrus' approach.

"You fool. If we kill them, we can both cross."

"I will not kill a child." Aegeus shook his head.

"They are not even human," Cyrus spat.

"Anthea, Diana, fly across the river. Get to safety. Go. Now," Aegeus shouted.

With a shout, Cyrus lunged for Diana, who was closest to him. He caught her as she began to take off. Wrapping his sinewy hands around her throat, he squeezed.

Aegeus threw himself at the struggling pair slashing at Cyrus' arm with the dagger. With a yelp of pain, Cyrus let go of the girl. She was unconscious, but alive.

"Anthea, can you carry her?" Aegeus lifted the limp figure up trying to help.

A flash of silver caught his attention. He watched in horror as the dagger descended towards Diana's back. Cyrus had picked up the weapon Aegeus had dropped in the struggle. With only a split second to decide, Aegeus turned to shield the girl with his body and felt a searing pain as the knife hit muscle. Again and again the knife plunged into his back as he held the girl up for her sister to take her. Anthea swooped in on her purple wings and pulled her sister to safety.

"Enough," the voice cracked across the sky.

A moment later, his pain gone, Aegeus found himself lying on the packed earth back in the circle. Cyrus, Diana, Anthea, and Ginny were there as well.

"Aegeus, you have proven your honor, and have passed all of our tests. There have been many who have not."

As Ginny spoke the grass began to evolve into sirens, hundreds of them, in their winged form. Many had wicked talons gleaming in the sunlight.

Aegeus felt himself being lifted to his feet. He hoped passing the test meant he would be allowed to live.

He could feel his face flush. He was not used to being praised. Ginny stepped forward and placed her hand gently on his reddened cheek. Her hand felt cool.

"Well done, my protector. You have passed all our tests. From the moment you awakened here on the island, you have been tested. Your kindness to the youngest of us, your thankfulness for the small gifts of vision and food set you apart from many men. Most of all, you proved your honor, when you thought that your courage and sacrifice would gain you nothing. Your willingness to die for my sisters was the ultimate test."

Ginny's voice turned icy as she turned to the other man in the circle.

"Cyrus, you have failed every single test we have offered you. You have no honor, and will die now, the death you deserve."

She lifted her hand and the sirens descended with a shriek. In seconds, Cyrus was ripped to pieces by their sharp talons.

Aegeus was stunned, but Ginny wasn't finished.

"You are now blessed of Poseidon, and will carry with you the Kiss of the Siren to protect you, as you have protected my sisters and me."

Ginny placed a thin golden chain with a fire red medallion around his neck.

"No one can remove this from your person unless you truly wish it to be removed. This medallion will also signal to both the sirens and the Gods that you are to be protected."

Ginny stepped back and handed him two vials filled with a pale blue liquid.

"These are the healing waters of Asclepius. Give them to your father and sister, and they will heal all their wounds and sickness."

Overcome with emotion, Aegeus fell to his knees and wept. "I could not have dared ask for such a blessing, Thanks be to the Gods. Thanks be to Zeus."

"It is men like you, Aegeus, who restore the faith of both men and Gods." A new voice echoed in his ears. "Since you have given thanks where it is due, you shall be rewarded beyond your wildest dreams."

Aegeus looked up to see the great Zeus standing over him. A glance at Ginny told him he was not dreaming, but before he could blink, the image was gone.

"Yes, Even Zeus has been impressed by your honorable actions. You have done well Aegeus. But the time has come to say goodbye. It is time for you to return home. Goodbye my protector."

Ginny leaned forward and gave him a kiss on the cheek, Anthea also ran forward to kiss him goodbye.

"I will see you again." Ginny's buttery voice echoed as the world began to spin and crack.

A moment later, Aegeus was standing in front of the door to his home. This time, when he walked through that door, arms laden with treasures, it was not a dream.

Long Course

Justin Herzog

He was waiting for me outside.

In his early fifties, a few inches below average height, with darkly tanned skin and thick forearms, his salt speckled hair was drawn back into a loose ponytail. Leaning against the side of a pickup truck whose fire engine sheen had long since faded to a muted citrine, he straightened at the sight of me.

"Marcus Aries?" he asked.

"Most days," I said. "Sometime I let loose and call myself Pete."

He narrowed his eyes. "What?"

"Never mind," I said. "How can I help you?"

"Do you have a minute to talk?"

"Sure," I said.

"Can we speak inside?"

I debated a moment before nodding. Turning back towards the front door, I slipped the key into the lock and made my way inside. The man followed behind me, favoring his right leg as he walked. Letting the door close behind us, I reached out and flicked on the light switch. The florescent lights came alive overhead, revealing a room the size of a large tennis court. Plate glass windows lined the wall closest to the parking lot, with blue and grey exercise mats spread out along the floor. Half a dozen heavy bags hung in the corner, along with various training mannequins.

"I didn't catch you name," I said.

"Jorn," he said, his dark eyes slowly taking in the room. "Elias Jorn."

"Pleasure to meet you, Mr. Jorn," I said, making my way over to the reception desk.

A martial arts instructor by trade, my school, The Dragon's Path Martial Arts Academy, was located a few blocks north of Kapaolono Community Park, in a peaceful neighborhood far enough from downtown to avoid the worst of Honolulu's ever-worsening traffic problem. Open six days a week, we offered a variety of self-defense classes for men, women, and children of all ages. Typically, classes were held Monday through Friday, with the final class ending just before nine P.M. Saturdays were a little different, in that we offered two morning classes, followed by a few hours of open floor time for any students wanting to squeeze in some extra practice. The final student, a black-belt candidate named Danny, had departed almost an hour ago, and I'd been hoping to slip out early, visions of swinging in a beachside hammock dancing in my head.

Alas, no rest for the weary. Business was good, for the most part, but it wouldn't stay that way if I started blowing off potential new students. Pulling open the top drawer, I rummaged around inside, quickly assembling a small file containing a short history of the school, the kinds of classes we offered, our monthly newsletter, and finally, our pricing structure. Arranging them into order, I stepped out from behind the reception desk.

"Here's some basic information to get you started," I said, handing over the file. "Were there any specific questions you had or were you just looking to get a feel for the place?"

Accepting the file, Elias gave it a cursory glance before extending his arm and laying it down atop the reception desk. "I'm afraid there's been a misunderstanding Mr. Aries. I'm not interested in joining your school."

"Oh," I said. "Alright then. In that case, what can I do for you?"

He didn't answer right away, dark eyes watching me closely, weighing me. "I hear things," he said. "Rumors mostly, but enough that I can't help but wonder."

"Wonder about what?"

"About you," he said. "About the kind of work you do when you're not here teaching classes."

A silent warning began sounding in my head, and I had to stop myself from stepping backwards. "You shouldn't pay attention to rumors," I said.

He grunted, the side of his mouth curling up into a half-smile. "Can't be helped," he said. "Rumors are my stock and trade. It's a professional hazard."

"And what profession is that, exactly?" I asked.

"I'm a bartender," he said. "Owner, actually, of a little place called Alibi's Lounge."

"Can't say I've ever been there."

He shrugged. "It's over near Waikiki Beach, but don't let that fool you. We cater mostly to locals. It's not really the kind of place that invites tourists."

"Good to know," I said. "Now, if you don't mind, could we cut to the chase? If you're not interested in taking classes, why are you here?"

"This is why," he said.

Reaching down into his pocket, he withdrew a piece of paper roughly the size of my palm. Handing it over, I accepted it cautiously, pulling back the folded edge to reveal a name, Abigail Brentwood, and an address.

"Who's this?" I asked.

"A friend," he said. "She needs help."

"What kind of help?"

"The kind that only someone like you can provide," he said.

"Can you be more specific?"

"She's in trouble," he said. "Backed into a corner and about to pick a fight with something dangerous."

Some*thing.*

Not someone.

The little voice inside, Mr. Gut I called him when feeling formal, whispered that Elias might be a little smarter than your average bear, which, while not exactly unheard of, was still enough to pique my interest.

Most people living on the island don't believe in the supernatural. They're all too busy being realistic. But most people are wrong. The world of the supernatural has always been there, since long before man first emerged from the ocean. The ancient deities and spirits aren't as visible now as they once were, but that doesn't mean they've ceased to exist. Life has a certain ebb and flow to it, and mankind's relationship with the world of the supernatural was no different. The arrival of the British at the end of the eighteenth century, followed by two hundred years of unchecked immigration, had done a number on the native inhabitant's connection with their spiritual counterparts. Most had abandoned the beliefs of their ancestors, choosing instead to immerse themselves in the digital age. Lucky for them, most of the supernatural beings inhabiting the islands were accepting of their choice, choosing to live peacefully along the uninhabited regions rather than risk provoking a confrontation.

I say most, because every now and then, you can't help but to come across a supernatural being that would rather rip some poor fisherman's head off than swim the other way.

That's where I come in.

In addition to running my school, I occasionally assist anyone who might have run afoul of the aforementioned supernatural baddies. Occasionally violence is involved, and I've got more than a few scars to prove it.

"It's best if she fills you in regarding the details," Elias said. "But you'd better hurry. The clock is ticking, and without your help, I've got a hunch she'll be dead before sunrise."

σ σ σ

I stared down at the piece of paper Elias had given me, then lifted my eyes to the sight before me.

"This," I said aloud. "Is not what I was expecting."

Located roughly thirty minutes east of Honolulu, in the small windward community of Waimanalo, Sea Life Park Hawaii was one of two large aquariums on the island. Hailed as a family-friendly attraction offering dolphin encounters, the park also provided tourists and locals alike the opportunity to interact with sharks, stingrays, and sea-lions. It was also the site of the Oceanic Institute, a subsidiary group of Hawaii's Pacific University dedicated to progressing the fields of marine aquaculture and coastal resource management.

Basically, it was Hawaii's version of Disney World, scaled to size.

Parking, I made my way up to the ticket counter, where I purchased a one day pass. I tried not to grimace as the lady behind the glass swiped my credit card. Money wasn't tight exactly, but there'd been talk among my wife and I that we would like to start trying for our first child. Ever since, I'd begun eyeing my checking account a little more closely. At least I got a resident discount.

Thanking the ticket attendant, I made my way in through the entrance gate. There was no line at this time of the afternoon, most people having arrived earlier in the day. Reaching down into my pocket, I withdrew the piece of paper Elias had given me, rereading the name one more time.

Abigail Brentwood.

Turning right past the entrance, I made my way past a Tiki statue the size of a man and down the ramp towards the Reef Tank area. The park was lightly crowded, and I stepped aside to allow a family of four to pass. The father, a heavyset man in his mid-forties, was holding his young son in one hand and pushing a stroller containing a small girl with the other. His wife trailed behind him, sunburnt shoulders chafing under the weight of a large backpack.

Catching sight of the gift shop at the bottom of the ramp, I made my way inside, where I politely inquired among the cashier's as to where I might find Abigail Brentwood. They conferred among themselves for a few moments before directing me to the dolphin exhibit. Handing me a map, the cashier closest to my left, an elderly lady with large glasses and short trimmed gunmetal hair, used her finger to trace me a path. Nodding politely, I assured her that I would follow it precisely. Exiting the gift shop, I headed north, past the bird aviary and sea lion feeding pool. I briefly debated detouring over towards the penguin habitat (I challenge you to envision any situation in which adding a penguin does not immediately improve it) but worried I might not make it back before closing time. Drawing close to the Dolphin Lagoon, I saw that there was a "Temporarily Closed for Repairs" sign slung across the entryway.

"Huh," I said.

Putting two and two together, it occurred to me that the dolphins, when not performing, had to be housed somewhere. Likely the same place they were trained. My suspicions paid off a few minutes later when I stopped by the Discover Reef Touching Pool and a stingray trainer directed me towards a second set of pools just outside the main park area. Exiting through the western gate, I spotted a large, if slightly less showy swimming pool area, along with an L-shaped building. Making my way up the entrance ramp, I found the front door unlocked. Swinging the door open, I took two steps inside and promptly crashed into a petite female about to exit.

In her early twenties, of Asian descent, with rectangular glasses and long dark hair drawn up into a bun, she let out a surprised gasp, dropping the box she'd been carrying and tumbling over onto her backside.

"Oof," I said, managing to keep my feet only by virtue of being twice her size. "Crap. Are you okay?"

"Ow," she complained, grimacing.

Bending down, I lifted the box from her lap. Something that sounded suspiciously like broken glass shifted inside, rattling against itself as I placed it down upon the counter to my right. Reaching down, I helped her to her feet. She rose slowly, gingerly, face tight and movements stiff.

"Sorry about that," I said.

"My fault," she said. "Probably should start looking where I'm going."

"I think I might have broken your box," I said, lifting it from the counter and extending it towards her.

"Oh," she said, accepting it. "That's not good."

"Sorry."

She gave a half-shrug. "The Wheel weaves as the wheel wills."

I blinked. Was it possible that I'd just stumbled upon another Robert Jordan fan? "Are you Abigail Brentwood?"

"Abby? No. She's in there." She motioned down the hall. "Second door on the left. I'm Jieun Chan. Everyone calls me JiJi"

"Pleasure to meet you Jiji," I said. "I'm Marcus Aries."

"Hi, Marcus," she said. "You can go on in. I was just on my way out." She hesitated. "Uh, you didn't by chance see anyone else in the parking lot, did you?"

"Like who?"

"Older lady? Short hair, dressed in an eggplant business suit?"

I shook my head. "Must have missed her."

"Consider yourself lucky," she said.

Flashing me a final smile, she slipped past me out the door, heading towards the parking lot.

I watched her go before moving off down the hall in the direction she'd indicated. Drawing up next to the second doorway on the left, I found it slightly ajar. Hesitating, I leaned in close, listening.

Something that sounded suspiciously like annoyed curses came echoing out through the cracked doorway after a few seconds, followed by the sounds of heavy items being shifted. Knocking twice, I stepped inside.

It was an equipment room from the looks of it. Dozens of wetsuits hung from the racks to my left, alongside vests, masks, flippers, and breathing hoses. To my right, a long row of lockers stretched half the length of the room, ending beside a large steel cage with the door halfway open.

"Uh, hello?" I asked, inching my way inside.

There came a muffle reply from inside the cage.

Moving forward, I slipped through the cage doorway, turning into a small alcove containing a large black locker. A woman was crouched down beside it. In her late thirties, medium height, with blunted features and brown hair dried out from too much chlorine, she was dressed in a long-sleeved black wetsuit along with a pair of khaki shorts. Crouched down on one knee, she was angling a pair of lock picks into the locker's keyhole.

"Can I help you?" she asked.

"Uh, maybe," I said. "Are you Abigail Brentwood?"

She grunted affirmative, grimacing as she struggled to turn the picks. "Most people call me Abby," she said. "Who are you?"

"Marcus Aries," I said. "Elias Jorn came to see me. He said you needed help."

She paused, glancing back over her shoulder. "You're the one Elias told me about?"

I shrugged, extending my hands out to either side. "Looks that way."

"Okay then," she said. "I appreciate you coming. Did you bring a gun or do you want to borrow mine?"

σ σ σ

I stared at her for a long moment to see if she was joking.

She wasn't.

"Come again?" I said.

Exhaling, she turned her attention back to the lock. "Duffel bag to your left," she said. "Center pocket."

I glanced over to my left, spotting the duffel bag sitting atop a waist-high stack of oxygen canisters, but made no move towards it. I've never been a big fan of guns. I harbor a healthy respect for those who've mastered their use, but know in my heart that I will never be counted among their number.

"Mrs. Brentwood," I said, slowly. "What is it that you need help with exactly?"

"It's Ms."

"Excuse me?"

"I never married." Straightening, she twisted the picks, and was rewarded with a metallic *click,* punctuated a moment later by the sound of the front door popping open. "Finally," she said.

"Ms. Brentwood then," I said. "Would you mind telling me why I'm here exactly?"

She blinked, glancing over at me. "Elias didn't tell you?"

I shook my head. "Just that you need help."

"Oh, lovely," she said. Drawing in a deep breath, she let it out slow. "Okay. Here goes nothing. I think something's trying to hurt the kids."

I blinked. "What kids? And what do you mean *something*?"

"I can show you," she said. "But first you have to promise that—"

"What's going on here?" demanded a voice from behind me.

Glancing back, I turned to find two figures standing in the middle of the room. I hadn't heard either of them enter. The first was a man. In his late thirties, he stood slightly hunched, the right side of his face dropping down in the manner of someone who'd suffered a stroke. Dressed in a pair of deep blue coveralls with the Sea Life Park logo, he clutched a dry mop in one hand, leaning against it almost like a walking stick. Beside him was a woman. In her early sixties, tall, with short cut moonstone hair and a pair of hooped earrings, she was dressed in an eggplant-colored suit with a black blouse and gold trim.

"I said, what's going on here?" she asked her voice raking across my face with all the sting of a bad-tempered cat. "Who are you?"

I frowned, feeling myself bristle. "Marcus Aries—" I began, but Abigail cut me off.

"Just taking inventory ma'am," she said. Straightening, she reached over into her duffel bag. For a moment, I feared the worst, but a second later she withdrew a clipboard with a pen attached to the edge.

The woman's gaze narrowed, which was impressive considering her forehead never moved. "That's the security locker. You shouldn't have access to that. Where's Harold?"

"He left early to watch his daughter's soccer game." Abigail said.

I assumed Harold to be the head of security, or possibly the maintenance supervisor.

The woman snorted. "Always an excuse with that one," she said. "As if the act of having children was some sort of free pass to get out of work. Not like Richard here." She smiled down at the man beside her. "Why, if left to his own devices, he'd worked his fingers down to the bone, wouldn't you Richard?"

Richard dropped his eyes, giving a single nod after a moment.

"That's a good boy, isn't it?" she said.

Beside me, Abigail's mouth tightened into a thin line, knuckles whitening on the clipboard.

"We already finished the initial counts," she said. "I'm just double checking the oxygen levels."

"I see," the woman said. "And you? Civilians are not usually allowed in here."

"I——"

"He works in the community ma'am," Abigail said. "Marcus Aries, this is Miranda Sakks, chief administrator of Sea Life Park."

"Hello," I said.

"Charmed," Mrs. Sakks said.

Abigail continued. "Mr. Aries has approached us about arranging a field trip next month."

"A field trip," Mrs. Sakks said. "More children. Won't that be...lovely."

She said the word lovely the same way you might say roadkill. Something unpleasant to think about, much less be near.

"Well, I'm afraid I must be going," she said. "See to it that you lock up securely before you leave. And in the future, inform Harold that I expect him to complete all tasks prior to leaving work."

"Yes, ma'am," Abigail said.

Flashing a cold smile, the woman turned and made her way out. The man, Richard, turned and lumbered off after her a moment later. Abigail waited for them to leave, then closed and locked the door behind them.

"That was too close," she said.

"No kidding," I said. "Who the hell is that?"

"Miranda Sakks," she said. "She's an evil bitch."

"You can say that again," I said. "And who was that guy—"

Abigail's eyes flashed, and she moved faster than I would have expected. Grabbing hold of my shirt, she jerked me close, leaning in until our faces were only inches apart. "Shut your mouth!" she said.

I blinked and stared at her. After a moment, she sighed and released her grip, all the anger leaking out of her.

"Sorry," she said. "It's just that Rich used to work here. He was a trainer, like me. There was an accident. They were able to resuscitate him, but…"

"Gotcha," I said. "Now that that's been made clear, would you mind telling me what this is all about?"

"I can do better than that," she said.

Slipping past me, she swung open the locker door, rummaging around for a moment, before withdrawing a heavy shotgun equipped with an olive-green shoulder sling and a folding stock. Shoving it down inside her duffel bag, she drew up the zipper before slinging it up over her shoulder. Motioning for me to follow, she headed towards the doorway.

"Come on," she said. "I'll introduce you to the kids."

σ σ σ

The "kids" turned out to be a trio of baby dolphins.

Roughly two and a half feet long and right around fifteen pounds each, the two females were light grey in color, their brother a darker shade of charcoal.

And they were cute.

Damn cute, if I was being honest.

But they were also afraid.

Hovering together, the two females remained closely bound, never more than a few feet from each other or the center of their tank. Their brother, on the other hand, came and went sporadically, shooting out to swim along the edge of the pool before zipping back to the safety of his pod, his agitation clear to see.

"*Stenella Longirostris*," Abigail said from beside me. She'd led me outside the building to the practice pools, then down the long ramp to a small, circular tank housing the trio. "More commonly known as Hawaiian spinner dolphins."

"I didn't know they would be so small," I said.

"They usually aren't," she said. "Dolphins typically give birth to a single offspring. Twins are rare, and triplets are virtually unheard of. But…"

"There they are," I said.

She nodded. "There they are."

"And you call them the kids?"

Her voice grew soft. "They're my kids."

"And you think something's trying to hurt them?"

Her face tightened. "I don't think, Mr. Aries. I know."

"How?"

"Because this is what I do," she said. "It's what I've spent my whole life doing. People don't realize it, but dolphins are more similar to us than you'd think. They're mammals. They breathe, they play, they love, and they feel fear. What you're seeing right now, that's fear Mr. Aries. They're terrified."

"Of what?"

She shook her head. "I don't know exactly, but two nights ago, something attacked them. See the way they're hovering near the center of the tank? That isn't normal behavior. They're afraid of getting too close to the edge."

"What about the male?" I asked.

"He's calling for his mom," she said. "Daphne."

"Where's she?"

"Gone," she said. "Airlifted over to the aquarium on Waikiki for medical treatment."

"She got hurt?"

Abigail nodded.

"Bad?"

Another nod. "Whatever came after the kids didn't count on Daphne, but dolphins are fiercely protective of their young. She defended them, but it nearly killed her."

I was quiet for a long moment. "What do the other trainers think of this?"

"They know something's not right, but they won't say anything. Miranda fed them some bullshit story about how the Finley must have gotten too rough while nursing."

I raised an eyebrow. "Finley?"

"The boy. Olivia and Clara are his sisters."

I grunted, taking a moment to gather my thoughts. Experience told me that Abigail believed what she was saying to be true, but it didn't tell me why. There were plenty of supernatural predators out there that would have relished feeding on a juvenile dolphin, but few would have expended the effort necessary to make their way into the park to do so. There were plenty of dolphins roaming the surrounding coastal waters, so what made these three special?

I didn't have an answer, which worried me more than I cared to admit.

"When do you think the next attack might come?" I asked.

Abigail opened her mouth to respond, but at that moment, the loud speakers overhead came to life, and a pre-recorded message rang out.

"Good evening ladies and gentleman. We hope that you have enjoyed your time here today, and regret to inform you that Sea Life Park Hawaii is now closed for the evening. We will reopen tomorrow morning promptly at eight o'clock. Here's wishing you a wonderful rest of your day, and we sincerely hope you will come back soon."

Turning, Abigail lifted her bag from the floor, bringing it around over one shoulder. "Got any plans for the rest of the evening?" she asked.

σ σ σ

I didn't, actually.

My wife was currently out of town. Her mother had taken her and her sister to the nearby island of Kauai for a spa-filled weekend. Husbands, of which I was the only one, were pointedly not invited. It was fortuitous in its own way, because it meant that I was free to stand watch over the tiny trio with Abigail.

So that's what I did.

The tourists and visitors emptied out shortly after the closing announcements, followed by the cashiers, and staff attendants. The park employed a lone nighttime security guard, but Abigail had offered him the night off and he'd leapt at the chance. Shortly after sundown, she disappeared into the locker rooms, emerging a few minutes later with a couple of bottled waters and some power bars. I helped myself to a peanut butter swirl. It tasted like a mixture of stale cheerios and plywood, but I was able to swallow it down with aid of some water before politely declining the second.

"So, do you do this often?" Abigail asked. We were sitting atop folding lawn chairs, perched not ten feet from the dolphin's tank.

"Sit out on a dolphin stakeout? Not so much."

"You know what I mean."

"Yeah," I said. "Every once in a while."

"How did you get into this sort of thing?"

I shrugged. "The same way you get into anything I suppose. A little bit of talent and a whole lot of training. What about you? How does one become a dolphin trainer exactly?"

She thought about it, then shrugged. "Talent and training."

"Amen" I said, lifting my water bottle in mock salute.

"It's more complicated than most people think, you know."

"Oh?"

She nodded. "Most trainers have some sort of life science degree. Marine biology being the most common."

"Makes sense."

"But that's only the first step. Next you have to get scuba certified, along with CPR and first aid. Then you have to train swimming. And after all that, you still have to gather enough experience to be considered trustworthy. Honestly, it's more of a calling than a job."

"I can relate," I said.

She glanced over to see if I was mocking her, but decided after a moment that I wasn't. "What I don't understand is why?"

"Why what?" I asked, though I had a pretty good idea what the answer was.

"Why would something do this?" she asked. "I mean, I understand the law of the wild. Freshly born prey is easier to hunt and take down, and Lord knows there are plenty of things that hunt dolphins, but not like this. I can't think of a single animal native to the island that would have done this."

"Is that what you told Elias?"

She shrugged. "Alibi's Lounge is an old favorite. Rich and I used to go there, before his accident. I hadn't been there for some time, but when I saw Elias, the whole story came spilling out over a few beers. That's when he said he might know someone who can help."

"I'm guessing that's when he came to see me?"

She nodded. "I think he hoped you might be able to figure out what was going on. Why something would want to hurt three innocent calves."

I considered it for a moment, taking my time. "Someone once told me that dolphins were the heart of the ocean," I said. "The embodiment of its spirit, made flesh."

"Who said that?" she asked.

"A fisherman," I said.

She thought about it for a moment before nodding. "I can see it."

"I can too,' I said, raising my water bottle. "To dolphins."

"To dolphins," she said, leaning forward to return my salute.

The moment our bottles touched, the lights went out.

Darkness came on rapidly, enfolding us in its embrace. Beside me, Abigail let out a startled curse, dropping her water bottle down onto the deck as she grabbed for her duffel bag. A string of furious curses slipped from her lips as she torn the zipper down, withdrawing the shotgun from between its folds. Chamber a round, the metallic ring echoed through the empty deck.

Rising from my chair, I let out a slow breath. I couldn't see, but I could hear, and what I heard was... nothing.

There was some ambient traffic noise echoing out from the nearby roadway, but nothing immediate, and nothing threatening. Abigail stood stiff beside me, evidently coming to a similar conclusion.

"Could it be a power outage?" I asked.

She didn't answer right away. Gripping the shotgun with one hand, she reached down into her pocket, withdrawing a small cylinder flashlight. The light flicked to life, its golden beam reflecting off the pools darkened waters to reveal three tiny figures moving beneath the surface.

"It's possible," she said. "There's a breaker in the utility room. Might be I could reset it."

I considered it for a moment, debating the pros and cons of splitting up before making my decision.

"Go," I said.

"I'm not leaving the kids here unprotected!"

"You won't be," I said. "I'll stay here and keep watch over them."

"And what happens if something shows up looking for them?" she asked. "What are you going to use, harsh language?"

"Oh, nice one," I said, in reference to her reference. "Look, if it's just a tripped circuit, you can get the power back on in a quarter of the time it would take me. Otherwise, we're just going to sit here in the dark, and that's not going to be good for anyone. Trust me."

She struggled for a handful of seconds before letting out a reluctant growl. "Alright," she said. "I'll go. Give me five minutes."

Gripping the flashlight and the shotgun, she started off, moving across the deck and up the long ramp towards the employee building. I waited until she'd disappeared from sight before drawing in a slow breath and bringing my inner spirit into focus. The power of the human spirit, mana, rose up within me, heralded by a soft blue light sweeping up the length of my body, illuminating the surrounding area.

Martial arts, true martial arts, is all about intention. It's a merging of mind, spirit, and body. Standing there, I held my hands out in front of me, fingers attuned to the surrounding energies, searching for any ambient vibrations that might warn me as to the presence of any supernatural predator.

A long moment passed before I felt it.

A slight tremor, just on the edge of perception, like a spider slipping down the strands of invisible webbing. Nearly imperceptible. Had I not been so focused I likely would have missed it, for it disappeared as soon as I'd noticed, almost as if it had felt my presence.

Seconds passed.

One Mississippi.

97 σ Realms of Fantastic Stories Vol. 2

Two Mississippi.

A scream broke the night before I got to three, followed by the sound of broken glass and punctuated by the roar of a shotgun. The blast echoed through the night, and I felt a lance of fear stab into my chest.

Abigail.

I remained frozen for a subjective eternity, wrestling with the dilemma of leaving the baby calves undefended against the desire to help with whatever it was that might be attacking Abigail. In the end, it was a second shotgun blast that made my decision for me. Whatever this thing was, it wasn't out here. It was inside, and Abigail was facing it alone.

Drawing in my focus, I took off, racing across the pool deck and over the long ramp. As I ran, I drew in my inner spirit, bringing all my will and focus to bear, drawing my energy around me like a protective cloak as I sprinted towards the building. I knew from having been there earlier that the doorway was on the eastern edge of the building, but I also knew that time was of the essence. Drawing in a heavy breath, I willed my body to be as hard as stone, my fists as mighty as battering rams. My skin began to tingle an instant before I leapt into the air. Drawing back my arm, a loud scream ripped out past my mouth an instant before I brought my arm forward, slamming my fist into the side of the building.

Wood and stone cracked, drywall and plaster shattering into a haze of thin, chalky dust. The side of the room imploded, the momentum from my jump carrying me through into what turned out to be an employee break room. Landing, I wasted no time, sprinting across the length of the room and into the hallway. Once there, a quick glance to my right revealed the utility room. Racing forward, I skidded into the room just in time to catch sight of two figures.

The first was Rich. Still dressed in his blue coveralls, the former trainer's mouth worked soundlessly, his mop drawn into a defensive stance. Abigail lay on the floor by his feet, unconscious, her shotgun not five feet away, expelled red shells lining the space around her.

Anger flared inside, wisps of red rising up to dance amongst the blue aura surrounding me. Setting my feet, I drew my arms back, preparing to strike.

"Get away from her you bastard!" I screamed.

Rich's eyes widened, and a wordless cry ripped out past his lips in the same moment that a couple of things dawned on me.

Firstly, there were no signs of the shotgun blasts inside the utility room, meaning they'd most likely been expelled out into the hallway from which I'd just entered. Secondly, Rich had his mop held lengthwise across his body in a *defense* stance, as opposed to an aggressive one.

Realization dawned in the instant before something leapt out of the shadows behind me. I started to turn, but something long and black cracked against the back of my skull, and I felt my feet leave the ground an instant before darkness overtook me.

σ σ σ

I woke up to Rich smacking my face.

"Up, up, up," he said. Gripping the mop by the handle, he slapped the dried cotton strands against my face over and over again, casting fervent glances over towards where Abigail lay.

"Augh," I said, waving him away. My head was pounding, my mouth dry. The lights were back on overhead, the fluorescent bulbs burning my eyes with painful clarity.

Retreating backwards, Rich drew back beside Abigail, motioning impatiently.

Realization came back with painful slowness, as I rolled over onto my stomach. Crawling forward, I came to a halt beside her, bringing one finger up underneath her throat. Her pulse was steady, but beneath my hand, blood lined the cement floor, not yet dry. Sucking in a soft breath, I gently turned her head towards me, running my fingers along the base of her skull until I found the cut. It was on the left side, halfway past the midpoint, just above her ear.

"Rich, I need your help," I said.

Rich stared at me, wide-eyed. Extending my opposite hand out, I took his wrist, guiding his hands over to the scalp wound.

"Hold tight," I said.

"Tight," he said.

I wasn't sure if he fully understood what I was saying or not, but he kept his hands in place, blood leaking through the space between his fingers. I swallowed, and shook my head, reminding myself that scalp wounds were the worst for bleeding. Shifting my hips, I reached down, searching through Abigail's pockets until I located her cell phone. I didn't know her passcode, so I pressed the emergency button and dialed 9-1-1.

A female dispatcher came on the line, and I informed her that we had an accident at the park. She clearly wanted me to remain on the line until the ambulance arrived, but a little voice in my head whispered that I couldn't spare the time. Dropping the phone down beside me, I searched around for some sort of towel, but there was nothing near at hand. Mouth tightening, I pulled my shirt off over my head, wrapping it around Abigail's head in a makeshift effort to slow the bleeding.

"Rich," I said, "I need to check on the dolphins. I want you to stay with her. Can you do that?"

"Stay," Rich said, nodding.

"That's right," I said.

Rising to my feet, I made my way back into the hall, then through the broken section of wall and out onto the pool deck. Crossing over the ramp, a part of me already knew what I would find, but I still felt a sharp stab of dismay when I arrived at the dolphin's tank to find it empty.

"Dammit," I said.

The kids were gone.

σ σ σ

The way I saw it, I had three choices.

Choice number one: I could stay here, assist the paramedics, and wait until Abigail woke to give her the bad news. Choice number two: I could call the police and report a dolphin-napping. I had some contacts in the police department, a couple of people who knew me well enough to believe what I told them was the truth. But then what? Once I brought in the authorities, it would all be out of my hands. I had no doubt that they would take a report, but I was pretty sure there was no standard operating procedure regarding the search and rescue of kidnapped marine life. It might be months before we found them, if ever.

Choice number three: I could get them back. Tonight. Now. They were still alive. At least I hoped so. Glancing into the pool, I saw no evidence of blood, which meant that something had taken them more or less uninjured. Which meant they'd taken them for a reason. Which meant I still had time.

But how?

I'd already concluded that the mortal authorities couldn't assist me, and there was no such thing, at least to the best of my knowledge, as a supernatural police force.

That being said… there was someone who might be able to help me.

It was a long shot, but if I could find him, he might be able to point me in the right direction. As luck would have it, I thought I knew where to start looking.

σ σ σ

Located on the southern eastern shore of Oahu, Halona Beach Cove was a small little stretch of sand surrounded by steep cliffs on three sides. It was no different than a hundred other spots on the island, save that Hollywood had filmed a movie here—*From Here to Eternity*—back in the fifties. Ever since, the little cove had been nicknamed Eternity Beach.

Parking at the edge of the lookout, I made my way on foot down the sharp, black rocks to the soft sand below. The water was relatively calm at this time of the night, and the full-moon overhead helped to illuminate the hunched figure sitting on the shore's edge.

Standing four feet tall, with a sloped, rounded body and wide, amphibian eyes the color of green fire, Darwin's skin was the color of driftwood, spotted with pearl and drooping at the jowls. Twisting, he inclined his head slightly as I approached, motioning for me to join him. Nodding my thanks, I kicked my shoes off, pushing them aside before lowering myself down into the sand beside him.

"Aries," he said. His voice was rich with the taste of the ocean, his words emanating out through a soft mist.

"Darwin," I said. "I trust you're well?"

He nodded, pearl lips splitting apart into a pleased smile. "The ocean sings tonight, the waves smooth. It is a good night."

"Not for everyone," I said. "I need your help."

"Help?" he said. "One of mine?"

I shook my head. "No. Nothing to do with the Gillispaw. At least not directly."

"Then, why?"

I drew in a deep breath. Then I laid it all out, bringing him up to speed regarding the trio of dolphins. "My only chance is to find them before whoever took them can complete whatever it is they're planning," I said. "I don't have much time."

Darwin hadn't said anything during my entire speech. Starring down, he slowly lifted one webbed hand, gently running his fingers through the soft white sand. "Dangerous."

"I know," I said.

He wasn't talking about just the dolphins. Supernatural beings placed great store in minding one's own business. To give aide was to become involved. That said, he was my only hope. The Gillispaw were among the more docile of supernatural creatures. They were nomads, fish herders, and as such, highly attuned to the surrounding ocean. If there was something happening in the nearby waterways, they would know about it.

"Growing old gives one new perspective on life," Darwin said, a gentle stream of bubbles sounding in his throat. "Learn to appreciate new life. Learn just how precious the young can be."

I nodded, but didn't say anything. I'd given him all the information I had. Any decision he made from this point on would have to come from him. It would have been wrong of me to try and coerce him further.

A full minute passed before he spoke up. "Manana Island," he said. "Were I in your position, I would begin my search there."

A sigh of relief slipped past my lips. "Thank you, Darwin."

He nodded, but there was a sadness to it. "Careful."

I nodded, rising from the sand. Collecting my shoes, I headed back towards the car. I had the place. Now all I needed was a boat.

σ σ σ

One plus side of teaching martial arts for a living is that you meet people from all walks of life. My students ranged from construction workers, gardeners, bankers, and even cafeteria ladies. You train people, and over time, come to learn about their lives. For example, I knew of at least three people off the top of my head that owned boats, and was pretty sure I could scrounge up a few more if necessary. Racing back to the school, I took to the phone. The first two students didn't answer, but the third did. He sounded like he was a few beers in already, but he offered to loan me his boat quickly enough when I asked. Driving over there, I found him sitting in the driveway. Accepting the keys, I thanked him profusely before heading down to the Ala Wai Harbor.

The largest small boat harbor on Oahu, the place was quiet at this time of night. Finding the right dock, I brought the tiny boat to life, heading out into open waters. Once I was clear of the harbor, I gunned the throttle, heading east and up around the island to where Manana Island lay.

A tiny islet off the eastern coast, Manana Island was almost a straight shot north from the Sea Life Park. In other words, it was an ideal location for someone who'd just kidnapped a trio of dolphins and didn't want to risk moving them too far.

Easing back on the throttle, I guided the boat onto the beach's edge, berthing it between a pair of volcanic rocks. Leaping onto the shore, I wasted no time, making my way up the steep ridge. Half a mile wide and shaped like a tuff cone, it didn't take long before I spotted a small clearing near the bottom of the western crater.

I'd read somewhere that the islet had been converted into a state bird sanctuary, but the night's sky was deadly quiet as I made my way down the steep rocky wall. Reaching the bottom, the low brush grew increasingly thick, catching my legs and feet as I struggled forward. I was maybe a hundred feet from the clearing when I realized that it wasn't the bushes grabbing for me,

It was webs.

Spider webs to be precise.

Silver strands, roughly the same thickness as fishing line, they blanketed the surrounding area like a heavy plush rug, pulling at me with every step.

Gritting my teeth, I summoned my inner spirit. A bright blue light sprang up around me, illuminating the complex web. Turning my focus inwards, I drew more and more, watching the strands burn away under the heat of my aura. Pushing forward, I left a clear path in my wake, burned webbing pointing the way as I drew up close enough to see a wooden pavilion located in the middle of the clearing.

Build in an open-air gazebo style, cobwebs lined the rooftop corners, the wooden floor wrapping around a small, Jacuzzi sized pool in the middle of the gazebo. Three small bundles dangled from the roof, suspended five feet above the pool. Wrapped completely in spider webs, the full moon overhead allowed me to estimate their size to be that of the dolphin trio. My gut whispered that I was in the right place.

Stepping forward, I made my way up a trio of steps before purposely bringing my foot down atop the gazebo's edge. The minute my foot touched the wood, the shadows off to my left shifted, a petite figure dropping down to the floor.

"Hello Jiji," I said.

The petite girl I'd crashed into back at the water park was dressed in a midnight black wetsuit, the back unzipped to reveal ridged skin beneath. Dropping to the floor, she slid gracefully into a standing position, her movements soft and smooth.

"You knew?" she asked, her voice a mixture of surprise and skepticism.

"I figured it out on the way over," I said.

"I'm surprised," she said, drifting to her right. "I thought Mrs. Sakks a much more likely suspect."

"She might have been, had we not crossed paths earlier."

"What gave it away?"

"You did," I said, matching each step she took. "I saw you wincing when I helped you to your feet. I didn't think anything of it at the time, but something tells me that underneath the suit, you're probably a mass of bruises."

She barred her teeth. "A temporary discomfort."

I snorted. "Daphne really thrashed you huh?"

"Ignorant beast."

"She's a mom," I said. "And mothers protect their children."

Reaching up, she grabbed hold of the nearest pillar, leaping into the air and spinning halfway up its length. "It makes no difference. Her spawn belongs to me now."

"Like hell they do," I said. "What is that you want them for anyway?"

"They are to be a gift," she said. "For the one who sired me."

I was quiet for a long moment. Then I said, "You're a Jorōgumo, aren't you?"

She let out a pleased sound. "Very astute mortal."

I grunted. Jorōgumo were supernatural creature hailing from Japan. Spiders in the shape of women, known for seducing men and then devouring them.

"What would a spider want with a trio of baby dolphins?" I asked. "After all, I thought you said they were nothing more than ignorant beasts?"

"For the moment," she said. "But that can be easily amended. You said so yourself, they represent the heart of the ocean, and as such, will make a fine gift."

"Wouldn't your sire rather have a lei? Or maybe a refrigerator magnet?"

She smiled, revealing sharp canines. "I have thirty-seven brothers and sisters to contend with," she said. "Sibling rivalry can be a rather tense affair, as I'm sure you understand. My sire demands unique expressions of affection, and can be most harsh on those who fail to deliver."

"Well, in that case, you might want to postpone your trip home," I said. "Cause there's no way in hell I'm going to let you hurt those dolphins."

"Let me?" she asked, sliding further up the column. "Foolish mortal, what makes you think you can stop me?"

"Try me and find out," I said. "The way I see it, you've got two choices. You can either beat it out of here and hope the plane home has SkyMall, or you can stay, in which case I'm going to force feed you your own webbing. Your choice."

"Perhaps I will present you alongside the trio. An amusement for my siblings to feast upon!" With a scream, she leapt from the pillar, arms stretched out towards me. As she cut through the air, her figure changed, the flesh of her back splitting open to reveal six dark, hairy arachnid legs.

Fear shot through me, and I drew in my inner spirit, the fierce blue glow springing up around me an instant before I brought my fist around in a looping uppercut. Light flashed, and a sound like thunder echoed out as my knuckled impacted against her chin. Jiji's head snapped back, and a cry of pain tore past her lips as she flipped backwards into the air. Completing the somersault, she recovered quickly, landing on the gazebo's floor and springing right back towards me.

Thankfully, I've had more than a little experience dealing with supernatural predators. Rule number one, never stand where they expect you to be. The moment my knuckles met flesh, I threw myself to the side, rolling once and coming up to my feet just as she landed.

Twisting on a dime, she righted herself, springing forward. Moving to dodge, my heel caught on a small strand of webbing. It wasn't much, but it slowed me down just enough that her thick, hairy leg struck me high up on the shoulder.

Pain exploded down the right side of my body, and I crashed to the floor, feeling my breath expel. Warnings began sounding in my head, and even though I was only out for a second, it was enough.

Cutting through the air, Jiji landed atop on my chest, raking at my face with long, black fingernails. Lines of fire took form even as I brought my arms up, catching her underneath the chin.

I was bigger than her, stronger, but I only had two arms, whereas she had eight.

Not good odds, and it showed.

Her spider limbs swept around, catching my wrists and pinning them to the floor. A pleased sound slipped out past her lips as she leaned forward, her face only inches from mine.

"Now that I think on it, perhaps I'll keep you for myself," she said, her breath washing over me. "I am old enough to birth my own young. Perhaps, after I've used you for your seed, I will watch as my children devour you. Yes, I think that would be a fitting end to a brave, foolish mortal."

"Never going to happen," I said through gritted teeth. "You know why?"

"Tell me."

"Because spiders are solitary creatures," I said. "Whereas mortals aren't. When the chips are down and things get bleak, we look for help from our friends."

Jiji blinked, her confusion lasting right up until the moment she heard Abigail rack the shotgun chamber behind her. Snapping her head to the side, she had a perfect angle to see the dolphin trainer as she stepped onto the gazebo platform and took aim.

"Get away from him, you bitch!" Abigail snarled an instant before she fired.

The side of Jiji's head exploded, blood, brains, and gore erupting outwards to cover the gazebo. Still positioned atop me, her form went limp, and a relieved exhalation slipped out past my lips as I rolled her off and rose up to my feet.

σ σ σ

Abigail took the dolphins back to the Sea Life Water Park. Turns out she'd refused medical attention, going instead to my school, where she'd broken inside and proceeded to star-sixty-nine the last three telephone numbers I'd called, eventually getting hold of the student who'd loaned me the boat. From there she'd returned to Sea Life Park and commandeered one of their vessels, circling the island until she spotted the boat. Upon making berth, she'd followed my trail through the spider webs to the clearing and the gazebo.

After she was gone, Darwin helped me clean up Jiji's remains, promising to dispose of them far enough out that they wouldn't accidently wash up onto shore. Once that was finished, I set fire to the gazebo, watching from a distance until it burned itself out.

Then I left.

The sun was beginning to rise as I pulled into the Ala Wai Harbor. Tethering the vessel, I made my way over to the school, duct taping the window Abigail had broken to get inside before heading home to sleep. Later that night, I got a call from Elias, inviting me to Alibi's Lounge for a drink.

A pale green building with dark tinted windows and a Spanish cedar bar, I walked in to find Abigail waiting for me already. Siding up beside her, I ordered a beer before inquiring about the kids.

"They're okay," she said. "I talked to the chief veterinarian at the aquarium. Daphne is scheduled to be transported back in two days."

"Good," I said. "Kids need a mom."

"They'll have one," she said.

Shifting in her seat, she glanced up as Elias appeared, holding a trio of bottles in his hand.

"I hear you did good," he said, placing the bottles down in front of us.

"Better than good," Abigail said. Taking her bottle, she held it up salute. "Here's to Marcus Aries, defender of spinner dolphins and bane of spidery bitches!"

"Here, here," Elias said, raising his own bottle.

Clinking my bottle mouth against theirs, I felt a low blush rise up in my cheeks, but a smile split my face that lasted the rest of the evening.

Destination Bermuda

K.A. Meng

Week One
Pilot

"I'm Alexandra Porter, the daughter of explorer, Dax Porter, who vanished six months ago. In dedication to my father, we're continuing his research by solving the mystery of the Bermuda Triangle," I said from the deck on the expedition vessel.

"Cut," the director yelled for the twentieth time.

"What's wrong with this take?" The muscles in my face ached from the smiling I was forced to do. How many more times did I have to redo each scene until it was Mr. Carter perfect?

"The tears in your eyes smudged your mascara. Makeup! Get someone over here." He glanced at me through the glasses on the bridge of his nose.

I didn't know I was crying. Reaching up, I wiped the evidence away. Couldn't he give me a break? This was my first time hosting a show.

My father was the big reality TV star and brought me on set before I could walk. At eighteen, I left my old life behind for college. Now, here I was three years later, trying to prove I could do what he did and failing miserably at it.

"You'll be okay," Gisela Brace said. In one hand, she carried a big concealer brush and in the other a large dark bag. Besides makeup, she had crystals inside the container.

"Did your spirit guides tell you that?" I asked. My father swore she was a gifted medium. I wanted to see her abilities for myself. She was the paranormal expert to prove or disprove our theories.

The network executives paid for an expensive cast, including a theoretical physicist, a weatherman, and an astronomer. If I didn't produce ratings, the show would be canceled, and I might never see my father again.

"You're a strong girl. You'll get through this," Gisela said. Her smile widened, showing her pearly white teeth except for the one in front tinged yellow. "Remember, you're here to find your father; the show comes second."

"I'm ready," I said to everyone. It was time for me to leave the scared girl behind. I dug my fingernails into my palm and cleared my throat.

"Good girl." Gisela fixed the smear in my mascara and stepped away.

Resuming my position in front of the camera, I rattled off my lines again. My heart beat wildly, and everyone turned the director, Carter Carter. What kind of parents gave their child the same first and last name?

"Scene change," he hollered. The rest of us breathed a sigh of relief.

We hoisted the anchor and the motor revved. After a couple nautical miles, we were at the next location. Dark waves rocked the boat, and only a single cloud marred the blue sky. The view was incredible, breathtaking.

"Three, two, one," said the conspiracy expert Jameson Rayz, who also held the clapperboard. He lifted the clapper, set it back down, and shuffled off camera. We worked as the film crew too.

"Despite the tranquil Atlantic Ocean behind me, we've entered the most dangerous place on Earth, the Devil's Triangle," I said, pausing for dramatic effect. "Welcome to Destination Bermuda."

"I didn't care for the ad lib," Carter said. He tightened his hold on a rolled script and waved it around. "I must admit you're finally acting like Dax Porter's kid. Keep it up, but nix anything not written here."

"Yes, sir. Will we be redoing the scene, sir?" My tone was filled with sarcasm. I stood at attention and even saluted the man. I wasn't a child; I was twenty-one years old. Jerk.

"No, what you said works better. You'll be interviewing our two professionals on why this place is special." He removed his glasses and wiped mist off the lens.

"We need to talk about the mechanical failures first," Dr. Waldo Krewal insisted. The boom mic he held fell onto the deck with a thud.

"Don't be ridiculous. Everyone knows aliens created the Bermuda Triangle," Rayz said.

"Is there something wrong with you? Aliens don't exist. I can't have a theory that isn't real on my show. I'll look like a laughing stock in front of my fellow scientists." Dr. K's face turned as red as a tomato.

Rayz's rebuttal was lost as I tuned them out. They had been arguing since everyone met on dry land, a week ago. Putting the Bermuda Triangle, the B.T., expert together with the biggest conspiracist in the world was not the smartest idea. With their opposite views, one scientific and one just bat shit crazy, they fought a lot.

"Alexandra will interview Dr. Krewal first," director follow-the-rules decided after the yelling died down.

"Dearie me, where do we begin?" Dr. K asked, stepping forward with a smug look on his skinny face. He picked up the boom mic and handed it to his nemesis. "We can start with the newest theory of underwater gas explosions or perhaps the issues with compasses."

"Ours are fine," Rayz, the owner of the website Conspiracy Daily, said. Saying the ideas on his site were nuts didn't do them justice. He claimed the government created purple elephants to confuse the locals when they invaded Grenada in 1983. Give me a break.

"Don't worry, Jameson. You'll get your turn later," Carter promised.

"How about we discuss issues with compasses since the collaborating specialist for gasses won't arrive until later?" I suggested. I blew a strand of raven hair out of my face. This would be a long day.

"Good show," Dr. K said. He smiled and pulled out a compass from his breast pocket. A long pause followed as he stared at the gadget. His brow scrunched up as he shook it and tapped on it.

The rest of us glanced at each other. Something wasn't right with his compass. The director motioned at the cameraman to begin rolling. He gave me the signal to speak.

"I'm here with Dr. Waldo Krewal, the leading expert on the Bermuda Triangle. What's one of the theories for people disappearing in this mysterious location?" I asked him.

"Compasses. In the Bermuda Triangle, they don't work, and mine is acting strange," he answered.

I glanced at the compass. The needle spun around, trying to locate the magnetic field. I stepped out of the way so the cameraman could get the shot. Why wasn't it working? Did the same thing happen to my father's?

"Does the steering compass have the same problem?" Krewal asked, glancing at me.

"I don't know, but we should go see," I answered. Our feet pounded on the hard wood deck as we sprinted the seventy meters. My pulse quickened and adrenaline filled my veins. My father loved doing reality shows because they were a rush.

The ladder slowed us. I climbed to the fourth level and waited for everyone. My frustration mounted. This could explain why my father, an experienced seaman, was lost. As soon as the cameraman readjusted his equipment, we burst through the bridge doors. I ran over to the large domed instrument. Peering down at the compass, the needle pointed true. My heart felt like it shrank ten millimeters, and my stomach clenched.

"Where's the fire?" the captain asked.

"Dr. Krewal's compass isn't working. We came up here to check on this one," I answered.

"There are many reasons why navigational devices have issues here." He motioned for the object and Dr. K. handed it over. After a quick glance, the captain gave it back.

"What do you think?" I asked him.

"To start, you need to know the difference between true north and magnetic north."

"Hold on, we should film this," Director Carter said in between breaths. He grasped his sides. The little jaunt we did must be the most running he had done in weeks.

The crew moved out of the way, except for the captain and me. The cameraman gave us the thumps up.

"Can you tell us the difference between true north and magnetic north?" I asked the captain, after introducing him.

"The first is the geographic North Pole. The other is the magnetic north where the compasses point. The distance between these two points is over one thousand kilometers," he explained. We continued the interview, and he listed off several ways navigation devices could act up while I demonstrated them on camera. The conclusion for Dr. K's was simple, it gave a faulty reading. My father always kept his equipment in perfect working condition. A malfunctioning compass wasn't the reason behind his disappearance.

Our group returned to the stern, except for the captain. We cleaned up the small mess we left behind in our haste. After we were in position, Director Carter motioned for the interview to start again.

"Dr. Krewal, can you tell us what the other scientific explanations are for the Bermuda Triangle?" I asked him once the clapperboard was out of the shot. The wind whipped my hair around my face.

"As you can see, the weather could be a factor. Storms, typhoons, or rogue waves," he answered.

"What else is there?"

"The Gulf Stream, methane hydrate, a mascon, or plan old human error could be the cause of the missing ships and planes."

"Cut! We should talk about the atmospheric conditions," the director said.

"Shouldn't I speak to our weatherman about the storms?" I asked to get out of this line of questioning. He was my least favorite person right now. I wouldn't have time for the captain with the other two interviews left.

Carter rubbed his jaw and his grip tightened around the script. My idea wasn't in there, but it was good because we wouldn't waste the little daylight we had. This was his first directing project. The guy never left his lab.

"I do know about the violent weather patterns found in this area," Dr. K said, trying to be helpful.

"We should leave the talk to the expert," I said. My voice was even and I plastered a grin on my face. I wanted to kick the good doctor in his shins for his unwarranted comment.

"We'll wait for the weatherman," Carter decided after five long minutes.

I breathed a sigh of relief and turned to my interviewee, asking, "Are you ready?"

"Whenever the cameraman is," Dr. K answered. We turned to the younger guy, and he gave us a thumbs up. Most of his face was buried behind the lens.

"Dr. Krewal, what is a mascon?"

"A denser material below a mass causes an increase in the gravitational pull. A boat or a ship could be trapped inside and sink within seconds. I can show you what I mean."

"Sure, the viewers at home would love to see a demonstration."

Dr. K left and returned with a glass of water. He placed a crumpled piece of aluminum foil into his cup. The objected floated on the top until his finger forced the small ball to submerge.

"The increase in gravity wouldn't come from my finger. It would come from below," he said, knocking the bottom of the glass.

I lost the ability to speak, thinking about how a mascon could have taken my father. Without any warning, his boat would be on the seafloor. This could explain why he didn't send an SOS.

"What are the signs a mascon has happened?" I asked once I found my voice. My throat was thick and a pain developed inside my chest.

"If the event was on the ocean, we'll never know unless we find the wreckage or big waves."

"Thank you for your time." Tears formed in my eyes. I stared out at the water while I worked to compose myself as the conspiracist took his position.

"Here you go," Rayz said. He handed his clapperboard and the boom mic to Dr. K. With his chest puffed out, he joined me at the rail.

"Jameson Rayz, what are the paranormal theories behind the B.T.?" I asked him.

"The biggest one is aliens. With their advanced technology, they could take boat or an airplane." He bounced on one foot to the other, and his muddy eyes sparkled with excitement.

"What else?"

"Ghosts could cause issues out here. The city of Atlantis would not want visitors. A rip in the space time continuum could cause a vessel to sail or fly right into it, never to be seen again."

We talked more about his theories. When we finished, the horizon was red and orange. I needed to do one more thing before the crew of the *Tranquil Seas* finished for the day.

"For you viewers at home, we'll do something that has never been done on television," I said. Taking a deep breath, I imagined the web address flashing on the screen. "You'll decide what we'll investigate next from the information we presented today. The poll with the top ten theories of the Bermuda Triangle is on this screen now and on our website. The voting will remain there for the next twenty-four hours."

I already knew what America would decide. The reason was everywhere: TV shows, movies, books, and social media. If they wanted something else, I would be surprised.

Week Two
Searching

The next morning, Carter didn't look too good at breakfast. A shine of sweat appeared on his forehead, and his cheeks were a little green. The rocking of the boat had worsened overnight. He went to bed until his body adjusted to the motion.

By the time the sun was high in the sky, everyone dropped off with seasickness, except for the captain and me. The urge to grab a jet ski to search for my father was strong, but instead, I held back, helping my crew. In between plotting my dad's last known location against ours, I brought them bottles of water to keep them hydrated throughout the day. I refused to clean their vomit. They stayed in bed, which worked for our schedule. Our episode didn't air until later in the week.

On the following day, I cooked a light breakfast for everyone. My father made sure I could create an edible meal, sew, and change a tire before I left home. He also taught me to navigate treacherous storms, suck venom from a bite, and read hieroglyphics, among other things. In a big city, those other skills weren't useful.

"Morning," Carter grumbled as he walked into the mess hall. His hair was tousled and some of the color had returned to his face. He poured himself a cup of coffee.

"You need to eat something," I told him, setting a tray with broth, crackers, and a bottle of water in front of him. The perfect meal for those with an upset stomach.

"I can't." Pushing the plate away from him, he made a face and scratched at the motion sickness patch under his ear.

"Drinking coffee won't do you any good. You need water and fresh air to feel better."

"Why are you helping me?"

"I didn't come on this show for fun. The sooner you and the rest of the crew are on their feet, the faster we can take the stock footage," I answered, leaving out my real goal on purpose. Everyone knew why I was here. I planned to spend every available moment searching for my dad.

"Thank you," he said. He nibbled on the end of a cracker.

The rest of the cast strolled into the room one by one, and we ate in silence. Once the meal was over, I washed the dishes while listening in on the plan for the next few days.

"Kyle, you'll need to take the photographs the network execs requested. I can't stand on a speed boat now," Carter said. He sipped his water. The coffee at his side was untouched and cold.

"Whatever you need," Kyle Drowling, the cameraman, said. He glanced over at me. "You'll be with me for the day, right?"

"Most of the shots will include her. I want you to make sure everything is done properly."

"Okay." Kyle climbed out his chair and joined me at the sink. A wide grin formed on his handsome face. "Need any help?"

"You can dry," I answered. My heart always raced around him. This wasn't the time for me to develop any feelings for him. The next moment, guilt seeped into my pours. I was here to find my father.

"I need to grab my gear," Kyle said once the dishes were done. He dried his hands and set the cloth down on the counter.

I watched him leave before I packed us a lunch. Afterward, I headed to my cabin to pick up my things. I carried my bag and shoved my map into the back pocket of my shorts.

Kyle waited with his bags for me by the stern. He jumped onto one of the boats, and I handed him our stuff. After the last piece of equipment was loaded, he held his hand out for me to take. I touched his and he pulled me onto the boat. His hands moved to my waist to steady me when a wave rocked us.

"Be careful out there," Gisela called to us.

"We will be," I promised, moving out of Kyle's embrace. I turned the key and the engine roared. Despite not having been at a helm for over three years, I wasn't worried. Piloting was like riding a bicycle. He unfastened the rope hooked to the *Tranquil Seas*. I maneuvered the boat away. Letting off the throttle, I turned to him. "Have you ever captained one of these?"

He shook his head.

"Do you want to learn?"

"Yeah," he answered. His blue eyes danced and he shifted closer to me.

"Put your hand over the throttle. When you press down, our boat will move forward." He placed his hand over the control, and I laid mine over his.

"This isn't the time for playing around," Carter yelled.

"If I'm injured, Kyle needs to know how to bring us back," I said.

"He can learn some other time. We've already missed a day of shooting." Carter raked a hand through his hair.

"I don't care what you think. I'm teaching him."

"I don't want to be in the middle of your argument," Kyle said. He tried to remove his hand from the throttle, but I wouldn't let him go.

"Alexandra's right. The lad does need to know how to steer a boat," the captain said. His eyes narrowed in on

Kyle and me. "He doesn't need to stand so close to be taught."

"We're fine," I told him. Turning my attention to Kyle, I directed him to our next move.

Kyle pressed the throttle and the boat sailed on the water. Within minutes the *Tranquil Seas* was a speck on the horizon behind us. He released the speed control.

"Are we far enough away? I sensed you wanted some distance from everyone," he said.

"This will work if it is okay for your photographs. What pictures do we need first?" I asked.

"We'll need generic images, like shots of the water and you at different times of the day. I like this spot." Pulling the script out, he read through the first page. The photographs would be used for promotional campaigns.

"Where do you want me?"

"Near the back of the boat. Put your hands on your hips and look fierce." He lifted the camera to his eye, snapping a picture. "Beautiful."

We worked until night fell. My body ached from the different poses, and I didn't have a chance to search for my father. Kyle and I did the same thing for the next three days. On the fourth, I couldn't take another picture.

"Do you mind if we quit early today?" I asked Kyle. Carter couldn't make our little jaunts, yet. Every morning his appearance was better and he would join us soon. Any chance of me sneaking away from the group would be gone. The jerk watched me like a hawk did a mouse in a field of long grass.

"Tilt your head to the side and smile," Kyle instructed, instead of answering. White puffy clouds stretched across the sky, and one moved in front of the sun. They played with the lighting all morning. He pressed a button on the camera, and it clicked and flashed. "What do you have in mind?"

"I want to search for my dad."

"Carter warned me you might try this. He told me not to allow you to leave on your own."

"What will you do if I take off?"

"I'll go with you," he answered. He rubbed the heel of a palm against his solid chest. "I can't imagine what losing a parent feels like and not knowing what happened to them. I've taken extra photographs so no one will know we stopped early."

"Thank you," I told him. My lips twitched as I tried not to smile, and my voice was hopeful for the next question. "Are you ready to go?"

"Give me another thirty minutes of bossing you around, and we'll be fine for the next two hours." He ordered me to do different poses. Once we wrapped up, he joined me at the helm. "Where are we headed?"

"To my father's last known location." I steered the boat fifty-two nautical miles away. With the help of my compass, I found the spot.

"Are you sure we should be this far out?" Kyle sounded nervous.

"We're fine," I said. I calculated the reading on the fuel gauge and the consumption rate for the distance we were away from the *Tranquil Seas* in my head, another skill my father taught me. Our boat had more than enough diesel for what I planned. I cut the engine and let the anchor drop.

"Why are we out here? No one is around," Kyle said.

"I'm checking Dr. K's theory of a mascon taking my father's vessel." I opened a storage compartment, pulling out my scuba gear.

"Sneaky, I was wondering why you wanted to use this boat instead of the other one."

"Are you coming with me or not?" I dressed in my wetsuit and zipped it up.

Instead of answering me, he lifted the lid to the container and grabbed the other diving suit I had stashed.

We helped each other slide on our tanks and donned our masks. Once we were ready, we sat backward on the edge of the boat.

I closed my eyes, allowing myself to fall. The moment my body touched the surface, I was pulled under. The shock of the cool water seeped into my bones. I shivered and floated back to the surface.

Kyle copied my movement. In less than a minute, he swam his way next to me.

"Why did you bring your underwater camera?" I asked him. My voice sounded hoarse from the breathing apparatus.

"If we find something, I want to document it. We may want to come back later. What's the plan?" he asked.

"We'll swim to see if we can reach the bottom." Some parts of the Atlantic Ocean reached to twenty-eight thousand feet. The most recommended depth for a human was one hundred and thirty feet.

As we descended, the light from above vanished and the darkness encased us. The blackness could play tricks on the mind. My heart beat steadily. We flipped on our flashlights, and Kyle turned on the one for the camera. Visibility was a few feet in front of us.

My depth gage read one hundred and thirteen feet below the surface. The ocean floor was another thirty at least. I glanced over at Kyle to see if he wanted to risk further downward movement.

"I trust you," Kyle said. Bubbles flowed out of his breathing apparitions as he floated next to me.

"We'll go down another five yards and stay there. When the sediment settles, we can move and look for any wreckage," I said, not wanting to put his life in peril.

When we reached our destination, a cloud of dust encased us. The strong desire to flee swept through me, but I stayed. My diving partner rubbed the back of his neck. Being nervous was expected in our situation. If a shark came at us, we couldn't see it. We couldn't do anything, except wait for the particles to disappear. Once the area cleared, I spun around, feeling the direction of the current and heading with the flow.

The ocean floor was full of life. A beautiful silver parrotfish ducked inside its home, and a school of yellowfin goatfish swam in a massive group, too many to count. They scattered when we were overhead. The reef could be anchored on a rock or debris. We wouldn't know unless we removed the coral. By the sheer density of growth, whatever it rested on wasn't my father's vessel. His would have sunk only six months ago, not enough time for this large community.

Kyle grasped my arm, scaring the crap out of me. I turned to give him a piece of my mind, but he pointed off to the side. A large black shadow rested on the seabed.

We hovered in place to see if the object moved or not. Something this big could be a shark, a whale, a ship, or some other massive creature. Once we were sure the unknown thing was resting there, we swam toward it. A boat lay on the ocean floor.

My mouth went dry. The feeling of dread filled every cell in my body. Without thinking of my own safety, I kicked my flippers, zooming ahead. The bow held little to no plant or animal life. This vessel must have sunk within the last year. I searched for a name, but a huge hole in the side damaged any words written there. The other half of the ship was missing.

Tears filled my eyes and I blinked them away. My sorrow wouldn't give me any answers, and crying under the water only fogged my mask. I thought about the name for this craft. After my father disappeared, I read about every plane and boat missing around this area, even the ones in the small hometown newspapers. I searched for clues to what one this could be.

A twisted metal rail was on the starboard of the ship. My father's did also. The anchor was not released, and the location of it was another similarity. Panic rose in my chest and I hyperventilated. I forced myself to gain control over my breathing. If I didn't, I would run out of air. The wreckage wasn't my father's boat. I refused to believe it was.

"Are you okay?" Kyle asked, concerned.

"I'm fine," I answered. I was far from being okay.

"Is this your father's yacht?"

"I don't know."

"You do, you remember every inch. Tell me what his ship should look like." Kyle's gloved hand gently touched my cheek, and he steered my face to his.

"The bow is long, it has a rail, and a crane to release the *Bluefin*," I said, closing my eyes.

"This doesn't have the last thing you described. I see a huge chimney that broke off," Kyle said.

Relief washed through me. My father's didn't have a stack, the thing Kyle spoke about. I opened my eyes and we swam toward it. A possible name for this boat came into my mind. At least some other family would have answers. I would be in a lot of trouble for disobeying orders, but I must report this location to the Coast Guard no matter the consequences.

"Shark!" Kyle cried out.

For a moment, I thought he was joking until I saw the great white for myself. The silver monster glided fast in our direction. My mind went numb.

Kyle kicked toward the surface, and I grabbed his leg, yanking him down. "Let me go," he pleaded.

"You can't out swim a shark to our boat. Hide behind the stack," I said. Laying on our bellies, we covered our heads with our hands. No bubbles escaped our air intake. We didn't dare breathe while the shark swam by us. I peeked and checked the length, over twenty feet. Yowzah.

"Is the great white gone?" Fear was etched in his voice, twenty minutes later.

"The circling ended a little bit ago."

"Why are we still here?" He glanced at me and through our masks, our gazes met. Terror reflected in the blue pools in his eyes.

"I wasn't sure if the monster would come back," I said.

"We need to go," Kyle said, reading his tank gauge. He showed me his was in the red like mine.

"What about your camera?"

"Damnit, I can't believe I didn't film the shark." He picked up his equipment, which had slipped from his hands when he attempted to escape.

"Don't be hard on yourself. You might have gotten the beast as it swam over our heads."

"I won't know until we watch the video up there," Kyle said, pointing to the surface.

"We better go then before our friend returns. This may be her feeding ground," I said.

"How do you know she was a female?" He swam next to me.

"To begin with she is much bigger, and she doesn't have a clasper. The males use it to help hold the female during copulation."

"Your dad has taught you a lot."

"He didn't teach me how to live in this world without him."

Week Three
Aliens

I woke feeling exhausted. Kyle's and my near-death escape wasn't the cause of my physical drain. The director and the network executives weren't pleased with our little voyage. They threatened to pull the plug even with the shark scene. Being at sea sucked. I couldn't turn my TV on to see if the show aired two days ago. The crew and I waited for word if we would continue.

"How did you sleep?" Kyle asked me, the only friendly face. Everyone else was mad at me.

"I couldn't," I admitted, sitting next to him in the mess hall. Men and women in suits would decide if I would find my father. What little money I had couldn't pay for a boat. By the time I received an inheritance, my dad would be dead.

"Everyone can tell." Kyle hid his smile behind a piece of toast.

"Jerk." I knocked him in his shoulder.

"Good to see you can joke around at a time like this," Carter said to me, snidely. He sat in the chair across from me, sipping a bottle of water. The noise ended and everyone turned to listen to us. He must know our fate.

"Why can't I? You and the network execs can't replace me," I asked, pretending to be egotistical. My heart hammered in my chest.

"You can be."

"How many other children of missing world-renowned explorers do you have ready to film? I'll have another show by the end of the week."

"Much to my objection, the producers agree with you. They aired our episode. We took the number one slot, and the world is talking about us. Everyone wants us to solve the Bermuda Triangle."

The captain clapped first. The rest of the crew joined in, including me. Kyle wrapped his arms around me and I hugged him back. This was the best news. No one could stop me from finding my father with the planet watching.

"What did the viewers decide?" Kyle asked, once the celebration died.

"Guess," Carter said.

"I hope not methane hydrate or the Gulf Stream. I don't want to go in the water so soon after the shark encounter. Are we seeking ghosts?"

"What do you think?" Carter shook his head and his attention turned to me.

"Aliens," I muttered, unhappy. I would've preferred searching for the lost city of Atlantis, myself.

"Little green men are correct. You're a lot smarter than I give you credit."

"Same to you." I grinned at him, holding my cup of tea in cheers.

Carter folded his arms and fumed at me.

"Alexandra has her mother's spunk," the captain said. He chuckled afterward.

"I never met Amelia Porter. What was she like?" Rayz asked, curious.

"A hurricane and a tornado rolled into one. She knew how to make others do what she wanted for the camera."

"After she screwed them," I said.

Coffee exploded from Rayz's mouth onto the table. He grabbed a napkin, cleaning the mess. His face turned bright red.

"I never witnessed someone as good as Amelia for shows besides Dax. They made a great couple. Their daughter comes from legends," the captain said.

"She's not holding up to their images," Carter noted.

"You wait. She hasn't found her stride yet. Once she does, you'll see why her nickname is Alexandra the Great."

"Those words do not compute for her."

"I agree with the captain," Gisela said. Her lips formed into a smile at me. "Your father loved talking about you whenever we met."

"Are you letting them discuss you? Where's the lady I know with the fire?" Kyle whispered.

"Old fogies have the habit of doing so even if you complain. They get worse; just ignore them," I said. They always gossiped on set. Although, Carter wasn't much older than Kyle and me. With the crew no longer hating me, breakfast was much more enjoyable. We ate in relative silence for the rest of the meal.

"After the dishes are done, we'll strategize the next three days of filming," Carter said. As soon as the last of the silverware was put away, we adjourned to the library and conference room. We fit at the large oak table with room for one more. "Rayz, where do we find extraterrestrials in the Bermuda Triangle?"

"All of the four hundred thousand square miles of the B.T. is rumored to be a landing spot," Rayz answered.

"You mean five hundred thousand," Dr. K corrected.

"We don't have enough time to explore everything. Do aliens visit a place more?" the director asked.

"I'll grab my notes," Rayz said. He hefted himself out of the chair and left the room.

"Alexandra, bring your father's journals here too. They might contain some clue to where we need to search first."

I nodded, leaving the group. My dad kept notes on the places he researched. He was old fashioned, but his quirk worked in our favor. I unzipped my emergency bag and pulled out five spiral bound notebooks. He numbered them one thru six. This collection was missing the last volume.

"Some of the Bahamas, the Bermuda Island, and the center of the B.T. are the hot zones," Rayz said, reading over his notes at the meeting table.

"My dad's journals confirm those conclusions," I said without looking at them. I knew every word by heart. These were my clues to finding him.

"What do you suggest we do?"

"Give me a minute," Carter said, taking a moment to think. He nibbled on his bottom lip and glanced at Krewal. "Do you know any of the last known locations for the missing ships or boats?"

"There are several theories, but nothing concrete. For example, the *USS Cyclops* sinking is believed to have happened somewhere between Barbados and Baltimore, Maryland," Dr. K answered.

"I need to chart everything out." Carter pulled a world atlas off the bookshelf. He flipped to the correct page. Overlaying a transpracy film, he mapped the B.T. and the *USS Cyclops* path.

"The airplane, NC16002, was reported to have vanished within fifty miles of Miami."

"The plane isn't near the path of the ship. What else is there?" He tapped the end of his marker against his work.

"The fate of Flight 19 went in this direction instead," Dr. K said, grabbing the marker. He drew out the newest theory.

"Off the coast of the Grand Bahama is where we'll search. Both airplanes at some point should have crossed there," Carter said after checking out the map.

"This is my cue to leave. At our top speed, we will arrive there in three hours. If you need me, I'll be at the bridge," the captain said.

"Don't you want to stay and hear our plan to find aliens?" Carter asked.

"I'm not into the hocus pocus stuff. I was paid for our safe journey and to speak about the weather." The captain left the room, heading to the helm. Our ship sailed a hefty U-turn as it changed course.

"Does anyone have any suggestions to finding aliens?"

"If no one has any ideas, we may be able to use some of the work I've done with paranormal investigators," Gisela said. When no one complained, she continued. "A lot of the time, we provoke the spirits for a reaction."

"How do we aggravate extratresstrials on the ocean?"

"We'll need a way for them to find us, but I don't know how."

"We're one tiny boat on a massive ocean. We'll have to send out a signal. Is anyone here a radio atronomier?" Dr. K asked.

"The network didn't spring for that speciality. They figured we can make due with the six scientists we had," Carter answered.

"I know a little about radio signals, but we'll need a much bigger array in order to send out a signal into deep space," Kyle said.

"We can't do it from here?"

"Nothing we have is strong enough. I'll try to rig up something."

"Go, take the reality show princess with you." Carter waved his hand to shoo us away.

"Hold up. Does anyone see anything wrong with this plan?" I asked, pausing by the door.

One after the other, they shook their heads. Kyle turned around and tapped his foot.

"Do we want something with advanced technology coming after us?"

"I thought you'd be willing to do anything to find your father," Carter said.

"I am, but are you?" No one said a word, and I left with Kyle to help him.

σ σ σ

Our ship drifted at the center of the B.T. at night, waiting for an UFO to appear. With a sigh, I leaned against the railing. Nothing was out here but us, the moon, and the stars. I saw well over a dozen constellations since there was no light pollution. Cities didn't have a view like this.

"We come in peace," replayed over the loudspeaker from the voices of the crew. We used every different language we knew, including elfish as if aliens spoke our tongues. Kyle had jerry-rigged it to broadcast on the satellite dish. I helped him, five days ago. We hadn't found anything since then. Carter decided to move our location to the middle of the B.T. This was the last night of filming before we sent the footage into the network.

"Don't forget to look to the sky," insisted Rayz. He shook his head to get his bangs out of his eyes. His light brown hair was already thinning. He wouldn't have to wait long for it to be nonexistent. "Christopher Columbus reported stars that spun or moved in 1492."

"What else did he see?" I asked, using my host voice. Playing the role became easier every day.

"He once saw lights flashing on the bottom of the ocean, rising above the water in a disc shape, the brightest he had ever seen."

I searched my mind for answers. The light might have been a new form of technology. Submarines didn't exist back then to explain what he saw. An illness was the most probable cause, but which one? Fevers created hallucinations. I wondered if the crew reported the UFO, or was it just him. My father noted in his journals the ship's logs were lost, and someone else wrote about the lights. No way to prove or disprove their accuracy.

"Look up there, a UFO," Rayz said, breaking my train of thought. He sounded excited.

I glanced to where he pointed. A light swept across the sky. Shooting stars left trails, but this one didn't. What could it be? My stomach felt as hard as a rock. One thing I never wanted was for my father to be taken by aliens. With their advanced weaponry, humans wouldn't stand a chance.

"You're looking at a satellite," said the world-famous astronomer, who was also our cameraman.

"How can you tell the difference?" I asked. I was glad there were no aliens. For a minute, I almost believed. This show rattled my nerves. For some reason, I enjoyed it.

"Satellites will move across the sky and don't twinkle as much as stars."

"We should get this information on tape," Carter said, motioning for Rayz to pick up one of the night vision cameras.

"I don't know how to use it," he objected.

"You point at them and hit the red record button on the side. The camera will focus on its own."

"Here take this. I can't do everything." Rayz handed over the clapperboard to his nemesis, who grumbled. The conspiracist picked up the heavy equipment anyway, lifting it on his shoulder. The thing weighed as much as he did. He swirled toward the director. "Don't blame me if everything is dark."

"We can try again later tonight." Carter turned toward me and motioned with his hands to begin.

"Something has appeared in the darkness of the sky. I'm here with Kyle Drowling, an astronomer," I recited the lines about seeing an alien.

"A lot of the time, UFOs can be explained without them being extraterrestrial," Kyle said. His lips formed into a delicious smile; even in the dim light I could see it. The man was good-looking. Too bad the viewers at home saw the green casted images of him from the night vision camera.

"What are we seeing?"

"The bouncing around is from a satellite in Earth's orbit. The object running across the sky with a tail now is a shooting star."

"Breathtaking."

"Alexandra, do you want to make a wish?"

As I was about to answer, the *Tranquil Seas* trembled and groaned. The movement felt like it crashed into something.

"What did we hit?" Carter asked. He untangled himself from the other bodies in a pile.

I grabbed the rail and managed to stay on my feet.

"Or something hit us," Drowling said.

"Aliens? The mothership has landed," Rayz yelled.

"Like what?" I asked Kyle, ignoring the panicking conspiracy theorist. We hadn't seen anyone out here for miles.

"I don't know. Whatever happened came from the bow." Kyle wiped a trail of blood off his chin.

We glanced at each other and said nothing as we ran single file toward the front of the ship. The director led, followed by me, Rayz, and everyone else. I almost jumped out of my skin when someone landed in front of me.

"It rose from the ocean," the captain stuttered. His face was ashen as if he had seen a ghost or something. "I couldn't stop us in time."

One thing I knew, hitting anything in the middle of the ocean wasn't a good thing. The hull could be breached. The ship might be taking on water. We could sink in seconds. Visions of the Titanic flashed before my eyes.

The director must have gotten the same idea as me. He turned around and ran the short distance to the bow at full speed.

When he stopped, I bumped into him. Words were lost in my throat. I held my breath. A massive ship was right in front of us. Where did it come from?

Water flowed over the sides like a downpour. Heavy plant and coral growth covered a small portion of the deck railing.

"Ships don't rise out of water, like a submarine," Krewal said what I was thinking.

"If I hadn't seen this vessel with my own eyes, I wouldn't believe it to be true either," the captain said.

"You have to be playing a joke."

"Are you calling me a liar?" This was the first time I had ever heard him sound angry.

"Never, sir. I was wondering what we should do." Dr. K wiped the sweat off his brow.

"See if anyone is alive on the ship and call the Coast Guard."

"I'm not going on that." Krewal paled and looked ready to toss his cookies.

"You don't have to go over there. We can try and radio them."

"What if they don't answer? Or someone is hurt?" I asked. My chest burned and I clenched my jaw. I was worried and scared, but most of all, I needed to do something.

"Hold on before we make any rash decision," Carter said. He turned to the B.T. expert. "What ship is this?"

"I'm not sure. Too many markings to make it recognizable," Krewal answered. He was right. The ship had a sail, metal foremasts, a wooden mermaid figurehead, and a wing. He fidgeted in his spot. "I'll have to check at my notes."

"Go get them." After he left, the director paused and rubbed the back of his neck. The poor man must have a headache because this wasn't in the script. "Robert, try and hail them. If they don't answer, see if you can get the Coast Guard on the horn."

"Wouldn't it be easier to read the name?" I asked.

The two men turned to me.

"We should be able to see the name if we move to either side or the stern," I pointed out.

"We need to check for any damage before we move," Captain Pike said.

"I'll have to go into the water." I grabbed my scuba gear from a bin and started to pull it on.

"Where do you think you're going?"

"I'm checking out our ship before we become another tragedy of the Bermuda Triangle. I'm certified."

"I can't let you go. The water isn't safe," Pike said.

"I can handle myself. My father taught me well," I said.

"He wouldn't want you to put yourself in any unnecessary danger."

"Who else besides me can go? You need to hail for help."

"I'd prefer anyone but you."

"Just because you feel guilty about not taking the job with my father doesn't mean you can order me around."

He opened his mouth and closed it.

"I'm leaving. You can't stop me," I said. I stuffed my feet into a pair of flippers and glanced around for a tank.

"Checking out our ship is our top priority, but she can't go alone," Carter said.

"You can't come. You don't know how to dive. You'd hinder me more than help." Despite sounding like a brat, I was right. Someone who didn't know how to scuba dive shouldn't at night.

"I wasn't planning on helping you." He ran a hand through his blond surfer hair.

"I'll go," Gisela volunteered. She had been quiet for most of the night. I figured she was mad at me. Without another word, she took off her life jacket and changed into her wetsuit.

"Go with them," Carter said, turning to the real cameraman. "Check the hull out first and then the other ship. I want footage."

Kyle nodded and ran back to the stern to grab his underwater equipment. He carried everything with him unless something made us move fast.

While he retrieved his gear, I helped Gisela into hers, making sure everything was fastened. We pulled on our tanks and waited by the rail for him to return.

"This is a high jump. Is it safe?" Gisela asked, peering into the water below us.

"The drop isn't as bad as you think. The next person waits until you reach the surface," I answered.

"I promised your father—" the captain said to me, grabbing my arm.

"I don't need your protection," I cut him off. My blood boiled. Turning to the only other woman, I wanted to leave our ship. "Let's wait for Kyle down in the water."

She grabbed a dive flashlight and jumped over the side. I waited for her to bob back to the surface before I took my turn.

"Captain Pike isn't bad," Gisela said once I floated near her. "He cares about you and feels guilty about what happened with your father. Robert thinks if he was there, he would have saved them somehow."

"He isn't the only one." I swam away and turned on my light. Okay, I didn't think he was responsible now. At least he was here, helping me.

"Shouldn't we wait for Kyle?" She caught up to me.

"He still needs to put on his gear. I'll check our damage and see what we need to do." I stuck my mouth piece in and dove under, kicking my way to where we hit.

The hull had a small spider crack like a windshield would have after being hit with a rock. We would have to patch it tonight. The inside of the ship needed to be inspected to see if we were taking on any water.

Once I surfaced, I called up to the ship and told them what I had found.

"I'll go below and see what is there. Can you repair the ship?" Carter asked.

"With Pike's help, we should be able to do some type of patch work. He'll need to see the full extent of the damage to confirm my assumptions," I answered. Last time I helped repair a boat was five years ago, with my father. I wasn't an expert.

"Kyle, grab some shots of the wreck and investigate the other ship."

"Yes, sir," Kyle said, saluting the other man. He had joined Gisela sometime during my dive.

"You ready for this?" I asked him.

"As long as you keep the sharks away." In the darkness, his white teeth flashed as he grinned at me.

"My father did say I have the Devil's Luck, bad things will happen around me. At least the viewers will love the action."

A chuckle escaped his lips, thinking I was joking with him. I wasn't. Before I could tell him the truth, he disappeared under the water. Oh well, he would learn soon enough.

I sank below the surface, showing him the way. He filmed everything we needed and signaled me when he was done. With a few kicks, we broke through the waterline.

"This is *Tranquil Seas* is anyone out there," Pike's voice blared over our loudspeaker. We waited while he hailed them again. Frustration rose in his voice with each signal to the other ship.

"How long has he been trying?" Kyle asked after the sixth time.

"Since you left to check our damage. What should we do?" Gisela asked, sounding worried.

"We need to identify the other vessel." He swam away and I trailed behind him.

"I'm scared. How can he be so gung-ho?" Gisela asked me as she kept my slower pace.

"People may be hurt and he understands. We have to determine what boat hit us," I answered. I searched the ship for words on the port side, but there were none. I swam on despite the ache in my arms and legs.

"How far are we going?"

"Until we see something." I glanced upward. Across the stern was a name I recognized, but the ship wasn't listed as missing in my father's journals.

Week Four
Atlantis

*A*tlantis. I gasped and swallowed a mouthful of salt water. Sputtering and coughing, I worked to gain control of my breathing. Bobbing up and down didn't help me.

"Is this ship a missing one?" Gisela asked after reading the name.

I shook my head. Turning my attention to Kyle, I motioned for him to begin filming. He raised the camera and pointed it at me.

"We've just collided with the *Atlantis*. This isn't a lost city like everyone assumes. It's a ship." Glancing over my shoulder, I imagined Kyle capturing my every word. Each letter in the name was different, reminiscent of a poorly done ransom note cut from a newspaper. I cleared my throat. "Stay tuned as I explore this vessel."

"Are you crazy? We can't go on there," Gisela said once Kyle indicated he was done filming.

"The only thing stopping me from getting on that boat tonight is the darkness." Two things prevented me from climbing onto it. The first was going onboard now could put myself and the crew in danger. We didn't know how much damage there was. I wouldn't risk their lives since we didn't know if anyone was alive. If people were on there, they should have come to the railings by now. The *Tranquil Seas* also needed fixing. I swam back to our boat and the other two followed me.

Carter met us at the stern, helping us pull the equipment over the side. He reached his hand out and gave me a boost.

"How's our damage?" he asked. I was surprised he didn't ask about the other boat first.

"We need repairs. Are we taking on any water below?" I answered.

"I found something, but I'm not an expert."

"Has Pike looked?"

"He's been trying to reach the Coast Guard, but our radio isn't working."

I shrugged out of my tank and pulled off my wetsuit with Carter's help. Running around with my equipment on would make the deck wet. I'd been given the task of cooking and keeping our ship seaworthy. Yay me.

"I'll stow your gear." Gisela took the tank and mask from me.

"Thank you," I muttered, before Carter and I took off. He led me through the different levels. The deeper we went the more my stomach churned. Some parts of the haul could never be fixed.

We ended on the second to the last floor. The spot where we hit held a mark on this side. The double wall kept it from cracking the hull further. We needed to repair the damage before water flowed through. The fracture held, but with the pressure from the outside, it might not last long.

"How's my girl?" Pike asked about the ship when we joined him and everyone else on the bridge

"She's holding, might not be for long. What does the Coast Guard say?" I asked. What Carter said about the radio had to be a fluke. Our equipment was the best the networks could afford. I made sure of that.

"I can't reach anyone because this thing isn't working." Pike picked up the VHF marine radio microphone and tried again. Static came across the line. He tossed the mic down. Cell phone reception range ended yesterday. The satellite connection was spotty at best. Anytime Carter wanted to call the network, we sailed closer to land. The rest of us waited for bars on our phones.

"The compass is out too. Robert thinks we are in a magnetic field," Carter said.

I glanced at the big doomed navigational device. The needle spun around. Removing the one my father gave me from my pocket, the apparatus couldn't find a direction either. Pike's assumption was correct.

"What hit us?" Pike asked.

Kyle told him before I could.

"*Atlantis* isn't possible," Krewal interjected. He held up a blue folder. "The Bermuda Triangle has never taken a ship with that name. I know every missing vessel in the region."

"The footage is right here." Kyle patted his camera.

"We have to watch it now." Krewal reached to snatch the equipment, but Pike grabbed it first. The cabin wasn't very big with the seven of us in here.

"The ship repairs come first, then the show. Alexandra and I will fix the inside and then the outside," Pike said.

"Kyle, will film you," Carter said.

"As long as he stays out of our way he can."

Carter opened his mouth to object, but I shook my head. We needed to be safe, not stupid in this situation.

Pike and I worked on the inside patch first then the outside. To say fire underwater was cool didn't do it justice. I stuck on a piece of metal to cover the crack. He welded the part onto the ship. After we finished, we swam back to the surface. Kyle filmed everything.

"The patch will hold us for now, but we did a temp job to get us to port," Pike said as he trudged to the ladder. I suspected he directed those words at me. We climbed onto the deck.

The sun had risen sometime during the repairs. Despite the lack of sleep and all the swimming I had done, I was anxious to climb aboard the *Atlantis*.

"Stay here and help me guide our ship back," the captain instructed much to my annoyance. He walked the short distance across the bow to the ladder that led to the bridge.

I waited for him to enter the room. After he did, I moved onto the tip of our boat. This was a long way to fall. My heart beat steady. I closed my eyes and extended my hands out, pretending I was flying. For a moment, all my troubles were gone. The next second the spell broke, I glanced at the big windows behind me. Pike was at the wheel. I motioned for him to begin backing out. He eased us enough backward. Once he finished setting out distance further away, we met on deck to check on the crew in the dining center.

"We reviewed the footage. You'll watch it while you eat," Carter said. His tone didn't reflect his feelings for once. I wasn't sure how to take it. Was the video even on there? During paranormal events, sometimes cameras lost data, like a magnet wiped it clean.

Someone had cooked a full breakfast. I assumed Gisela had, not because she was a girl, but because out of everyone who remained, she was the least egotistical. Everyone else might argue why they shouldn't have to prepare food.

The smell of maple syrup made me queasy. My stomach growled, but I couldn't eat anything. Grabbing a cup of black coffee instead, I sat down next to Gisela to watch.

The first scene rolled onto the screen. Our boat rocked after we hit something. Confusion was on everyone's faces until the looks turned to determination as we ran to the bow. Rayz kept the camera leveled, but it bounced around. I couldn't help noticing my butt. The rest of the events proceeded. Kyle switched out the flash card for the underwater one.

"This footage doesn't change what we need to do. We have to check the ship for survivors," Pike said after

145 σ Realms of Fantastic Stories Vol. 2

examining everything. He bit into his pile of scrambled eggs smothered in ketchup.

"We don't have the gear for something like this. We're not salvagers. I sent our footage to the network. We should wait until they tell us what to do next." Carter stood and paced the length of the two tables.

"Doesn't matter what they say. The code of the sea is to help those in need. I swore to live by it whenever I captained a ship. What if we were stranded?" Polishing his coffee off, Pike stood, set his dishes in the sink, and exited the room.

"We're leaving in ten minutes with all hands-on deck," I told those in the mess. I waited for someone to object, but no one did.

"I can see why she's called Alexandra the Great," Dr. K muttered.

"You have nine minutes and forty-five seconds remaining. Tick tock. Better get a move on." I left them there and searched for supplies. By the time we were ready to go, I had almost everything marked off my list.

"Everyone take a pack. Two people will go grab the rest in the hall," I said, setting three down on deck.

Without a word, two men retrieved what remained. Once they returned, everyone else pulled one on. Mine was already on my back.

"Does this need to be so heavy?" Krewal complained. Beads of sweat collected against his forehead, causing the dark hair on his widow's peak to stick up at strange angles.

"Do you want to survive over there?" I asked. A sigh built inside my chest, but I didn't let it escape. I gave him a moment to think about my question. After he didn't speak, I took off my bag and unzipped it. "Everything in here should work in an emergency."

"I won't ever be alone. Why do I need to carry something?"

"You may not be with someone at some point. We can't account for everything with the unknown. We need to prepare the best we can. You're taking a damn backpack, and so is everyone else."

"Where's your sense of adventure?" Kyle asked. He glanced at me and smiled, the blue in his eyes brightening.

"I'm leaving my imagination here." Dr. K stomped his foot and pointed at the ground.

"No one's splitting up." Pike tossed his stuff into one of the small boats.

"I don't think checking out the other ship is a good idea. The network hasn't responded to my inquiries. We should wait to see what they say," Carter said. His voice held his nervousness; he was stumbling over his own words.

"The satellite reception may be down."

Carter paled at the captain's words.

"Be a man. We are out here and the network execs are not. You need to decide what to do for yourself. I'll be searching the *Atlantis*," Pike said.

"Me too." I set my belongings in the other craft. Pulling my black hair back, I fastened it into a ponytail. The wind picked up and the sky darkened. In a few hours, a storm would arrive.

"We'll go and make sure everyone is okay," Carter said.

The captain clapped him on the back. He approved the director's change in attitude. He jumped onto his craft afterward.

"Can I speak to you a moment alone?" Carter asked Kyle.

Kyle followed the director. They whispered for longer than I would have liked. I figured they must be talking about filming our little jaunt.

"If you don't get your ass in this boat, I'm leaving without you," I yelled at our cameraman. Whenever my emotions ran high, I had a potty mouth.

The captain laughed and started his engine. He waited until the annoying director was with him before he pulled away from the *Tranquil Seas*.

"I'm sorry," Kyle muttered an apology to me after he stepped onto our vessel. His hand touched the back of my chair, he bent closer, and his voice dipped low for me to hear. "Carter wants me to film everything."

"Duh," I said.

"Please don't be angry with me."

"I'm not. We're in for a storm, look at the sky. We need to search a massive ship and return to ours." Staying out there wouldn't be a good idea. We didn't know what condition the ship was in. Large waves rocked our boat as I closed distance between us and the *Atlantis*. I released the throttle and brought us parallel to it. Our current location was as good a spot as any to board.

"No ladder is down. One of us must scale the side," Pike said, pulling alongside us.

"I'll go. This will only hold my weight," I said before he could object. Opening my bag, I grabbed the grappling hook I'd made.

"Can you even lock the rail with your thing?" asked Krewal, in a rude tone.

"You'll have to wait and see." I hooked the rail in two throws. With a tug to secure the grapple better, I climbed, using the side of the ship as a walking platform. About two-thirds of the way, the material under my feet changed into rotted wood. I slipped and one of my legs fell through. Pain shot down my arm where I bumped my funny bone.

People below me yelled. With the roar of the wind, I couldn't hear what they were saying. Grunting, I pulled myself out of the hole and continued. This time I watched my steps. The ship was made from metal and wood, as if the shipbuilder fastened it together with spare parts. No one would do a crappy job like this on purpose.

On the starboard side, I jumped over a hole for a weapon. I first thought the *Atlantis* was a humongous schooner because of the sails. With the five cannons on this side, it could be a war sloop. The other one wasn't outfitted for weaponry.

I lifted myself over the rail and checked the deck before plopping down onto it. The climb zapped my energy. Breathing heavily, I rested for a minute. Once I could stand, I searched my bag for a rope or something to throw to the others to join me.

The captain and Kyle scaled the side. The rest tied a rope around their waist, and those onboard hoisted them upward. Once everyone was here, I glanced around. The deck was in as bad shape as the side of the boat. Everything was either metal or wood, which shouldn't be possible because the two materials blended together without being fastened.

"Is anyone here?" the captain yelled.

"We're here to help," called Carter.

No one responded.

"Something isn't right," Gisela said once she could talk.

"What do you mean?" I asked.

"We shouldn't be here." Her lip and chin trembled. She rested against the rail for support. "There are hundreds of ghosts."

Week Five
Ghost Ship

Krewal laughed. Until he realized no one else was. He clamped his mouth closed and stopped.

"What are you feeling?" I asked Gisela.

"This is hard to describe." She closed her eyes and her eyelids fluttered. "There are a lot of ghosts trying to talk to me at once."

"What are they saying?"

"They are telling us to leave. We're in great danger if we don't go immediately."

"You gotta be kidding me. Spirts can't communicate with someone," Rayz said.

"For you, they can't, but with me, they do."

"Make them do something then. I'll believe you and jump right into the water." He lifted his leg over a rusted railing. He shouldn't pick on someone because he didn't agree with them. The ideas from his mind were crazier.

A window shattered. Any objection to Rayz's statement died on my lips.

Pike ran in the direction of the noise. His movements were calculated, missing the rotted wood and bad metal.

I would have followed him, but the cameraman's peril caught my attention instead. I pushed Kyle away from a bad part as he chased after the captain. We landed on our sides next to each other.

"What are you doing? I need to film what happened with the window," Kyle said. His tone was filled with anger.

"You don't want to fall through," I told him, pointing to his left.

He turned his head in the direction and a gasp escaped his lips. A hole was where he would have stepped. He might not have died, but he could have fallen through a level or more.

"Thank you," he said. He rolled onto me and wrapped his arms around me.

"We shouldn't lie in the same spot. I'm not sure if the deck can hold our weight." I hated that I spoke those words. Why couldn't I hug him back instead? He removed himself from me and helped me to stand. "Is your camera okay? I'm sorry if I damaged it."

"This one doesn't have a mark. I'll have to test it to make sure." Lifting the device, Kyle took an image of me. He glanced at the picture. Once he was done, his gaze returned to me. He licked his lips and a yearning look passed through his eyes. "My camera is fine."

"Good." My heart raced, almost exploding out of my chest.

"Did the wind break the window?" Rayz asked, sounding nervous.

"I don't feel any, do you?" Kyle held out his hand to test the air. "With the storm approaching, we should have air currents." The eerie calmness was beyond strange.

Rayz shook his head.

"Jump right in, Jameson," Dr. K joked. A nervous bubble of laughter escaped his lips.

"No one's leaving the group. The window broke because it was already cracked. We were at the right place at the wrong time. Tell us what your feel happening here," Pike said when he returned. He bent down in front of Gisela.

"The spirits are terrified like something bad happened on this ship. Give me a moment to catch my breath," she said.

As we waited for her to recover, I wandered over to the figurehead, playing a game of hopscotch with rotten wood and rusted metal floorboards in the process. The mermaid was handcrafted, in great condition, exquisite, and over two hundred years old. Her hair flung around her in every direction, giving the effect that she was floating. How did she land here?

Attached to her head were the bowsprit riggings. The sail was closed. This setup made no sense to me. If I opened the white cloth, I bet it would work. I reached up to test the strength of the cords, but a hand grabbed mine. I almost jumped out of my skin.

"Best not be playing with the sails. We don't want the ship to move," Pike said.

"Do you think they'll work?" I asked.

"I'm not as old as the first sloops, but these should do the trick. With the storm on the horizon, we'll have heavy winds soon."

"Why don't we have any now?"

"I don't know."

I glanced upward, tracing the riggings and seeing how it attached to the first mast, which was part of a set.

"She's a beauty, isn't she?" Pike asked, staring at the mermaid.

"She's one of a kind. That's for sure," I answered.

"Come and help me check for an anchor. We don't want to lose our boat's location and be lost at sea."

Kyle moved forward. I motioned for him to stay put while I followed the captain to the stern. The walk to the back was at least eighty feet. Our cameraman would slow us down. The anchor was rusted but still in working condition. The chain was more burnt brown than silver.

Pike pulled the string for the engine, which released the metal links. A sputtering sound came out, but it wouldn't turn over. The gas tank could be dry or something else might be wrong with it. Since we didn't have the right tools to fix the device, we removed the pin to release the chain. The anchor lowered into the water, descending until the ship jerked. We reset the clasp.

"This should keep the vessel steady for now. We should search for any survivors. Gisela and everyone else have rested enough," Pike said. We tiptoed back to join the group.

"Where did you go?" Kyle asked, pointing the camera at us.

"To set the anchor. Everyone needs to watch their steps. These floorboards aren't safe. Follow behind me or Alexandra if you're unsure where to go." Pike cleared his throat.

Our group moved in two lines across the deck with him and me leading. We headed toward the ladder and climbed two more levels until we were outside the door to the bridge.

"Wait. Before we enter, Alexandra should check if anyone is in there," Carter said. He motioned for me to step forward.

"Hello, is anyone here?" I asked. When no one answered, I tried again.

"This part of the ship is like the *SS Cotopaxi*," Krewal noted, stepping into the shot. "It vanished in December 1925 along with a crew of thirty-two. A radio distress call reported she took on water after a tropical storm. She was never seen again."

"I don't remember the name."

"This area is not the same. It doesn't make any sense." He scratched his head.

"What do you mean?" the director asked, forgetting about the camera.

"Ships are not thrown together like this," Pike answered. He explained further on how everything was different. Krewal chimed in when he could.

"What are you trying to tell us?"

"We shouldn't be here," Gisela said. Her lower lip trembled and she pressed her elbows against her side. She appeared smaller than her already petite size.

"Don't tell me. You believe the stupid ghost crap," Krewal said. He grabbed the knob, but the door creaked open before he could clasp it. Stumbling, he fell backward onto his rump. A look of horror flashed across his face.

For a moment, I lost the ability to speak. Once I could talk again, I called out the same words as earlier.

"No one's home," I said after a minute of silence.

"How do you explain the door?" Dr. K's nostrils flared with his anger.

"The lock is rusted." Gisela held out her hand to help him stand.

I walked onto the bridge and stopped in my tracks. Everything was wood. Someone bumped into me, and I shuffled out of their way. A large desk was off to one side with a lavish, red leather chair, like a captain's quarters on a pirate ship. The wheel was in front of stained glass windows. I glanced out of them, but I couldn't see anything. A ship wouldn't have them here since they were useless. I left the area, wiped the grime off the glass, and peered inside. The room looked like a more modern-day bridge with electronic screens. What the heck was going on here?

Scratching my head, I was about to enter the room, but someone grabbed my shoulder, startling me.

"What are you staring at?" Kyle asked. His hand dropped off my shoulder. The director must have instructed him to stick to me like glue.

"See for yourself," I answered.

He shifted his equipment and pressed his face against the glass. His next act was to step inside the bridge. Once he was done, he touched the base of his neck and opened his mouth to speak to me. No words came out. A dark look passed through his eyes. He stared behind the camera, repeating the same movements.

"Everyone will think this is a trick," he complained once he was done.

"The important part is we know it's not," I said.

"How can one room be different on the inside then the outside?"

"I've been to some of the strangest places on Earth, and I don't have a stinking clue."

"Alexandra and Kyle, get in here. We need to find the ship's logs," Pike called. We spent the next thirty minutes searching for them. A few pieces of paper turned into dust when we touched them. Other scraps were fine. None of them told us about the ship's voyage.

"The books might be somewhere else," I said, sounding hopeful and knowing Pike wanted them. To be fair, I wished to see them too. It might explain what we were seeing.

We left the bridge and searched the lower three decks. I swore there was only two before. I must have imagined it. Each room took us to a different ship's area. The last floor was the mess hall, which was the length of a basketball court. Two rows of tables were down the middle for seating. The kitchen appliances were a mix of old and new.

"How can the food area be this huge?" Krewal asked, scratching the stubble on his chin.

"I don't know, but each of our bags should have ten feet of rope. We should measure the outside and the inside," I said. We worked in two groups. The interior was fifty feet wide by one hundred feet in length, and the exterior was just ten by ten. The sizes didn't add up.

"Is there a reasonable explanation for the differences?" Dr. K asked on the balcony. He glanced over at the conspiracy theorist. I wanted to laugh at him for seeking advice from his nemesis first. When science couldn't explain anything, they went to the unknown, the paranormal.

"Your guess is good as mine," Rayz said. He held the map he drew of the measurements and returned to staring at the drawing. His lips moved as he spoke to himself.

"Okay, we're done figuring this on our own," I said. Everyone turned to me with puzzled looks on their faces. "Time for our director to do his job."

"What do you mean?" Carter asked

"You're talking on camera." With my cue, Kyle pointed the device at him.

"I'm not in the script, unless we see a black hole." Carter pulled the rolled stack of papers from his back pocket.

"Does your precious writing have anything on what to do when we encounter a ghost ship?" Without waiting for him to answer, I continued, and Kyle swiveled the camera at me. "I'm here with world-renowned theoretical physicist, Dr. Carter Carter. We measured the mess hall and the outside of it, but they are not the same size. How could this happen?"

"I don't know. I need to see more and search my books back on our ship," he said, stuttering. Despite his lack of confidence, his blue eyes twinkled, like he was holding something back.

"Do you have any idea what could have done this?"

"Or something," Rayz said.

"Mr. Rayz, are there any conspiracies that match what we are seeing here?" I asked, knowing what he would say. At least, the viewers would be happy.

"Just one… aliens."

"We'll find a better explanation than an extraterrestrial, but we must finish checking this ship from deck to hull. Someone may be injured and can't come to our calls," Pike said.

"How would we know if this phenomenon was created by aliens?" Dr. K asked. His gaze bounced around; he wouldn't look anyone in the eyes. "I'm saying just in case. I don't actually believe."

"If we were in a crop field, the stalks would be bent at odd angles. Since we're on the ocean, any sign of unusual patterns or things that can't be explained is the work of aliens," Rayz answered.

"Like the floor?" Krewal's face paled and his cheeks were a little green.

"The way the metal and wood merged together could be considered out of this world. As far as I know, those materials are not found like that in nature."

"I don't think an alien designed this," Carter said.

"What are your theories then?"

"I don't have any, yet."

"Considering what we are standing on has the design of a shipwright, we know it isn't a UFO," I said.

"No human could construct this craft," Rayz said. A triumphant grin stretched across his lips.

"Then I decree what we stand on is a schooner-of-war."

Kyle barked a laugh but sobered the next second. The smile didn't leave his face.

"If everyone is done talking, I suggest we start searching. We'll lose daylight soon," Pike said. Without waiting for anyone's input, he walked ahead while watching his steps.

"Are you okay?" I asked Gisela a few minutes into our quest. I lifted a flap from a lifeboat from this century and glanced inside. Nothing was in there. The one next to it was several centuries older.

"I'm fine," she answered. Beads of sweat dotted her forehead.

"Do you want to return to our ship? Someone could take you back if the ghosts here are too much for you."

"I can handle them."

"Please tell us if you can't. I don't want you to be a liability." Did I believe Gisela's capabilities? I didn't know, and I didn't want to find out if they were true. Fighting an entity wasn't part of the things my dad taught me.

"I'll let you know." She lifted her chin, returning to rummaging around the lifeboats with me.

We cleared them and the crew swept the rest of the deck. I bet the area was one hundred and fifty feet or more. We didn't find anything more out of place than the usual. I couldn't wait to head inside. Pike urged us to take a break though.

"These markings could be alien," Rayz said as he bent down and rubbed the paint at the stern.

"Those are the signs for a helicopter pad," I informed him.

"How can you tell?"

"Give me your notebook and I'll show you." Once he handed it to me, I drew an H and a circle. I kept sketching until the illustration was the same what was by our feet.

"Your work is remarkable." He glanced at what I had done and the floorboards, comparing them.

"Why would someone keep drawing the marks here?" Krewal asked.

"I'm not sure," I answered, knowing he meant something other than the obvious. Any normal person would clear the paint before they created a new image.

"I'm starting to believe the alien theory."

"Me too." Unless someone has a better idea. I glanced over at Carter.

He stared at a spot in front of him. His lips moved as he muttered to himself. What did he know or think? His occupation worked to figure things out, like what we were witnessing.

"Everyone ready to head inside?" Pike asked. His gaze focused in on Gisela.

"I'll be fine. You don't have to worry about me," she said. When she stood, she lost her balance.

"Use my arm and I'll walk with you." He offered his biceps for her to hold onto. They were the first through the door.

On the first level below, we stumbled across a room with six backpacks. Five sleeping bags were rolled out and one was in the corner. We searched everything, trying to figure out who owned them. When I was on the last bag, I pulled out a journal. The writing was familiar.

Week Six
Lost

I flipped through the pages in disbelief. The notebook was the one missing from my father's collection on the B.T. He had taken it with him on his voyage.

Someone could have taken his work. I checked over every item in the bag, remembering a few of the shirts he wore. I had bought some of them. His dark blue satchel could have been stolen. A red towel was rolled different from everything else. I unfolded the ends and a photograph of me was wrapped inside. I pulled the frame out. My father always carried this with him. No one else would have it. A chill ran down my spine; this was my dad's duffel bag. If he left his belongings here, where was he? He wasn't the type to leave anything important behind.

Holding my breath, I opened the journal to the last section. The date from two days after my father and his crew reported in was written across the top. He wrote that the ship wasn't natural. He wanted to leave before the crew couldn't anymore. Everyone else wished to stay to find Jakobe, the pilot. The man disappeared sometime during the previous night.

"This can't be his," I muttered, reading everything over again. My dad never left anyone behind. Tears filled the corner of my eyes.

"What did you find?" Kyle asked, coming to me and setting his camera down.

"I discovered my father's bag." I stood and clenched the notebook to my chest. My father was alive. He could be on this ship right now. I must search for him. He could be hurt or worse. I couldn't bring myself to say the four-letter word.

"You're not going alone," the captain said. He placed a hand on my shoulder, stopping me from bolting out of the room.

"I'm looking for my dad with or without you." I shrugged off his hand and showed him the picture along with the notebook.

"I'm not preventing you from leaving, but you don't know anything about his or our situation. Your dad would want you to be safe." Pike's voice was soft and much to my dismay he was right.

"What will we do?" I sighed, giving in to him. We could argue, and at the end of our conversation, I would bolt out of the room. He would lock me up once he caught me. I could hold my own for a few minutes at best with him.

"We'll take two groups with Alexandra and myself as the leaders. I want Krewal and Gisela with me. The rest are with the young explorer, who will stay with her people," the captain said, glancing at me.

"I thought you said we're not splitting up," Dr. K complained.

"Since we found evidence of survivors, my plan has changed. My team will search the even floors and the others will do the odd We'll report back here in an hour, no matter what."

"I should go with you. We need footage," Carter said.

"I'll document everything because we might miss something, not for your stupid show." Kyle handed Pike a spare camera.

"We're moving out," Kyle told my group. He grabbed my hand and squeezed.

"Dad," I yelled, once we were in the hallway. The fear of not finding him was in my voice.

My people searched the rest of the floor. We didn't come across anyone or any clue to my father's

161 σ Realms of Fantastic Stories Vol. 2

whereabouts. Each area was different than the last. If I wasn't good at direction, we would have been lost. I found a staircase and we headed to two levels below this one.

A red carpet ran along the hallway. Dozens of doors were on either side. Probing the rooms one by one would take forever if we did it together. We needed a better plan.

"Pair up," I said, deciding on the faster route. We might be fine with a buddy system.

"Do you think your idea is safe? Robert told us to stick together," Carter said.

"Pike's not here. I'm the one in charge." I leaned against the wall next to a portrait of a man in a naval uniform. He was in his late forties or early fifties.

"If you say this is for the best, I'll believe you. Kyle is with Alexandra. Rayz and me will go together." Carter's tone sounded as unsure as I felt.

"Don't move far away from the other partners. If you find something holler at me, and I'll come check it out." At least we should be safe if everyone was close.

Kyle and I cleared the first room and moved onto the second. By the time six places were marked off, sweat beaded my brow. I wiped the liquid with the back of my hand and stared at the naval captain from earlier. On his breast were a lot of insignias and badges. With my limited knowledge of the United States Navy, I could only name a few.

"I swear I know this guy from somewhere," Kyle said, pointing at the man.

"Now that you mention him, he does appear familiar. He could be the captain of this ship," I said. My mind couldn't place where I knew him from. Shrugging the thought away, I opened my bag and pulled out a bottle of water. I took a small sip, already rationing myself. Old habits were hard to break.

"Are you ready for another room?" Kyle wiped spittle off the corner of his mouth and stuck his water bottle into a side pocket of his bag.

I nodded. We entered the nearest door. This place was oddly reminiscent of the *Tranquil Seas* lounge. Three large leather couches and two chairs were pushed together in a small space. The coffee table in the center was filled with papers. I searched the mess for any clue to my father and the ship log. Finding nothing, I left the room.

Kyle opened the next door for me. We stepped into a gym, like a room we searched before. I didn't find it odd because everything was strange on the ship. Most of the equipment couldn't hide anything. A quick sweep checked off the fitness area.

I returned to the hallway first, stopping in front of the painting. The guy kept on appearing everywhere we went, but his location was always near a port window. I tried to open it, but the frame was warped around it. No light came through the glass. I couldn't see through the porthole.

"What are you doing?" Kyle asked.

"I don't know. We'll wait here until everyone finishes their spot," I answered. Something was wrong with the portrait, but I didn't know what.

"Shouldn't you be searching?" Carter asked after he and Rayz joined us in the corridor.

"We're taking a break," Kyle said.

"If you are, so can I." He yanked out his bottle of water from his backpack and gulped it down. The amount of liquid remaining wasn't much. He should ration himself.

"Has anyone seen the guy in the painting before," I asked, pointing at the art work.

"He does appear familiar. I may have some notes on him, but Krewal would know who he is," Rayz said. He took his glasses off, cleaned them, and examined the image more closely.

"I'm not talking about him being a victim of the B.T. Kyle and I have walked by him at least a dozen times."

"Maybe more," Kyle added.

"If you have seen the same man a lot, we could be trapped in an infinite cycle. I've heard of them. They are almost impossible to break. We'll loop forever," Rayz said. Not a good thing considering there wasn't a place to eat on this floor.

The sensation of everything moving too fast for me to process flowed through my brain. I needed to get a handle on my emotions. I thought about what I should do next while keeping the fear building inside me at bay. An idea formed inside my mind. Not the best one I had, but it would have to do.

"Since we believe we're stuck here, does anyone have any yarn in their bag?" I asked.

"What will you do with it?" Kyle asked. He pulled out a purple ball and handed it to me.

"Checking Rayz's theory." I tied the string to a door handle. With me leading, our gang followed the hallway until we returned to the yarn again.

"How do we break this?" Rayz asked, terrified. His next words out of his mouth were incoherent. I swore he said something along the lines of conspiracies weren't supposed to be true.

"You need to calm down," I told him.

"Okay, give me a minute."

"We don't have the time. How do we leave an infinite loop?"

"I don't know. I've only read about them. Why do you think I was freaked out? We'll die here."

"We have some of the brightest minds in the country. One of you needs to think of something." I glanced at the men, one was an astronomer and the other even smarter. Rayz and I were the odd ducks out.

"Everything I deal with is in theories," Carter said.

"If I had an answer, I would tell you. Out of everyone here, I believe Alexandra can help us. You have an amazing ability of getting us out of tough spots," Kyle said, scratching his head.

"I also wind up in bad situations because of my impulses," I said. How could he forget about the shark incident? We needed to leave the way we arrived on the floor, remembering the stairwell was near the painting. A solid white wall was in the doors place. "I have an idea."

With no time to be scared, I ran to the gym. I picked the bar for the weights off the posts. The equipment was heavy and should do the trick.

"Why do you need a barbell?" Carter asked. His brows furrowed and his lips curled into a frown.

"We're busting out of here. Everyone, grab something you can use to hit," I answered. With both of my hands wrapped around the end, I wielded the bar like a samurai. The wall would fall.

Swinging at the barrier, chucks of the plaster broke off as I hit the wall. It reacted, filling in the small hole. I held back a scream of frustration and fear. The barbell banged into the divider a lot as I found my rhythm. Material rained on my head. The infinite loop would not win.

Exhausted, I stopped for a moment. My shoulders heaved from my heavy breathing. I felt like I had run with the bulls all over again. The metal door was a quarter of the way free, but the edges of the void were filling in fast. No matter how much I wished I could take a break I couldn't. I raised my fake katana above my head. Out of the corner of my eye, I saw a flash of metal.

Carter stood next to me, pounding away with a dumbbell. Rayz and Kyle joined him. We chose our spots. The taller men worked at the top while I took the bottom. The plaster fell away and a door was revealed. I grabbed the handle, yanking it open. We tumbled through and landed in the stairwell.

"We need to go." I scrambled out of the way and stared back at the entryway. The hole vanished in a matter of seconds. Standing, I flew down the steps to the fifth floor with the three guys. We might not be safe if the loop reacted to us leaving.

"I can't believe we made it out of there alive," Rayz said, sounding impressed. He bent over and tried to catch his breath. Once he could speak, he turned to me. "Thank you for saving my life."

"You're welcome," I said. Running a hand through my hair, bits of mortar fell to the ground. Sometime during my exercise, I had lost my scrunchie. I didn't what to check myself in a mirror. I had to be a mess.

"Do you want to try the buddy system?" Kyle asked.

"We better. We were trapped for three hours," I answered, glancing at my watch. Pike could wait in the return room until we finished our search.

"Lead the way." Kyle held his hand out for me.

The first room was three stories and filled with shelves of books. No sea vessel or airplane would have this many. They would be too heavy for cargo. For some reason, I believed the ship's log was buried in this mess.

"Why are we not searching here?" Kyle asked.

"We don't have time," I answered. Every room was different from others on this level and the next. Floor eleven was the hull. We entered a walkway over a large storage space. This was the end of our path, and we had found nothing. I hoped the other group had better luck. We returned to the original room and waited for the rest of the crew to arrive.

"What took you so long?" Carter asked once they joined us.

"We couldn't open a door and spent most of our time trying," Krewal answered.

"Did you find anything?"

"By the look of this place, no one has been here in years. Well, no one alive." He snorted and nodded at Gisela.

Carter told him we came up with the same, minus the spirit thing. He warned everyone to stay away from the third floor.

"Where's this door?" I asked curious. Clues might be behind it.

"We'll show you in the morning," Pike said. He held his hand up, stopping me from speaking. "We should either go back to our ship or camp here. I want to check on the approaching storm."

"You can do whatever you want. I'm staying until we have answers." I turned to Krewal. "Where's the door?"

"I'm not sure if I should be in the middle of this." He glanced between me and Pike.

"She is the host of the show," Kyle said, coming to my aid. My knight in shining armor. "You'd get more film time."

"I'll lead the way."

"Don't do this," the captain said. He stood in the doorframe and folded his arms across his chest.

"If we all try, the door will open," I said.

"You look like your mother when you're angry." He studied me for a moment then his face softened.

"I wouldn't know." I fingered the locket around my neck and waited for a better response.

"You have your father's tenacity. We'll try and dislodge the door for ten minutes. If we can't open it, we'll equip ourselves better tomorrow." He led us to the eighth level.

The door at the end wouldn't budge with the seven of us pulling on it.

"Time's up," Pike said, glancing at his watch.

"We need more leverage," I said. Those words reminded me of something we could use on level seven. Without waiting for a response, I ran back and pulled a piece of rail that looked like a crowbar off the wall. When I returned to the group, I showed them the metal. Pike didn't object so I wedged the hook into the gap. No matter what happed, I was opening this door tonight.

"Alexandra wait," Gisela called, placing her hand on my shoulder. "I've been wanting to tell you since we were on this ship. Your father isn't in this room."

Week Seven
Answers

"What are you saying?" I asked Gisela. Even as I spoke those words, I knew the truth. Tears filled my eyes. I couldn't turn around; their sad faces would make me cry.

"He's gone. Your dad, Dax Porter, died here. I can feel his ghost," Gisela said.

"Opening this door won't hurt me then." The muscles in my back tensed. I worked to gain control over my body and my emotions. If my father was dead, I needed to see him for myself. I wouldn't believe it otherwise.

"Seeing his body after he's been missing this long isn't good for you. He wouldn't want you to remember him that way," Pike said, in a gentle voice. He covered my hand with his own; his grip tightened around mine.

"Move your hand or I'll take it off." My tone came out harsh, despite what I felt. A pain developed inside my chest, my head spun, and I saw black spots. My whole world was about to break.

When Pike released his hold on me, I resisted the urge to scream. I returned my focus to the crowbar and the task before me. The thin metal end that held the screws fit between the wooden entrance and the jamb. With one quick thrust, the lock pried out, falling to the ground. The railing landed next to it with a thud. The door creaked open. I held my breath in anticipation of the worst possible scenario.

The eight-by-eight foot room was empty. A laugh escaped my lips and my shoulders sagged in relief. My dad wasn't dead. Gisela had to be mistaken. My chuckling died when a strange pull came from inside. I grabbed the door as the movement took hold of me. Pike's hand snaked around my waist before I was taken. His watch broke off in the strong vacuum, and the necklace I wore tore off. They sailed through the air into the center of the gravitational vortex, disappearing with a pop.

The next second, a single item crashed to the floor behind us. They had combined into one. Everyone stepped away from the door and it slammed shut. After I recovered from the initial shock to what we had witnessed, I pushed past my shipmates, running to my locket.

"Don't touch anything. We don't know if the object is toxic," Gisela said by my side.

I scooped up the necklace-watch combination with the hem of my shirt. The face of the clock had my mother as the background. The band stretched enough to the point where I could wear it around my neck.

"Three hours have passed," I said, reading the time.

"Let me see," Pike said. I handed it over to him. He didn't put on any type of protective wear, and nothing happened when he touched it. If the vortex had another reaction, we might be too early to tell. After he inspected the necklace combo, he gave it back to me. "You can keep this now. I can't take something with your mother's face on it."

"What the hell happened in that room?" I pulled the large locket over my head. My mother wasn't dead. She was out of my life, her choice not mine. She hated me after I told the court I wanted to live with my dad rather than her. I chose him after she screwed a cameraman. The show my parents were on was canceled, and our family was ruined. My life was better without her. Part of me loved her, which was why I carried the locket around.

"I don't know, but something on the fourth level might give our theoretical physicist some answers to figure everything out."

"What are you talking about?" Carter asked, narrowing his eyes and staring at the captain.

"You'll have to come and see. I can't explain what we saw." We trudged down the hall and climbed the stairs. Level five wasn't there anymore. Pike stopped outside a set of double doors. He opened them both, stepping inside.

I glanced over at Krewal for a hint of what to expect. His face lacked any emotions. For him to be speechless and expressionless, whatever was in there was serious. I entered second to last. What I saw wasn't anything I could have ever imagined.

A UFO in the shape of a diamond sat near the port windows. My heart thudded in my chest. On weakened knees I drew closer. The object appeared to be more like an airplane, but everything about it was wrong. A chunk of metal was missing from the hull, like the thing had crashed years ago, and the ship fixed itself around the aircraft. The wing sticking out of the side finally made some sense.

My chest tightened and a flutter formed inside my stomach. What I saw confused the heck out of me. Little green men didn't exist. Space travel was to advance for the technology on Earth. Science should have a reason behind the flying saucer. Maybe, I should have expected the unknown here. Four of us had survived being inside a time loop.

"This is the proof I've been waiting for my whole life," Rayz said, excited. He skimmed a hand across the top of the spaceship, whipping out his cellphone and taking pictures.

"This isn't even the most interesting part," Krewal said. He walked over to a tail section with white numbers on top of each other.

"Why do I recognize these?" I asked. The numbers twenty-eight, thirty-six, eighty-one, three, and seventeen were familiar.

"This is *Flight 19*. The five TBF Avengers that disappeared without a trance along with their fourteen crewmen in December 1945 in the Bermuda Triangle." He sounded giddy.

"Didn't a PBM Mariner disappear as it searched for them?" The words in my father's journal followed through my mind, and I scratched my head.

"Not anymore." He pointed at a large wing that had fallen off.

"How can you tell this section came from the PBM Mariner?" I asked. Everything was smashed together.

"The gull wing has a cantilever design, which means it is fixed to the aircraft. The markings are like pictures of those planes. Besides those two things, not many airships were lost in the B.T. like this one," he answered.

"Do you think Amelia Earhart's airplane is in this mess? I would love to find her and give her family some peace," Gisela said. She toed at a piece of scrap metal.

"The *Electra* disappeared on its way to Howland, near the Solomon Islands, on the other side of America," Rayz answered. He sighed afterward. For a conspiracist, he knew a lot of history. He might have to know the past to create a fake future.

"We're forgetting the most important part," I said. The crew turned to stare at me while my gaze was on Carter. He had to have a theory of what happened here. Whatever he was holding back, I wanted to know now. "Since you've seen everything, what happened to my father?"

"From what I can tell, the *Atlantis* is a natural phenomenon in which things of a matter are combined," Carter answered, choosing his words with care.

"Then my dad's still alive." Happiness flooded my heart.

"The ship is absorbing the airplanes. A human being would take less amount of time to disappear. I'm sorry, but he's dead."

"Will the event happen to us?" Pike asked.

"We would become one if we stayed here long enough." He nodded, solemnly.

"If what you say is true, we need to leave."

"Hold on, some things aren't combined," I said. The big UFO in the room was my proof.

"Have you ever tried to fit a lot of items inside a suitcase?" Carter asked. He licked his lips. "At some point, you can't shove anything else inside. The anomaly works the same way. Matter shouldn't be condensed like this."

"Could the ship explode?" More than once I had over packed a bag, the zipper was destroyed and my clothes popped out.

"A detonation is possible."

"I'm not abandoning anything until I find my father."

"This place takes bodies; nothing is left of the person. You'll never find him."

"Gisela, can you contact his ghost?" Pike asked, glancing at me.

"I've been trying since we arrived, but my ability hasn't been working right." Gisela held out her hand for me. With some reluctance, I set mine in hers. When she touched me, a stronger connection to the deceased was formed.

"What do you feel?" I asked. My throat tightened.

"He's here with us, but I can't get him to speak to me." She closed her eyes and called to my father.

"What's he saying?" Pike asked.

"He has to find Jakobe. Who is he?"

"He's the helicopter pilot."

Krewal scoffed.

"What she's saying is true. He's listed in my father's journal if you want to read them," I told him, holding up the notebook. Gisela confirmed to me her abilities were real. Only I had read his last journal entry.

"Try again," Dr. K muttered.

"Dax, I have your daughter here," Gisela said. She stopped, waited for a minute, and tried again. "He isn't answering. He keeps trying to find Jakobe."

"Have you ever not connected with someone before?" I asked. An ache formed in my heart, and I worried about what her not reaching him meant.

"I was unable to twice. The ghost didn't know they were dead. The second event involved a spirit meeting a tragic demise. They were trapped in their own death loop."

"Can you break him out of the first?"

"I can try." She closed her eyes and spoke to my father. "Dax, I'm here with your daughter. We want to help you, but we need your assistance. Can you please communicate to us?"

"Dad, I'm here. Please talk to Gisela, you remember her after she did the reading for you on your last TV show. You liked her," I said, trying my best. A shiver developed at the base of my spine. I never felt this cold before. Could I be feeling a ghost or was I afraid to lose my father? The worse part of my situation was that I didn't know which instance was true.

"Dax, you're trapped inside your death spiral. Jakobe is already gone; you can't help him," Gisela said.

"You need to wake up. You've done your best to help your crewmate." My heart was breaking. My father would never leave anyone behind. Jakobe was dead.

"What we are saying isn't working." She opened her eyes; her eyebrows furrowed together.

"Have you been able to force a ghost to realize the truth?"

"Yes, when I spoke to them. I'm confused. Why isn't he responding?" she asked.

"What do you think is wrong?" I asked.

"I don't know. This vessel has too many spirits. They are interfering with me. Once we are off, I'll try again. The distance will give me some clarity." She shook her head and released my hand.

"Fine, we'll leave here." Contacting my dad's spirit was the only way to figure out if he was alive or not. I was forced to leave for now. He wouldn't have a body to find here anyway.

Pike led us to where we left the boats, but one was missing. I darn well knew he had tied it. The anomaly must have taken it.

"This might be happening sooner than I thought," Carter said. His face was pale as he stared down at the single vessel below us. Panic was filled in his voice. "We need to leave now."

"What do we do then?" Kyle asked.

"Jump," Carter said. The director went over the side of the ship. Everyone else followed him. He struggled to swim, but Pike helped him onboard.

With everyone on the remaining craft, we sped away. We loaded everything onto the *Tranquil Seas* and set out. I wanted to keep the other ship within sight just in case we needed to return.

Week Eight
Finale

I was exhausted. Every muscle in my body ached. Zero sleep the night before caught up to me. I was ready to lie down and nap for a day or two.

"Come here, Alexandra," Gisela commanded. She yawned, her shoulders drooped, and she couldn't keep her eyes open. Dealing with the spirits must have drained her.

"What do you want? Can this wait until morning?" I asked.

"Don't you want to know about your father?" She shook her head and held out her hand.

Walking to her, I set my hand in hers. These last few months of not knowing the truth about my dad had had almost killed me. I was more afraid to know now.

"I don't feel him," she said after a few minutes.

"Since you can't reach him, is he alive?" I asked, hopeful.

"I think so." She didn't sound too sure.

"What do you want us to do?" Kyle asked me.

"Check out the ship again, but we need sleep," I answered. Dark waves rocked our boat and the sky turned gray. We were in for a heck of a storm. The water surrounding *Atlantis* was crystal blue. If the weather was too hard for us, I would suggest sailing into the calmness. Although, we might be safer away from anything turning us into each other. I would hate to become like the director.

"You can go to your cabin. I'll put everything away."

"Thank you for your help." I gave Kyle a hug and a kiss on the cheek.

"I have to contact the network. They haven't heard from us for well over six hours," Carter said. Worry lines appeared in his forehead; he bit his bottom lip and took off in the direction of his room.

"Resting is the best plan, but I'm worried about the coming storm. We'll take shifts watching the horizon," the captain said. He stifled a yawn.

"You shouldn't go first," I said. He had less sleep then me.

"Someone with experience needs to be awake."

"I disagree with you. We'll need you in tiptop form if the beast heading our way becomes worse," Krewal said.

"Are you agreeing to go first?" the captain asked him.

"Heavens, no."

"I'll volunteer," Rayz said. Everyone turned to him in disbelief. He wasn't a team player. "What? Two of the crew members with the most experience are dead on their feet. I want to do my part to help out."

"What is your real reason?" Dr. K narrowed his gaze at the other man, and a wrinkle formed in his brow. Seeing him accuse someone of something was strange. He was the type to help. Usually Rayz was the pain in the butt. Maybe, I was too tired to think straight.

"My blog needs a new post, and since I'm too full of adrenaline to sleep anyway, I figured aiding those who worked hard is the best use of my time."

"We have a plan," Pike said. He clapped the other man on the back in approval.

As I left the stern, I bumped into Carter. For once, he didn't yell at me. He must be sick or extremely tired.

"Wait, come with me. I have to show you and the rest of the crew something." He waited for us to follow him and hurried to his quarters. Piles of books were scattered around. Papers were on the floor and strewn across the desk. He pushed everything aside, picking up his laptop.

Unplugging the cord, he held the screen for us to see. "You need to see all these emails. We've been missing for four weeks."

"No, we were gone at best several hours," Rayz said. He removed his pocket watch, reading the time. "Your device has to be wrong."

The one on my neck was off. I didn't bother to look at it. Pulling out my cellphone and turning the screen on, the date jumped from when we first boarded the *Atlantis* to twenty-eight days later.

"My cell has the same date. We've been gone for a long time. Could the natural phenomenon also be a time loop?"

"I would say the evidence is right here," Carter said. His emails were darkened from when he read them.

"What did you tell the producer?"

"Nothing, I didn't know what to tell her without sounding nuts. What we witnessed hasn't been named yet."

"The Carterdox works for me." Part of me liked being a smart aleck. The other needed the comic relief. I didn't want to think about the event and my father.

Kyle and Rayz laughed at my pun.

"This isn't something to joke about. We witnessed something serious," Pike said.

"What do you want me to do? Cry? Run away?" I asked with a sharp tone. Heaviness formed inside my chest. "My dad has been trapped on the *Atlantis* for a long time. What if he can't ever leave?"

"We'll find him. Your father is a smart man. He left the event. He's safe now, waiting for you," Kyle said. He wrapped an arm around my waist and hugged me as I cried.

"Thank you." I wiped the tears out of my eyes and stepped out of his embrace. The minute I needed to cry until my heart was content vanished. I was ready to find my dad.

"Should I contact the network?" Carter asked, sounding nervous. He rubbed the back of his neck. The show's owners hadn't heard from us in a while. They must be worried.

"What have you told them so far?" the captain asked instead of answering.

"I informed them we had hit something, and we were repairing the damage. I was supposed to report in after we completed our task, but the mission to the other ship sidetracked me."

"They might think we sank."

Carter paled and his gaze darted between us. He was more anxious then I had ever seen him.

"The producer would have sent a search party, right?" Kyle asked.

"They would give our last known location to the Coast Guard," Pike answered.

"Where was that?"

"Carter's last email sent has our GPS location in the signature," I said. Using the computer mouse, I opened the message on his laptop.

"The Coast Guard has been looking in the wrong spot," Krewal said.

"No, they've been searching in the wrong time. How long would it take for them to give up finding us?"

"The longest anyone has been at sea has been one hundred and thirty-three days."

"We haven't been gone for too long. The Coast Guard will be out here looking for us," the captain said. He frowned and ran a hand through his hair. "I need to think. No one contact anyone, yet. I need sleep before I can formulate an idea to tell everyone."

"Us returning from being gone should boost our ratings," Rayz said, giddy.

"If we have a show left," I muttered. The media might think us missing was a hoax. I went to my room to sleep. Instead of going to bed, I used the satellite phone to call my dad. He didn't answer. My mind was to foggy to think what him not there meant. He must be stuck within the loop. I laid my head down and fell into dreamland.

σ σ σ

"How did you sleep?" Kyle asked me when I entered the deck, ten hours later.

"Alexandra, get up here," Pike called over the speaker.

I climbed the four levels to the bridge. When I entered, he pointed over at the microphone. I glanced at it, confused over what he meant.

"Mayday, this is *The Alexandra*. Can anyone hear me, over?" My father's voice came from the radio.

I couldn't believe what I was hearing. I pinched myself; this wasn't a dream.

"Mayday, this is *The Alexandra*. Can anyone hear me, over?" Dad repeated.

"Dad, it's me," I said into the mic. Heat radiated through my chest. He was alive, thank the stars. He was alive.

"Baby girl? What are you doing out here?"

"I've come to rescue you. Where are you?"

He gave us his coordinates. Pike steered us in their direction. Within a few minutes, his ship was a speck on the horizon.

"Can you see us?" I asked.

"Barely," he answered. We stayed on the radio until his boat was within shouting distance.

I helped direct Pike so the two ships didn't collide. Once we were next to each other, the other crew came over to ours.

I ran up to my dad and tossed my arms around his neck. He bent to pick me up since he was six feet and two inches tall. This time, happy tears filled my eyes. He hugged me back.

"I'm glad to see you. What are you doing here?" he muttered into my ear.

"You've been missing for seven months. Of course, I'd come find you," I answered.

"Has it really been that long?" He scratched his head.

"*The Alexandra* was bone dry of fuel," one of his people said.

"Only days have passed though."

"I have a theory. It's a pleasure to meet the famous Dax Porter," Carter said, stepping forward. He introduced himself, shook my father's hand, and explained the *Atlantis*.

"If we were trapped in a time warp, wouldn't we have fuel left?" Dad asked. He ran a hand through his short auburn hair.

"Depends on when the event decided to let you go. We were on the vessel for a maximum of seven hours, and four weeks were gone when we returned to the real world." The *Tranquil Seas* didn't run out of gas because the captain turned off our engines and not much evaporated within the big tanks for the month we were away.

"I don't think we should tell anyone what happened. I don't know if the world can take this phenomenon. But I must discuss this with Lucinda," my father said.

"You lost Jakobe?" Pike asked, referring to the husband.

"We didn't actually lose him." My father glanced over at his captain. "They are now one. I don't know how I'll explain the transformation."

"Wait a minute. I thought you were dead. Everyone on your ship was, according to our medium," Krewal said.

"I was wrong. What I felt was Dax's energy. The ship must have absorbed it. When a moment is emotionally charged, it leaves a portion behind. That was why I couldn't contact him," Gisela said.

Her explanation made sense. Being stuck on the boat and being combined with another person would have been terrifying. I was glad that my crew was okay. Although, Rayz had become much nicer like Krewal. Not a bad thing for him considering he had been such a jerk before.

"We should tow *The Alexandra* to port. We'll have to go slow since our vessel was damaged," Pike said. He turned to leave. My father followed him.

"Wait," I called over to him. Before he could ask me what I wanted, I gave him a hug and a kiss on his cheek. "Thank you, Robert, for everything."

"It's about time you called me by my first name."

Pike and I tethered the smaller ship to ours. He promised to get us home within the next two days and left the rest of us on deck.

"How are you feeling about not helping the ghosts on the *Atlantis*?" I asked Gisela, knowing she wanted to save them.

"I don't like it, but the ship is to dangerous," she said. She gave me a small smile and left.

"You brought everyone here for me?" Dad asked, sounding impressed. He wrapped an arm around my shoulder. "I didn't know you wanted to be in the family business."

I didn't until now. Nothing would ever keep him and me apart. This world contained plenty of other mysteries and myths for us to solve.

Jane's Kingdom

E.B. Sullivan

Chapter One

As if I were a child on Christmas morning, anticipation bubbled within me. While dressing in my best clothes I couldn't believe I would soon be a princess.

Of course, I understood, since the castle housed fine art, rare antiques, and a collection of priceless objects, I could only take a few items with me.

What did I want?

A gray haze covered my surroundings. The last few days were too hectic for me to do chores. To be perfectly honest, wanting to focus my attention on the future, I chose not to make cleaning a priority. The sheets were in a jumble on the bed. Dirty dishes crowded the sink. Clutter described the entire space.

Just looking at the messy place made my heart ache with sadness, but I couldn't put my finger on why I was teary eyed.

Like most people would be, I felt thrilled by the idea of moving to a royal court. I felt sure I wouldn't miss anything about my dingy abode.

I shifted through lots of stuff and grabbed a few appealing objects. They each sparkled in a unique way assuring me each piece would enhance the palace.

Before the royal chauffeur came to pick me up, I was waiting at the curb. I was more than ready to say goodbye to the broken hamlet I was powerless to fix.

I slid into the back seat of the impressive vehicle. I leaned my head against a side window, and watched the landscape change from an urban slum to pristine countryside.

The car turned onto a long driveway lined with trees.

Blossoms painted in pastel hues greeted me by shaking their pretty faces. Leaves dotted with freckles beckoned us forward. Pointed branches directed the way.

Acknowledging their friendly gestures, I repeatedly nodded.

As we snaked up a hill, a flock of white doves escorted us through every twist and turn.

Pride swelled within me as I relished my upcoming role as a princess.

When the car came to a stop, I waited patiently for the driver to open my door.

Reaching for my hand, he said, "Your Highness, you've arrived."

Along the footpath, flowers, some yellow, some white, displayed their bliss by dancing on green stems.

I lowered my head to smile at them and heard a host of violin strings playing in synchronized rhythms.

My feet fell in step with the familiar classical tempo. I waltzed in a circle. My heart beat with delight.

Almost hidden under a leafy canopy I noticed an orchestra of fairies dressed in all the colors of the rainbow.

Careful not to hurt their delicate ears, I whispered, "Bravo, Brava!" Softly, I clapped my hands.

I walked over the narrow moat and leaned against the latticed wall. A school of spotted goldfish swirled through the clear water. Concentric ripples spelled out a warm salutation.

The second I stepped under a columned portico, large doors slid into its framework.

One by one, my staff dressed in cheerful, printed fabrics bowed.

A lady in waiting, robed in a blue garment took my hand. "Welcome to your kingdom."

Sensing the weight of a jeweled studded tiara resting on my head, I beamed with elation.

Allowing me to take in the immensity of the castle, she silently led me through a labyrinth of faintly lit passageways.

We stood before a golden portal. When it magically opened, I followed her into a mirrored box and glanced at my radiant image. I stood tall ready to shoulder the awaiting responsibilities, no matter how daunting.

With the touch of a button, the box propelled us up a high tower.

In a quiet hallway, we strolled over an indoor lawn. My feet quietly sank into its lushness.

The maiden paused at a tall window.

I peered at a formal garden in the foreground and undulating hills in the background.

I exclaimed, "How magnificent."

"From now on, this land is yours."

"What are its boundaries?" I asked.

"As far as your eyes can see and beyond."

She opened a nearby door and ushered me into a regal bedchamber.

She triumphantly declared, "Your private space. You'll note it has the same panoramic view of the grounds. I hope it meets with your approval."

"It's indeed very pleasing."

Reaching her hand over a bed covered with a purple coverlet, she fingered a red ribbon. "Your Majesty, when you want assistance pull this string."

My heart soared.

It was true.

My childhood dream of being a princess was now a reality.

Chapter Two

Fatigued by the events of the extraordinary day, I stripped out of my clothes and crawled under the sheets. Their silkiness reminded me of my elevated status. Ensconced with contentment, I closed my heavy eyelids.

While dozing, dark images from a tragic, familiar opera haunted me.

Demons cast their shadows over me. I tried to run away, but my legs felt tied together with constricting twine. I projected my body in one direction. Then I jettisoned to another. I felt disoriented. I didn't know if I was moving up or downward.

The evil ones chased me. Their long tentacles caught me and held me. They submerged my body into a dank swamp. Their razor sharp fangs were about to pierce my skin, when I suddenly sat up, wide-awake and covered in cold sweat.

To calm my nerves, I reminded myself, I was now a princess.

Still, I trembled.

I staggered into the en suite's shower and let warm water cascade over me. I rubbed a sweet smelling gel on every inch of my skin. The luxurious substance burst into white puffy foam. Iridescent bubbles floated through the fog. Magically, my fears evaporated. The horrific nightmare fled from my mind.

I realized being royalty had special benefits.

A resounding voice echoed in my head, "It was true. I lived in a castle far, far from the perils of my past world."

In my protected environment, I sighed in relief and felt safe for the first time in a very long while.

With a lighthearted step, I explored my room. The walls glowed with muted rosiness. The furnishings trimmed with gold were quite elegant. The velvet drapes held back with embroidered ties added a depth of richness to the space. Tassels hung from jeweled knobs reinforcing the classic regal ambiance.

Gilded comb, brush, and manicuring tools rested on a silver tray.

Taking my time, I used supplies on a vanity table to fix my face and style my hair.

I winked at my reflection in a mirror framed with a climbing vine. Delicate lily of the valley dangled from branches. I inhaled a heavenly scent and felt uplifted.

I opened drawers. From one, I pulled out undergarments, from another a pair of stockings. While my fingers skimmed the satiny fabrics, I noticed each item embossed with a crest. On closer inspection, I recognized it as my family crest.

I peeked in the closet and was pleased to see it filled with lovely apparel. I chose a smart frock. It wasn't too fancy, but its demure lines made it just right for my first dinner at court.

From a rack, I picked a sexy pair of shoes.

I sashayed back to the chest of drawers and allowed myself time to stare at the sparkling items I had brought with me. A deep satisfaction caused my lips to form a broad grin.

Totally prepared to meet my subjects, I tugged the red ribbon.

After a short wait, someone knocked on my door.

I opened it and stared at another lady in waiting, this one dressed in red.

She asked, "How can I be of assistance?"

"A rumbling in my tummy tells me it's dinnertime."

We traveled down the tower in the mirrored box. I glanced at my image. I straightened my back ready to discover whatever was ahead.

She led me to a banquet hall.

The sounds of a harp playing ethereal notes glided toward me.

Understated crystal chandeliers illuminated the space.

Tables set with bone china and sterling silver announced my kingdom's wealth.

Fresh flower arrangements emitted lovely perfumed scents.

Handsome men and stunning women sat in many of the chairs. Their well-designed clothes led me to believe my kingdom was prosperous.

While elongating my neck, I held my head high and presented an air of confidence.

I thought, *Beautiful Princess Jane now replaced my plain Jane's former persona.*

As I passed, hands reached out for mine. With each touch, I glimpsed a tip of each soul and catalogued my observations.

I smiled and repeated, "Thank you. I'm so happy to be here."

My lady in waiting sat me at the head table.

A round of applause from the members of court welcomed me.

Neatly dressed servants offered us food. Most seemed happy giving service.

By the way others frowned, placed the plates askew, or rattled the dirty dishes; I knew they resented their jobs. To make my kingdom run efficiently, I'd have to speak to these disgruntled employees and assist them in finding work more suitable to their interests and abilities.

I redirected my focus on the meal. Each course, while looking tempting, tasted bland. The exception was desert. It was sickeningly sweet.

No one complained, but I made a mental note to visit the kitchen staff, speak to the head chef, and discuss ways to make pleasant tasting offerings.

Then I scolded myself. Even with a mother who was a gourmet and gladly shared her secrets, it took me years to master the art of cooking.

I decided to be patient with the staff and give them time to develop their skills.

While we ate in silence, I studied the assemblage.

Goodness oozed out of the majority of these people.

I felt proud to be their princess.

Their auras twinkled before me. Beyond the dazzling displays, regardless of color, I detected a gentleness bordering on frailty. There was also an underlying sorrow, a great deal of fear, and a familiar confusion.

Recognizing their problems from my nightmares, I understood why they chose me to be their princess.

My heart filled with an urgent passion.

I wanted to give these folks hope.

I wanted to help them find peace.

I vowed to devote all my time and draw upon whatever knowledge I possessed to strengthen my people and infuse my kingdom with the spirit of love.

Chapter Three

Following a breakfast consisting of dry cereal and fruit swimming in syrup, intent on further exploration, I left the banquet hall alone.

Occasionally, melodious chimes wafted through the corridors. I wondered if swirling fairy dust was responsible for the lilting sounds.

When I passed individuals huddled together, wanting to respect their privacy, I tried not to listen to words, phrases, or sentences. Nonetheless, I couldn't avoid hearing the tenor of the majority of conversations. Repeated refrains often not going beyond small talk, made me wonder, *Did my subjects have meaning in their lives?*

From the depths of one of the chambers, I heard crashing objects.

A female voice shouted, "You #### witch leave me alone. Don't think I'm fooled by your pleasantries. I know you're part of the plot. I don't trust you or any of your wicked crew. I won't do anything you tell me to do, not now, not ever.

"Get out. Get out."

A man dressed in viceroy attire ran in front of me and disappeared into the room.

I hastened to the source of the disturbance, but lingered in the doorway watching.

When I spied the ranting person's robe, I knew she was a noblewoman.

A lady in waiting acknowledged the viceroy with a nod of her head.

He advised the agitated woman, "Please calm down, relax, and take a seat."

As if his presence and the sound of his voice conveyed a serious threat, she cowered and a look of compliance replaced her show of bravado. She quickly retreated by sitting on a tufted throne.

Silence filled the space.

Feeling the time was right, I held up my hand and ordered, "Leave us."

After the pair brushed passed me, I closed the door.

I stood in front of the countess.

"I'm your new princess, Princess Jane. And you are?"

While she pondered which to do first, rise or speak, I lowered my hand and observed her lovely face framed with short curls. Her skin was as pale as alabaster.

She extended her hand. Her fingers skimmed my ring. It housed the gemstone of my family crest.

She said, "I'm Marie."

I told her, "You have extraordinarily soft skin."

"My Mario would always tell me that."

"Is he here at the castle?"

She placed her hands in her lap. "No. Sadly, he left a long time ago, but he's protecting me from afar."

I assumed he was a knight stationed on the borders and fighting in the endless war.

"Tell me, why are you upset?"

As if ashamed, she lowered her head. She seemed so meek, so frightened. Yet, moments ago her eyes had conveyed the wild frenzy of a caged animal. I wondered if given the chance she could be dangerous.

"You're safe in sharing your secret with me. I promise your words will go no farther than this room."

She sniffed.

From the pools collecting in her eyes I knew she was on the brink of crying.

I knelt before her. "I'm your princess. You can tell me anything. Maybe I can help."

Her halted words slowly left her mouth. "I... I'm tired... tired of fighting."

Her speech accelerated. "They're all out to get me. I'm crazy with fear of what they'll do next. They banished me from my homeland, brought me here to this foreign place. They stripped me of my possessions. They used my money. They hate me, and I don't know why."

A look of fury flashed across her face. "I'm tired of taking orders… tired of obeying orders. I want to steal one of their cars and drive far away."

She clutched my hand so tightly I had to summon all my self-control to prevent myself from wincing.

From the corner of my eye, I noticed something sparkle.

As I turned my head, my free hand pointed. "Tell me about this. Why is it special?"

She released my hand, rose, and caressed the twinkling object. "It's mine from before. I'm afraid they'll take it."

"I won't let them have it."

"Promise?"

"Yes. I promise. And even if it were gone, no one can take away why it's important to you. Can they?"

A peaceful countenance brightened her face. "You're right. There're thousands of important memories I hold inside me."

"And no one has any idea what they are. They belong to you alone, now and forever."

"Indeed."

I requested, "Tell me what you're feeling."

"There's a certain protocol for a woman of my station. I must speak softly and never challenge others. I must act appropriately, politely, hide my feelings."

"Not with me."

"But what will you think of me, if I let my hair down and explain how I see the world?"

"I'll think you're honest. There's no harm in you sharing the truth with me."

"Really?"

"Really. In fact, I encourage you to tell me what you're thinking and what emotions are twirling deep within you."

She put the object on the table. She placed her hands on her hips and looked me in the eye. Her voice was loud. "I'm angry. I feel rage for all the wasted time I blindly obeyed the rules, denied myself fun, was polite to the degree of hiding my opinions. I resent the ones who expect me to be the same obedient woman I once was. I'm fed up with being nice. Nice made me take a back seat to life. I missed out on way too much."

She sobbed.

I patted her shoulder.

"Maybe there's still time to find what you want right here in this kingdom?"

"I hate it here."

"Why?"

"Because I'm surrounded by my enemies. Haven't you seen them? They lurk in every corner and hide in every crevice. They can pop up, scare you, overtake you, or kill you in a few seconds."

"Listen," I suggested. "What do you hear?"

"Nothing."

I told her, "I hear wings flapping."

"Really?" She sat on her ornately covered bed.

"Don't you see the angels all around us?"

Her gaze scanned the room. "I don't see anything, but I know the evil ones are hiding."

"Close your eyes. Look into your heart. Tell me what you feel."

She lowered her head on a fluffy pillow. She stretched out her legs. She shut her eyelids. After a few minutes she said, "I feel safe. Did you bring the angels?"

"I only reminded you they're always with you."

Noticing her breaths slowing I realized she'd soon be asleep.

I whispered, "No matter what happens, the angels are always ready to protect you."

Chapter Four

After leaving the countess, in order to get an overview of how my court functioned, I roamed the castle's halls. I whiffed the air infused with floral scented beads, but beneath the enchanting aroma, I detected the smell of cleaning solutions.

Members of the staff scurried about like mythical elves doing chores I myself had done in my former position as an ordinary citizen.

This work, although not too strenuous, because of endless repetition, became laborious. Over time, I resented doing jobs that took me away from the things I preferred doing and considered important. I mourned the hours I wasted performing mundane duties instead of showering attention on the people I loved.

I tried to calculate the hours I spent dusting furniture, vacuuming carpets, doing laundry, washing windows, scrubbing bathtubs, and making beds. The numbers escalated into the thousands.

I tried to remember the times I felt appreciated for making my environment tidy and attractive, but couldn't think of any.

A tear slipped down my cheek recalling incidents when disrespectful individuals tracked mud on my floors, spilled liquids on my counters, left dirty clothes scattered about for me to pick up.

In gratitude for relieving me of distasteful tasks, I smiled broadly at each uniformed individual.

To acknowledge the staff's efforts, I made it a point to thank everyone.

I praised, "Good job. Nice work. Looking good."

I recommended, "Open the windows. Don't advertise your mission to rid the castle of germs. Let the outdoor freshness steal away the underlying antiseptic fumes."

I offered reassurance, "I'll do my best to respect the results of your labor. Moreover, I'll try to make good use of the time your diligence affords me. I've made it my quest to rule my kingdom fairly."

In their humility, the staff quietly absorbed my compliments and listened to my suggestions.

I knew, regardless of my behaviors, the loyal ones would devote their time and skills in keeping my palace immaculate. I also knew the slackers wouldn't be influenced by my opinions or follow my advice.

Face to face with an unhappy employee, I didn't censor my words. "Why are you here doing a job you hate?"

He stared at me.

"I repeat. Why are doing work you detest?"

"I need the money. Without a job, I can't pay my bills, feed myself, or buy things I want."

"But why this job? Why not earn a living doing what you like?"

"Your Highness, you wouldn't understand."

"Do you take me for a simpleton? I didn't get to my station in life without becoming aware of a few things."

I questioned, "What do you like doing?"

My comment must have gotten his attention, because he answered, "Having fun."

"Doing what?"

"Playing hockey, watching football games, going fishing, and kissing my sweetheart."

"And?"

"Whatever I like to do won't earn me enough dollars to survive."

"I find that hard to believe. You seem like an interesting person. I'm certain you have varied interests.

Many of which could be profitable. Tell me about your passion."

He was quiet.

"Surely something excites you."

"You'll think me silly."

"Why? Do you crave power? Do you want to trade places with me? Do you want to be king and rule my kingdom?"

His head snapped back as he snickered. "Hardly." He cleared his throat. "I think such a position would be overwhelming."

"Then what is it you enjoy doing?"

"I like working on computers. You know tech stuff."

"Have you thought of finding employment in that field?"

He shrugged his shoulders.

"Would the pay be comparable to your present salary?"

"I don't know. I don't make much money doing janitorial jobs around here. But I'd have to get certified or something. I'd have to take classes and pass tests."

"So?"

"That would take time especially if I went to night school. Then I'd have to get experience working as some kind of apprentice or assistant. I'd be middle-aged before I could benefit from any real training."

"Won't time pass anyway? Two years from now, won't you be two years older even if you don't go to school? Whether you attend school or don't go, five years from now, won't you be five years older? Won't you wake-up one morning as a middle-aged man regardless of your chosen profession?"

He looked surprised. "You have a good point."

"How do you think it would feel learning more about computers and spending more time tinkering with them?"

"It would be great. And it would be fun talking to other geeks like me. It would be thrilling finding out the latest advances and …"

Listening to his growing exuberance, I felt sure he would pursue his dream. Although still a new princess and feeling my way into the role of mentor, I felt encouraged to speak to the other discontented ones working in my kingdom.

Chapter Five

At a relentless pace, fierce monsters pursued me. Some were tall and slender. Others were round and squat. Fire spewed from their ears. Venom dripped from their tongues.

They soon discovered me hiding under my covers. Their oversized claws ripped off my blankets and pulled me up to a sitting position. They hissed at my eyes freezing them open. My neck like the rest of my body couldn't turn or move in any direction.

There I sat forced to watch videos containing scene after scene of my most wretched mistakes.

My heart broke for the children I had wounded and the adults I had injured.

Remorse mixed with self-disgust spilt out with my anguish cries.

I begged, "Please let me go back. I now know how to do a better job.

"If I can't return to the past to make things right, I don't deserve to be a princess.

"Take away my kingdom and throw me in a dungeon.

"Chain me in irons next to the damned."

With my heart rapidly beating, I awoke with a hunger for sunshine.

As pressing as was the need for air, I gravitated toward the window longing for natural light. Grabbing a robe and flinging it over my shoulders, I answered the call to leave the castle.

Once beyond the guarded exits, I skipped down the garden path with my face turned upward. I soaked up the rays and felt rejuvenated.

Fairies surrounded me. Their impish expressions made me smile and restored my equilibrium.

A miniature voice advised, "To help others in the future, live in the moment."

I thought of the countess. Like her, I, too, had frazzled nerves.

Shaking my body, I tried to rid it of a too familiar terror.

To assist my subjects, I needed to lead by example. I needed to conquer my demons by making each day of the rest of my life count for something important. Although future deeds, no matter how great, would ultimately be insufficient to rectify what I had done or failed to do, there was a chance one intervention might benefit at least one person.

I sucked in the fresh air, held my head up high, and turned until I located the trellised arch laced with budding white flowers. Under this lovely canopy I spied my outside, copper, patina throne.

I ran to it, stepped up, and sat on the formal seat. Spreading my robe in a flared fashion, I awaited my audience.

A stranger, a man, was first to arrive. He bent from his waist to kiss my cheeks.

I cordially greeted him, "Thanks for stopping by. Nice to see you."

He babbled about people he knew. He updated me on anticipated births, upcoming weddings, and a recent funeral.

I wasn't acquainted with any of the individuals he mentioned.

Frankly, I wasn't interested in them not because they were mean or bad, but because I now resided in another kingdom. Since I'd never return to his world, I no longer had the ability to meet any of them, hug them, wish them well, or bid them goodbye. Thus, I didn't want to invest my emotions in their lives.

Trying to keep the subject matter impersonal, I suggested we go for a stroll. Along the way, I pointed at astounding bushes and astonishing trees.

"Can you hear the magnificent tunes performed by our bird population?"

He didn't respond. He seemed bored. I sensed he felt uncomfortable.

"How can I help you?" I asked.

He started to laugh, but stopped himself by saying, "Life's busy."

"Too busy to notice the beauty around you?"

Memories of him in my last life flooded me. Over the years, no matter how hard I tried to reach him, he made it clear he had no desire to understand me.

Today, like always, he ignored my comments. In doing so, he evaporated the worth of my words. Like always, I felt discounted by him.

Then I realized my past immature behaviors were deeply etched in his heart. He couldn't see beyond the many times I had failed him, let him down, embarrassed him. Locked into a view of me as a weak adult, no matter how many years past since his childhood, no matter how I evolved, he'd always see me as a foolish woman. I guessed he considered me the worst of fools, someone who acted like she knew everything. When in reality, she knew very little.

Loving him so, I hoped by devaluing me he gained self-value.

Realizing I created the chasm between us, I didn't blame him for not wanting to really know me.

Having no other choice, I accepted his indifference. It was what I deserved.

As if to prevent my broken heart from crumbling, the fairy population sent an entourage to accompany me.

Knowing this particular visitor hadn't cultivated the ability to hear the wee people, I didn't mention them.

Maybe as he matured, he would open his mind to their wondrous existence. Maybe someday they'd help him realize no matter how badly I had injured him, I always loved him and always would.

Another person came running toward us. She shouted, "Sorry. I had to take an important call."

When she came closer, I glimpsed her muddled aura.

While embracing me, she whispered, "Let's go back to your room. I'll help you slip into clean clothes."

Her insensitivity made me cringe.

Didn't she know as a princess I could dress in any way I pleased?

Didn't she know I was the one who set the standards in my kingdom?

Didn't she know I didn't have to follow someone else's ideas of what was decent or proper?

While wiggling my arms free, I thought of banishing her from my kingdom.

Involuntarily, I raised my hands in the air.

A fairy flew to my fingertips and held back my impulse to strike the insincere maiden.

Another fairy whispered in my ear, "You don't want to be like her. Do you?"

What I wanted was to be a fair-minded princess. How could I reflect justice if I ignored truth? The woman embodied greediness. She personified a selfish wife and a sham of a mother. She was of the passive aggressive ilk. While cloaking herself in self-righteousness, she secretly tormented those around her. She didn't have the power to hurt me directly, but by wounding innocent ones, she could slice my heart.

I felt confused. *Was I mixing her up with someone else? Was I tossing her into a group of people I had disliked in the past?*

The videos I watched in my dreams flooded my mind. Realizing my failings reminded me I had no right to judge anyone, not even this questionable woman.

Yet, she troubled me.

Hating to be in her presence, I wanted to run away and hide under my bed.

The fairies cautioned, "Your Majesty, your best defense is to tolerate her."

While I tried to act dignified, a glint in her eyes told me she lusted after my kingdom. She felt entitled to inherit my wealth and position.

I giggled and thought, *She didn't have the ability to recognize, let alone appreciate, my true treasures of loving others.*

Another thought entered my head, *If I didn't accept her then maybe I was more like her than I imagined.*

Despite telling myself I could love someone I disliked, a seething welled within me and threatened to explode in her face.

The royal fairies flitted around me.

Their wings tickled my skin.

I giggled.

My mood tempered.

I glanced at the man. He continued to be disinterested. It was obvious he felt bound by duty to be here.

And the woman, the self-serving one, was here to scope out what she hoped to someday gain.

Unlike the dangers looming over me in my past world, I was safe in my kingdom.

But I was wise enough to realize, my kingdom, in too many ways, was like my last home. Good, bad, and in between folks inhabited its fenced in walls of twisted barbed wire.

Chapter Six

After showering, I dressed in my favorite frock.

No longer bound by obligations, responsibilities, or expectations I felt free to give from my heart. As a princess, I no longer cared about what others thought of me. Acceptance or rejection took a lowly place compared to serving my court.

Intent on acquainting myself with members of my kingdom, I entered the great hall. Its abundant space decorated with flags, pendants, and crests, reinforced the power of my dominion.

It was a place for leisure activities, a social space, and the hub of my castle.

Columns set off cozy nooks. Cushioned sofas provided relaxed seating. Fabric covered chairs surrounded tables with marble tops infused with gold flecks.

The thick walls absorbed harsh noises.

Mingled voices sounded like a lyrical hum.

Some people were playing board games. Others worked puzzles. A few were making exquisite pictures using colored pencils.

As I drew closer and circulated among the many members, I waved and said good day more times than I could count.

From what I observed, I couldn't help but conclude my kingdom reflected the world I had left behind.

People gossiped and tore down others for sport.

I saw friends embrace, hold hands, pat each other on backs.

Folks bragged and exaggerated.

I listened to happy laughter and watched it spread from face to face.

A myriad of emotions filled the grand expanse.

Tears welled in too many eyes.

Sorrow and pain darkened moods.

Mourning the dead was another common theme.

I wondered, *Didn't these individuals believe in Heaven or did they fear Hell?*

I continued my tour.

Bitter ones dwelled on anger. Hate festered in them like ulcerated sores.

Forgiving ones focused on love. Radiance spread from them like sunbeams.

I gravitated to the ones concerned with other people's lives. I admired them.

I also knew I could learn from the introspective ones.

I marveled at the creative ones and turned away from copycats.

It felt like I was in a living classroom. Each person had many lessons to help me further understand myself.

The frightened ones allowed anyone and anything to exacerbate their fears.

The immature ones were critical and blamed others for their mistakes.

The dysfunctional ones lived from one crisis to the next never solving problems and seemed to thrive on the moment's drama.

The mean spirited ones took without giving.

The caring ones gave without expecting anything in return.

The ones who sat in their lounge chairs all day staring into space intrigued me.

I went to one man's side.

He was a duke.

I knelt next to him.

I took his hand. It remained limp. I realized he didn't want me interrupting his meditation.

From the corner of my eye, I glimpsed the countess.

Her wide, bulging eyes conveyed panic. Her arms flayed about. She shouted, "They've penetrated the walls. They're set to attack. They're going to torture us."

I spied viceroys rushing toward her.

I spoke up, "This is your princess speaking."

The countess paused to listen to my proclamation. "The angels are protecting us. They won't allow anyone, or anything to cause us harm."

She froze in place. Her eyes locked on mine. I waved, indicating she move closer.

I sat on the piano bench. Without thinking, I allowed my fingers to fly across the keys. As I played a melody, her high soprano voice accompanied me. A baritone stepped to her side. Together they performed a duet.

Soon members of the court formed a chorus. Their voices rang out and brought each of us to a happy place.

I felt pleased we could share beautiful moments from past worlds.

Chapter Seven

Days drifted by.

Weeks passed.

No matter how hard I tried, I couldn't stop some things from staying the same and other things from drastically changing.

In this new season, raindrops, laden with sadness, perpetually poured on my kingdom.

I watched rivulets of water travel down the glass windowpanes and pool in the nearby grasses.

Drenched plants shriveled into dormancy.

In order to avoid drowning, the fairies hid underground.

The outside gloominess seeped into the palace.

Unfortunately, like other such structures, this elaborate edifice lacked insulation from the elements.

I felt a constant chill. My thin flesh and old bones couldn't shake off the dankness. My only real warmth came from gazing at the giving souls in my midst, but it became harder to concentrate on them.

When I attempted to sleep, crude monsters spouted ugly stories of betrayal, estrangement, illness, and death.

I tried to shrug off the woeful warnings by telling myself, "This castle like others was plagued with mystery and intrigue."

At the entrances of private bedchambers, I watched as viceroys followed out medical directives by offering calming pills.

I stormed into the renowned royal physician's office and shouted, "Your job is to heal not to dull the senses of my court."

He responded, "I only give your subjects what they desire. There are those among us who would rather not feel at all than experience excruciating discomfort."

I finally faced the truth.

I didn't have the power to destroy the enemies dwelling inside my distressed subjects.

No more than I could hold back the dampness, I didn't possess the ability to ban the adversaries of light from permeating the kingdom's fortress.

Before I arrived at my kingdom, the notorious Alzheimer somehow invaded my head. He tenaciously held on to my gray matter and nourished himself on my brain cells. I irrationally believed, as a princess of a safer world, I could rid myself of him. I thought, in time, somewhere in the universe, someone wiser than I could destroy him.

The countess was correct about enemies seeping through the castle's walls.

Throughout my kingdom, I wasn't able to stop tortuous Cancer from inflicting lingering slow deaths. Years ago, on a far away battlefield, this formable foe had stolen my right kidney, but I was the victor. Others weren't as fortunate. I prayed someone smarter than I would one day annihilate him.

I couldn't prevent the bedridden from the hands of repugnant Pneumonia. Not even newer medications, more potent than penicillin, could stop his advances.

And I couldn't heal those who struggled from the aftermath of sudden blows from the infamous Stroke. Although some people recovered from his parlaying wounds, I couldn't forget this villain had debilitated the strongest person I'd ever known.

Sequestered in the castle I couldn't escape seeing constant problems eroding the spirits of those residing in my court.

With reluctance, I accepted that I couldn't eradicate gossip, hate talk, or dissuade people from vying for power regardless of how insignificant. I couldn't redirect folks from placing emphasis on little things in order to avoid facing big issues.

But wasn't that what I was doing?

Wasn't I avoiding the reality of losing my mind by hiding in a fantasyland, a make believe kingdom?

Within my private space, I fingered the sparkling picture frames I brought with me. I sighed as I thought of the strangers in the photographs. Were they members of my family? Was I looking at my son, my daughter, my grandchildren, and a wonderful husband?

I let myself sob.

It was best my loved ones, whoever they were, would no longer be with me. I couldn't care for them. I wasn't fit to be seen by them.

A distant recollection flashed before me. Without anyone's knowledge, when I started losing my memory, I applied for the princess position.

Low and behold, my childhood wish of becoming a princess came true.

Not wanting the ones I loved to miss a second of their happiness or see me deteriorate, I ordered them never to visit me in my kingdom.

Yet, I had vague recollections of being upset when they occasionally didn't honor my request.

Each day since I arrived in my kingdom, to bear the pain of leaving my family, I told myself, unless I severed the past, I wouldn't be able to serve my people.

My lofty quest helped me shift my agenda from my once upon a time home to my new vast domain.

Now it was time to make another dramatic detour.

I was at a crossroads. I could either pray for a merciful future or dwell on my past mistakes. Either way I was no longer interested in the present.

While I pondered my dilemma, I moved into another realm.

I was elevated to queen.

Devoted ladies in waiting performed my basic needs. Not permitted to lift as much as a finger, as if I was a baby, they changed my diapers, bathed me, dressed me, and fed me mashed up foods.

Like queens of ancient times, I wasn't permitted to walk. Caring ones wheeled me around in a silver chariot.

Without outward independence, I initially felt seized by fear.

Gradually, by searching my heart, I found peace.

I resonated with the old ones who sat in chairs staring into space. I concluded they were contemplative philosophers.

Like them, I continued to be introspective.

In addition, my new role was one of observer.

While I sat on an ebony pillow, a lovely lady in waiting dressed in turquoise steered my glistening chariot through the castle's grand doorway.

The weather had changed. Once again, the outdoors felt alive and inviting.

I turned my head up to the sunlight.

In the magic garden, I took deep breaths of fresh air.

Fairies surrounded me.

Flowers danced to birdsongs.

As a stoic queen, my heartstrings stirred, but my face didn't express any emotion. My lips didn't utter any words.

My personal lady in waiting took me over the paths around the castle. I noticed a new sign and realized a replacement princess must be in charge of my kingdom. I wondered why she chose to name her kingdom *Brookside Nursing Home*.

I felt the name I had chosen, *Comfort Castle,* was more fitting.

I reviewed my reasoning.

The ladies in waiting and the viceroys couldn't nurse members of the court back to health.

The royal physician couldn't restore memories.

Innovative therapies couldn't help us regain strength.

But the palace staff could be kind to me and my subjects, offer us soothing reassurances, and respect us.

My kingdom was akin to what the bigger world had been. It was a place of transition.

Unlike my last home, this one sat on the threshold to a permanent destination.

Although I no longer spoke, I constantly thought.

I cherished each moment I had lived.

I recalled a mixture of joys and sorrows.

Biblical wisdom reminded me life is fleeting.

I was growing weary and lacked the stamina to participate in the repetitive game of living in this world.

I'd already won my race.

Unfortunately or fortunately, I wasn't sure which, I lacked the power to help others reach their finish lines.

The message was clear.

It was up to each individual to run his or her own race.

Despite brief moments of confusion, deep within me, I knew I was about to enter a true kingdom, the Kingdom of God.

With each breath, I looked forward to seeing His peaceful, joyful garden filled with more beauty than I could ever image.

The Season of the Neuri Knight

Leigh Podgorski

Bridget Grace, her close cropped flaxen hair swept straight back from her wide high forehead, watched her father, Luke Stone, closely on the sixty-inch monitor. Something was off. His steel blue eyes were so dark they radiated black, the pools of his corneas swallowing his irises until there was no distinction between them. The deep golden tan burned into the crags and crevasses of his face from a summer spent by the sea of New Camen, New Hampshire, shimmered in fragments, trying desperately to break through the ghostly pallor that buried the sun. The jagged vein on the right side of his forehead jumped with the beat of his heart and the effort he was making to keep his mind closed to her.

And even after all these months in this forested wonderland of the Primeval Bialowieza under the tutelage of her shaman and the leader of all her people, Jadwiga, still, Bridget Grace did not have the power to unlock her father's mind—not when he chose, as he was doing now— to keep it closed to her. And at this moment, he'd wound it tight as Midas's fist.

They could communicate without speaking. In images, emotions, symbols, even plain words. She called it their "secret language." She discovered it when she was still a toddler—three, four? How delighted she had been to find this secret passageway to the father she so adored. But he was not delighted. He was reluctant. Discouraging. And as Bridget Grace grew, and as she discovered more gifts, her father became more and more discouraging. Not just with her, but also with himself. He had never been comfortable with the powers, the gifts bestowed upon him.

Still, he was allowing her some access. The access he chose. Images flew, swirling like icy flakes in a blizzard, spinning out from his mind to hers. Though his face remained placid on the screen before her, she felt the rage burning behind the mask, the inferno blazing deep inside him: raw, feral, thunderous. A ghostly shadow wavered amid the fire and ice. A tall man dressed in black, his silver hair sleeked back and shimmering in the storm. Armand. Of course. It could only be Armand Jacobi who would invoke such furor striking at the heart of Luke Stone. Armand, like a wisp of smoke, vanished. Armand, like the black magician he was, escaped. The image shifted. Her father, in his office, his head thrown back, howling. Her father, a man of infinite calm and control, ripping his phone from his desk, flinging his chair against the wall with such force it splintered, upending his desk and tearing it apart with his bare hands. But his hands were no longer human. His hands were transmogrifying: the fingers twisting, elongating, the nails blackening and curving into claws. He paced, wild, captured, his spine bending, fine fur covering his torso, his limbs, his mask extended, sharp teeth protruding, all, all of him transmogrifying until he stood nearly eight feet tall, a giant golden grizzly in the midst and wreckage of what used to be a precisely organized office.

"Luke..." Her mother, his wife, Beth, called out, reaching her hand out to him, softly, quietly, unafraid. "Luke... it's all right... Luke... come to me."

"I'll tell Jadwiga to get your cabin ready for you," Bridget Grace spoke as the images faded and fluttered away like dead autumn leaves.

"Good."

This was why he wanted to see her. He'd shape-shifted. Transmogrified. He was half Neuri, like most Neuri now in the twenty-first century, half Neuri or even less. He had been endowed with Neuri powers since birth, a healer, a tracker, a visionary unequaled, a warrior, and yet he had never shape-shifted. It was the supreme gift attained by but a few. No Neuri had ever been born with the ability. There was training, but no one knew for certain the sacred path, not even Jadwiga herself, keeper of all Neuri texts and secrets, keeper of the Bialowieza Village. Jadwiga, who was close to ninety, had yet to achieve this highest skill. At the age of fifty-five, in a situation of extreme emotional and psychological duress, her father had experienced a spontaneous transmogrification, which was exactly what she had done four months ago. And exactly as she had been, he was disoriented by the shift.

"Dad?" Bridget Grace spoke before they disconnected. "It's okay."

And for the first time, her father smiled. "I'll be there soon."

σ σ σ

From the Diary of Bridget Grace Stone
May 25

The Bialowieza Forest is the last of the primeval forests in all of Europe. A primeval forest is one that has suffered minimal disturbance by man. The forest has grown, developed, diversified, decayed, renewed, transformed, and transmogrified according to the laws of nature, the way only nature intended for it to do.

It is so exquisite here. I walk these woods and my soul sinks into my peace. Like the forest herself, I am renewed; I am transformed.

I don't remember much of my own transmogrification.

Jadwiga told me my experience was what was called a spontaneous transmogrification brought about by extreme emotional and psychological duress.

To which I replied, "No, shit."

The last thing I remember was Downing trying to kill my father. I remember him drawing his gun. I remember the gun glinting in the light of hundreds of lanterns. I remember the gun pointed at my father's heart, and the sound of the shot exploding through the forest. I remember this pressure ricocheting through my body—

this... force... ripping through me like a blast of dynamite in my soul, and I was being torn into a million pieces ....I remember a... rumbling... from the depths of my being... and this... intensity... of sight, of sound... of smell... I remember throwing my head back and howling into the wind. I remember a feeling of such vast freedom and belonging to the night and the wind... my hair was turning grey and beige and covering my body... fur... not hair... lifting with the soft breeze. My limbs were lean and strong and sure; my black claws unbending... I remember seeing Downing cowering... and I sprinted towards him... he tried to escape... but I was relentless... I ran him down... leapt upon him.... his screams filled the forest as I swiped at him with my mighty claw... leaving stripes of red blooming across his face, down his back, and blood spurting from his neck...

I remember hearing my father calling... as if from a great distance... as if from another world... I remember the calm settling over me like the sweetness of a summer night... he was safe... the bullet was not true...

My father approached me quietly as I paced, panting, before my prey, the vanquished enemy— Downing... low growls erupted as my father continued to move towards me invoking my name, calling me back from that world to this one...

I remember the woods... not Bialowieza, Michigan... deep within the Northern Michigan woods, the woods my father loved... I remember the words Downing had enticed me with... words of love... words of wonder and salvation and hope for all good things... I remember how deeply I loved him... how truly I believed in Armand...

I remember the feel of the cold stone marble as Downing and Armand placed me on the altar. I no longer believed in Armand Jacobi. I was no longer in love with Downing Shirley.

I knew by then they had used me. I had been set up as nothing more than bait. As nothing less than a lure for Luke Stone.

I remember the feel of the blood when I first touched that marble. It swept through me like fire. I knew what they had done. Who they had placed on this altar before me. And what they had done to those girls.

I remember guarding the dead body of Downing Shirley. I don't remember the journey back to… me. I remember gazing down at Downing and being naked in the woods, and taking the white silken cloth from the altar they had made me lie upon and wrapping the cloth around…

I remember my dad a few yards away from the altar, from where Downing now lay, pounding Armand Jacobi, his fists pumping like pistons… Armand wailing like a beast or a child… begging for mercy. I remember joining with the others, with my grandmother, Danuta, and Stan and Mike, the ex NYPD, who now worked for my father… all of us together, calling to him, reaching for him, trying to grab on to some part of him to hold my father back, but it was like trying to hold back that grizzly that lived inside him… finally, I spoke in our secret language… and finally he heard my voice…

We weren't going to lose him… not like that… after everything Jacobi had put us through… have my father then the one facing charges…

Stan called the cops. My father called my mother. And finally, my dad and I were able to go home.

I remember how it felt to be swept into my mother's arms.

In June, my parents and my grandmother brought me here.

σ σ σ

Every muscle in Bridget Grace's body throbbed in perfect rhythm with the pounding of her heart. Her head drooped leaden on her shoulders, feeling as heavy as the petrified tree stumps she stepped wobbly over as she made her way home. The deep cool green of the forest sparkled with the liquid gold drops of sunlight, inviting her to lay her weary load down and sleep.

But this she would never do. Instead, she squared her shoulders, lifted her chin, and forced her foot high over the fallen stumps. She reminded herself to *breathe.* The forest air was crisp and sharp, filled with the scent of spruce and pine and earthy peat, of thyme and wild rose, and primeval grasses. As she breathed in the manna of the invigorating air, she commanded her mind and body to rejuvenate.

She was not a healer—not yet— but she was mastering the ancient Neuri art of rejuvenation.

And, she thought with a wry anticipatory smile, she had a very good reason to knit herself back together as quickly as possible. Her smile broadening, she skipped up the wooden stairs to her cabin, her calves already screaming less painfully. Once inside, she hastily peeled off her work-out clothes soaked through with her sweat, and made a beeline for the shower. Milos.

Milos Drya was not only one of the few Neuri warriors in the forest village; he was a warrior leader and instructor. Her instructor.

Like her, Milos had not been born and raised in the village, but had come from outside though not nearly as far flung as she had. He came from Venta, Lithuania. And like her, he had grown up a freak. Milos, like all Neuri, was tall, athletic, and physically fit. He was charming, bright, and of high intellect. Unlike Bridget Grace and most Neuri, though, Milos was dark, his skin deeply olive and rich in tone, his eyes pools of liquid chocolate, his long hair tumbling down his back in a polished ebony jet. Like Bridget Grace, and like Luke Stone himself, Milos had been prone to "spells," as his parents had called them, visions, from as far back as he could remember. Sometimes, the visions were violent. His father, Jan, was most upset by these "spells," abandoning his family when Milos only eight or nine years old, leaving mother and child to fend for themselves. His mother, Olga, was a simple woman whose Catholic faith grounded and centered her life. As Milos grew older, especially as he approached puberty, just as had happened to Bridget Grace, his visions grew more intense and more gruesome.

Olga could offer nothing to her son but church and prayer. As the visions grew more frequent and ever more savage, she looked more and more to the priests and toward exorcism.

Though terrified by what was happening to him, in his core, Milos knew his visions were not from the hand of Satan.

And then one summer day as Milos worked his family's fields, a tall man with silver hair shimmering in the blistering sun called his name.

σ σ σ

Showered and changed into worn jeans and her favorite tee, a light orange with short sleeves and a butterfly in flight across the front, Bridget Grace pulled on her riding boots and headed for the stables, her heart pounding again ever harder as she drew nearer. But this time, it was not from physical exertion or mental preparation exercises that wore her nearly to a breaking point. And at just this moment, she couldn't be sure which one was worse. Her knees were weak and wobbly, her hands trembling. With every deep throb of her heart, her stomach flipped, filling her with exhilaration and fear. Would he be there to meet her?

She closed her eyes and wiped her mind clear as she approached the stables.

Now was not the time for doubt. Doubt of any kind. Now she had but one task before her. Ride.

Apolonia was the horse that had been assigned to her when she first came to the village. Apolonia was a Tarpan, descended from the original ancient breed, her lineage going back as far as the fifth century BCE. Many, most, in the outside world believed the original line of the Tarpan no longer existed, that the breed had gone extinct. But here, deep within their secluded village, these first wild horses of Poland thrived, nurtured, and were protected by the Neuri.

They were breathtakingly beautiful. Cream-colored with a thin black stripe riding down their spine, they sported a dark mane and tail. Their ears were long and set high upon their head to enhance their hearing for prey, predator, or enemy. Their necks were thick, yet graceful, impenetrable to sword or stake or snapping jaws. Their bellies were round and small, their legs lean; they were built lightly, and for speed. In the winter, their coats lightened to match the snows. The stallions were fierce in battle and their wounds healed as swiftly as they ran.

Bridget Grace spent weeks caring for Apolonia, walking her around the riders' circle, feeding and watering her, talking to her and furnishing her with treats of carrots and celery sticks, brushing her creamy coat until it shone before Milos, who was her instructor in this as well as her other physical feats, granted her permission to mount her. Once she was allowed to mount, this was all he would allow her to do until she thought she'd howl from the tedium, exactly what Milos wanted.

"Patience," he said to her in a tone that reminded her of none other than her father. "Patience and practice."

He would repeat the mantra to her when all she wanted was to soar. And so, she set about wrangling her spirit, tamping down her frustration, and amping up her patience. She gave herself over to Milos's instructions, and finally moved past mount/dismount, to walking astride Apolonia, then trotting, then advancing to cantering, all the while learning her horse, divining Apolonia's spirit just as Apolonia learned and divined hers. And so the endless repetitions were never just about the physical, Bridget Grace finally realized; the physical feats were a passageway to the melding of their minds, of the Tarpan with the Neuri, of Bridget Grace with her beloved Apolonia.

So the day finally arrived. The riding circle gates opened. Apolonia and her rider were set free upon the forested paths of Bialowieza.

At the stable now, Bridget Grace greeted Apolonia with her favorite treats. As she fed her she spoke to her softly, caressing her silken muzzle, smiling into her deep brown eyes, opening her mind and listening to her horse's spirit deeply. She brushed Apolonia down until her creamy coat shone in the sun-speckled stable. Then, she placed the saddle pad upon her back, patting it down. She grabbed the leather saddle and set it gently across her back. Next, she cinched the girth and last placed the bridle around her head and the bit in her mouth. She hated this part more than all the others, though she was fond of none of it. Milos had promised her once she demonstrated enough control, once she and Apolonia rode the wind as one, she would no longer need to weigh Apolonia down with any of the gear she was forced to use now.

She led Apolonia out of the stable, mounted her, and headed out towards the Narewka River and the meadow where she and Milos were meeting.

Astride Apolonia, riding through the rich forest smelling of balsam pine, ripe berries, and mushrooms calmed her jitters. How foolish she'd been to doubt him. She could not allow herself these continuous childish insecurities. Hadn't he proven himself already countless times? Every engagement they set up outside their regular class times was a high risk for him. For both of them, but for him, as her instructor, the consequences would be far more severe. No one at Bialowieza must ever know of these private meetings.

There was a strict code at Bialowieza regarding "fraternizing" between student and pupil. The protocol had been written and followed since the beginning of Neuri time. The Neuri demanded strict adherence to this code, as they did to all their edicts, but this one was guarded meticulously. Neuri gifts held great power; danger always lurked, the dark side constantly looming, patiently biding its time, seeking the optimum moment to strike. And there were always those who would succumb, now, before, and forever, to the temptation of the dark. One of the most dominant and accessible pathways to this temptation was the instructor student relationship. By the very nature of the relationship, the instructor held sway over his or her student. To charge that relationship with intimacy tipped those scales beyond redemption.

Milos and Bridget Grace knew the ancient code, having read and memorized all the codes during their initiations. Now, together, they shared their guarded amusement about this particular text. It struck them of Deism or Papistry. For the Neuri culture they embraced fully, indeed immersed themselves in, this code seemed... out of step... even bending towards the hysterical... towards fear and trembling instead of light and joy, which was more the Neuri way. The edict seemed, well, ancient, a command that might have applied to centuries past, but now? Here and now?

Besides, Bridget Grace *knew* Milos. She had been under his tutelage for four months, ever since she had arrived, a freak, lost in the world, her heart and soul wounded by the destruction she'd had a front row seat to rendered by Armand Jacobi and his minion, Downing Shirley. Bialowieza had been the home she'd always dreamt of. He—Milos—was the companion, the friend, the one her soul had been forever searching for.

Apolonia broke out of the forest. Bridget Grace saw Milos on his Tarpan, Zygmunt, in the distance. Like Pavlov's dogs, the sight of him caused her to react instantly: her mouth went dry, her palms sleeked with sweat, her heart leapt.

There would be a way. Together, they would find a way. Love always found a way. Neither liked the deception. Deceit went against Neuri code as it did against their own personal codes as Neuri Knights and Warriors.

Apolonia reared and sprinted forward.

Bridget Grace and Milos, their horses kicking up clods of thick sod topped with long strands of grasses, raced toward each other. He rode magnificently, his tall frame leaning forward driving Zygmunt, his black hair flowing behind like tendrils reaching for the sky, every muscle of horse and rider, of Tapan and Neuri primed and engaged. As Bridget Grace rode, she smiled into the wind, Apolonia's hooves clattering against the sod like the clattering of a thousand, thousand eagles. She bent forward, wanting to drive Apolonia even faster, but instead of speeding up, Apolonia slowed. Bridget bent down farther to speak into her horse spirit's ear, but it was as though her limbs were suddenly encased in ice. Time slowed.

Forcing herself back into an erect posture, she saw before her and all around her, the meadow was melting. The golden October grasses were twisting, the land itself uprooting as if pushed from below by a mighty earthquake. All about her, the grasses, the land, the wood that ringed the meadow bent and warped and melted until it melded into a flat dusty plain.

In the very center of that plain, clad in armor of silver and red with high arcs of wings stretching up and over his head, Milos sat astride a stallion of gleaming black, leading a battalion of thousands into battle.

The foe sat astride their horses, their armor of gold and black, their shields raised, their horses pounding in dusty charge. This battalion wore no arced wings; compared to Milos's army, his foe charged in relative silence.

It was the arcs of wings of the armor that Milos's battalion wore as they swept across the plain and down upon their enemy that clattered like a thousand, thousand eagles. A sound at once haunting and terrifying, of throngs of birds and dead souls, indeed, a sound of death.

She was flying.

The vision, now stretched out beneath her, began to twist and bend as had the meadow before, evaporating like mist or wisps of clouds returning to the golden grasses and pretty wood as she and Apolonia flew as one towards the sun.

Throwing back her head and howling with delight, Bridget Grace let loose the bridle.

But suddenly, the earth spun towards her.

Apolonia, her eyes wide and terrified, twisted her head toward Bridget Grace, neighing stridently.

Without warning, he was there, riding the wind beside her.

Milos.

Gently, he took the reins. Gently, he guided them back to ground.

Bridget Grace dismounted, patting Apolonia's neck, as she whispered into her silken ear.

Milos placed his arm on her shoulder, raising his finger. "I told you. Patience. Practice."

Though the moment of the sudden descent had terrified rider and horse, Bridget Grace had been exhilarated. Her heart pounded, still, the blood setting her cheeks afire.

She glanced up to answer, and suddenly startled.

She saw, sparking in his eyes, a sudden flash, like a quick strike of lightning that portended a storm. Abruptly, she stepped back. "I want to fly," was all she said.

"Oh, my darling," he said, "you will. Farther and higher than you can even dream."

He swooped her in closer, encircling her in his arms. He lifted her chin, and gazed deeply into her eyes.

There was no anger lurking in those infinite liquid pools. No hidden warning prowling.

The only thing she saw was love. The only thing she felt was desire.

His desire for her. And hers for him.

Upon which, no matter how foolish or old-fashioned they thought this particular Neuri code was, they would not act. Not now. Not until they found the resolution.

Reluctantly, they parted, pushing their desire down, containing the forbidden. Milos and Bridget Grace unloaded the saddle bags on Zygmunt and together they prepared their picnic, complete with books and study materials. If they should be seen, study would be the explanation.

They settled themselves, stretching out upon the blanket, attacking with fervor their picnic lunch prepared by the kitchen staff for their favorite instructor, watching the Narewka flow gently by. Still, that moment riding the wind continued to play in Bridget Grace's mind. He should have let them be. For even as she saw Milos gliding up beside them, she felt Apolonia rising. They had panicked, that was true. Both of them panicked—Tarpan and Neuri. But within that moment of panic, already, they were working to correct their mistakes. Working together, they would have pulled out of the fall and turned to the heavens; they would have soared. How far, how long before they would have returned to earth safely—without interference?

They had needed no assistance. Bridget Grace knew that to the depths of her Neuri soul.

σ σ σ

"No. It is not possible," Jadwiga was saying to Luke, Beth, and Danuta as they gathered in her office sipping herbal tea and snacking on recently baked lemon-blueberry muffins. Luke and Beth had just arrived, completing the arduous journey from New Camen, New Hampshire to Boston's Logan Airport to Krakow, and then driving to Bialowieza. The trek took nearly two days, and on Luke, it showed. Jadwiga knew it was not just the journey that weighed so heavily upon him. Bridget Grace had a training session this morning with Milos and a note was left for her to join her parents in their cottage later this afternoon. Jadwiga wanted this private session with them and Danuta before they met with Bridget Grace. "To commit such an act… a brother upon a sister… it is not only unnatural… it is so evil… so against Neuri codes of conduct… it would act as a poison upon him. It would turn his Neuri blood against him, on a cellular level, like toxic radiation, that eventually would destroy him."

"Not possible." Danuta repeated, dazed.

"It would have done the same to you."

Danuta looked at Jadwiga sharply.

"No matter how innocent you were, how unknowing, how unwilling."

"How drugged," Danuta added.

"So. Armand lied." Luke said. "For years. Decades. Torturing his beloved sister, his twin, with his vile concoctions. Surprising."

Danuta turned to her son. "But why? Why? Why would he do such a thing to me? …Insinuate… Make me doubt… believe… he had…?" She could not continue the thought.

Luke turned his ice blue eyes on her. "Because he is Armand."

Danuta rose forcefully. "That's not good enough, Luke."

Luke softened his tone. "You know the answer. Power and control. That is his essence."

"And fear," Beth added, turning to Jadwiga. "He cannot be Luke's father, then."

Jadwiga set down her teacup and rose, moving to the other side of the room to the large picture window that opened out onto the forest. "Not that way."

At this, Luke also rose, crossing to Jadwiga. "What does that mean?"

She sighed heavily, turning towards him. She laid her hand lightly upon his shoulder, then, took in the rest of the group. "There is another way Armand could have accomplished his desire…"

Jadwiga's oak wood door flew open and Bridget Grace strode into the room.

"Dad!" she declared as she rushed to him, throwing herself unexpectedly into his arms.

Luke smiled broadly at his daughter, and wrapped her in his arms.

"Hey, Beege," he spoke her pet name softly.

Beth crossed to them, placing her hand upon her daughter's back. Bridget Grace turned to her mother and embraced her.

Milos stood at the door's threshold. "I'm… sorry… I… apologize… I'm intruding…"

"Of course not," Jadwiga said. "Please… Come."

Bridget Grace broke from her mother's embrace. "Oh, Milos. I'm so sorry." She crossed to him, taking his arm, and leading him to her parents. "Mom, Dad. This is Milos Drya. He's an instructor here. He's my instructor." She blushed. Quickly, she turned from her parents to Milos. "These are my parents Beth and Luke Stone."

Milos stepped forward, taking Beth's hand and elegantly kissed it. He turned to Luke. "Luke Stone. I'm so honored to meet you, sir. I've heard so much about you."

Luke took his hand, turning his cool blue gaze on him.

"You're a legend here," Milos continued.

"You have to be very careful with those," Luke replied neutrally.

"Well, we're adjourned," Jadwiga said with a smile. "We will meet again tonight for dinner at my quarters, yes? Eight o'clock?" She turned to Danuta and Beth. "Beth, Danuta and I would love to show you the herbal garden and the lab if you're up for that now after such an arduous journey."

"Absolutely. I made some notes after we first talked I'd like to share with you."

"Wonderful." Jadwiga turned to Luke. "If you need my office, Luke, it's all yours."

"Thank you, Jadwiga" Luke replied.

"I'm already late for class," Milos said.

"See you later, then." Bridget Grace said to Milo.

"It will be my pleasure to see you all for dinner."

When the room had cleared save for father and daughter, Luke walked over to Jadwiga's desk and leaned his tall frame back against it, stretching his legs out before him. They fixed their eyes on each other, deep blue upon deep blue.

Bridget Grace could feel he was more open to her now than he had been in that initial phone call. Still, he was guarded. What was he keeping locked away from her? Of course, she, too, had secrets she wanted to keep. She wondered how successful she would be against her father's far superior skills.

Of course whatever he was keeping, it was about Armand. Armand Jacobi. It would always be about Armand Jacobi.

And they'd had him. They'd had him, and some young fool in the backwoods of Michigan let him escape.

"Walk with me," her father said, holding out his hand to her.

σ σ σ

As Bridget Grace held her father's hand, walking beside the Narewka River, images tumbled. He was using their secret language. There was so much he wanted her to know; spoken language would be far too cumbersome to convey the knowledge. She walked beside him silently, letting his images fill her world.

At first the images coming from him were familiar; things she already knew, had lived through, but he was showing her them with much more clarity. The night of her transmogrification, Armand's escape, the day of his own shape-shift—his wonder and his fear, the power of the beast that lay within—him—a golden grizzly. She squeezed his hand, her mind resonating with his, her shifting resounding with his.

He took her back further, to a place he'd never showed her, to the place of his childhood. They no longer walked beside the gentle Narewka; they were walking beside a wide green river flowing deep in the wood—the river of his childhood—the river, the wood that was his sanctuary.

The images came faster, like pictures from a film flashing across a screen, only these zoomed across the river, played out against the oak and the pine and the maple, in his eyes, and across his worn and craggy face. She held onto him tightly. These visions hurt. They touched upon a place so deep inside him, a place dark and wounded, scarred, healed over, but imperfectly leaving deep anguish beneath the scar. Her father's agony, the brutal images he now finally allowed her to see, struck at her core, doubling her over with grief. *It's okay... it's okay...* his mind whispered into the dark... *It's long over... it's past...*

A brutal drunken father, an absent mother... Danuta, his mother, her grandmother... locked away... drugged... terrified... warned to stay away or it would only be worse for him... savage beatings... momentary escape to the river... to the wood... to the North... to New York...a tall man with swept back silver hair shimmering...

I thought he was my savior... his mind whispered...

Escape... the woods... water... great bodies of beautiful endless water... sanctuary... a Cherokee Shaman... Shadow Wolf... Grandfather... My real father...

Her father stumbled.

Bridget Grace held him up.

His mind whispered... *there's more... not now... I can't... not now... do not ask... not now...*

The river and wood of his childhood dissolved, pixelated, and disappeared.

He was very pale, his limbs weak.

Bridget Grace led him to a grassy knoll atop the river bank.

They sat in silence save for the chirping of the birds, the wind in the tress, the soft flow of the river.

When her father began to speak, his voice was so low that Bridget Grace thought at first it was the flow of the river, or the wind in the trees.

"I cannot allow him to be lured here."

He turned his gaze to her. His eyes, always startling in their color and clarity, were so intense in their focus and purpose, she gasped.

"Do you understand what I'm saying to you?"

She rose and walked down to the river. Her father followed, standing behind her.

"Have you picked up anything?"

She shook her head.

Luke reached for her, turning her towards him, his eyes just as focused, just as intense. "Nothing? Nothing at all?"

"You think I wouldn't know?"

Those restless, ceaseless eyes searched hers, piercing deep. "Not necessarily."

He walked away, moving upriver, picking up stones, skipping them in the water, down, down, down the river. It was hypnotic how far he could skip stones. His pallor, his weakness from just a few moments ago was already gone; erased as if it had never been. His transmissions to her had lifted a great weight from him, but it was more than that. It was rejuvenation. Within minutes, he had rejuvenated. He had healed himself.

"His ways are many."

"You make him sound immortal."

"Not immortal. No." He skipped another stone. "Treacherous like black ice you never see coming, devious, like a snake you never know will strike until it's too late."

"I won't leave here."

He turned to her, fixing that disconcerting gaze upon her.

She walked closer to him. She took his hands in hers.

"These are my people. This is my home. Isn't that why you brought me here?"

He cocked his head to the side, studying her carefully.

"We need to get back," he spoke in a voice so quiet it blended with the gentle rush of the river and the swoosh of the wind in the trees. "Walk with me."

They walked silently side by side though each walked alone, each wrapped within his or her own world. Exhaustion now seeped into Bridget Grace's every pore with every step she took, her limbs growing heavy and more unbearable. It was not just the effort to mask her secrets from her father that was causing such weariness. It was the sum toll of the images he had transmitted. And knowing that still there were more to come. She understood now why he was holding back. The images she had already seen were devastating.

Oh! How often had she wanted to run! Be like one of those stones her father skipped down and down the Narewka. Only she would not sink. She would keep going, circling the world's waters without end, without care, without the responsibility of being Luke Stone's daughter, carrier of his name, his blood, his Neuri gifts. How often had she wanted to simply close her Stone eyes and follow the waters drift?

His hand gently touched her shoulder. "Your mom is in the garden with Jadwiga and your grandmother. Would you like to join them?"

She turned to him, her eyes grazing his not as a knight, not as a warrior, not as a protector or defender or usurper of kings, but as a daughter, a child grown weary, as weary as he, and as doubtful.

Tears filling her eyes, she glanced quickly away.

Her father placed his soothing hand on her back, rubbing tenderly. "We'll meet at dinner."

Like Apolonia when she reached the meadow wide and open before her, Bridget Grace sprinted away waving her hand behind her as she took her leave of him.

She would not let him see her tears.

σ σ σ

"The ancient healers are here, huddled together in this section." Bridget Grace heard Jadwiga saying as she found the small circle of women. Jadwiga, her mother, and her grandmother were in the ancient herbs and plant section of the bountiful Neuri garden.

Seeing Bridget Grace, both mother and grandmother smiled. Her mother took her hand as Jadwiga continued.

"Echinacea, also known as pink or purple coneflower, we grow here." She led them to a wide grassy patch lined with several bushes of plants. "No blooms now but in the spring and summer, this area is alive with purple and pink. As you know, Echinacea has been used since ancient times to fight infections, colds, sore throats, stomach problems, stress. It also has mild sedative properties." She led them a bit farther into the ancient herbs and plant garden. "Comfrey, here, fantastic bone-setter; Burdock… here, that one's a detoxifier."

"That's one of the slides I brought," Beth said.

Jadwiga stopped walking, acknowledging Bridget Grace's mother's words with a nod of her head. "Good. I'll want to see that one. And you mixed Burdock cells with the Neuri blood samples I sent?"

"Absolutely."

"The results were good?"

"I think you will be quite pleased.

Jadwiga sighed. "Good."

She surveyed the garden. The Neuri garden had always been a place of refuge for Bridget Grace. It flowed boundless, and in every season held secret delights of splendor.

"For centuries our garden has grown here. Now, we will need it perhaps more than ever." Jadwiga cast her eyes over the richness unrolling all about her. "This land we were given, our home, has always been so luscious. Beautiful and peaceful. The Neuri have always preferred tranquility. But tranquility is not always possible. Sometimes, for the tranquility we seek, we must conquer beasts." She turned back to them. "Let me show you the lab."

Inside the lab, Beth Stone was at home. The Neuri lab was spotless, gleaming, and state of the art. The slides she had prepared were projected on the wide screen before them.

"On the left, you see the initial slide; the original cells of the Burdock plant. We experimented with all parts of the plant, and in many stages: dried, green, blooming. We even steeped them and took the cells from the tea, also both liquid and dried. There are differences in properties, strength, side effects, and toxicity. I've categorized all of that for you in my report. What you are looking at here is dried Burdock root. It is the root that has been used for centuries, but, as I said, we did want to examine all parts of the plant to see for ourselves. Now, look at the second slide."

As the others turned their attention to the second slide a soft chorus of "ooohs" and "ahhhs" escaped them.

Jadwiga spoke softly, "Marvelous."

"The results are quite stunning," Beth echoed. "These slides on the right are the ones that have been mixed with the Neuri blood samples you processed. You can see how much they have changed, how much more vitality they have from the slide on the left."

"They're glowing," Bridget Grace said.

"That's the life force; the vitality of the Neuri blood." Jadwiga said.

"And look at the bonding," Beth added. "The elements of these two samples, the Burdock and the Neuri blood samples, bond perfectly together—each complementing the other; nothing detracting, nothing is sacrificed or taken away."

Bridget Grace stared at the slides.

Her mother continued her presentation, but Bridget Grace was focused on the slides, drawn into them. She heard the voices filtering in behind her: her mother, Jadwiga, Danuta.

How many were you able to do? Four... But when I'm set up here, we'll be able to do so much more... You'll get all the help you need...

Rejuvenation... that was what they were talking about... The Rejuvenation of her people. Strengthening. Building up. For what was coming.

He knew. Her father knew.

That was part of the secret he was keeping locked away from her.

But, of course, she knew, too.

As soon as she knew Armand Jacobi had escaped captivity, she knew.

Armand Jacobi was alive and well.

They should have let her father kill him.

They should have let Luke Stone loose to destroy the beast that night in the deep Michigan woods.

And now, Armand was unleashed.

Again.

And the black magician was on his way to wreak what havoc he could before he was stopped.

If this time, he could be stopped.

σ σ σ

Bridget Grace had agreed to walk to Jadwiga's dinner party with Milos that evening. He arrived at her cottage late and out of sorts. While she ducked into her bedroom to give a final brush to her hair and fasten a pearl necklace given to her by her father about her throat, Milos asked if he could brew some tea. The evening had turned sharply cold, the wind whining through the trees. The last of the balmy days of October were gone and winter was making her arrival.

"What has you so keyed up?" Bridget Grace called out from the bedroom.

"Really? You're asking me that?" Milos appeared in the doorway, a cup of tea in his hand.

"I don't know how much time we have for tea."

"Drink. It's good for you. An aperitif. Look." Milos took a long draught from his cup. "Drink."

Bridget Grace took a sip. "Well?"

"You mean besides the fact that your father's such a hard ass?"

"Milos!"

"You were there. Did you not see? Those eyes… those artic blue eyes… He hated me."

Bridget Grace laughed, a lovely light timbre, like the sound of silvery bells. She put her hand on his arm. "He only just met you. He had but a moment with you."

"You really don't know him at all, do you?"

"What?"

"Finish your tea. It gets very bitter if it grows cold."

"It tastes… funky."

"That's because you let it grow cold."

She finished her tea in a gulp, then, held her empty cup out like a child showing her parent. "All gone."

"Excellent."

"His mind is always a million miles away."

Suddenly, Milos's eyes sparked with tears. "I just… wanted him to… like me."

"Milos." She hugged him. "Patience."

"Ah." He brushed away his tears. "So, the student surpasses the teacher."

"That is the natural order, no?"

He grabbed her winter coat, and after wrapping it tightly around her, they exited the cottage for Jadwiga's dinner party.

σ σ σ

They were the last to arrive. Jadwiga's home glowed with soft warm light, candles, and muted lamps. A fire burned in the fireplaces in her sitting and dining rooms to ward off the sudden October chill. Her mother saw her immediately as she and Milos entered, and waving hello, moved to greet them, embracing them graciously, as she would. Her father, deep in conversation with Jadwiga, glanced up, and seeing them, also strode to them. He smiled as he embraced her, and then turned to Milos.

As soon as their eyes met, the air crackled with electricity—like bolts of fire passing between them. Bridget Grace stepped instantly back, her head whipping towards her mother, towards Danuta, towards Jadwiga. Time slowed, as if the moment had frozen, then suddenly, whooshed forward momentarily dizzying her. She shook her head, and when she looked back to Milos and her father, the men were extending their hands forward, exchanging simple pleasantries, her mother joining in, laughing softly. Across the room, Danuta and Jadwiga chatted easily as they gazed into the fire. The men dropped their hands, smiling still, but Bridget Grace could clearly see their smiles never reached their eyes.

Jadwiga called them into dinner. Milos offered his arm.

The meal progressed apace, course after splendid course, as the conversation flowed. But Bridget Grace was unsettled. She had no appetite though while walking through the woods to reach the party, she'd been ravenous. The room felt overly warm, stuffy, and the food too abundant, too rich. Everything was too bright, too brittle, as if it were about to crackle; the conversation was too loud as if everyone were playing a scripted part upon a stage.

Her father was asking about the training program, her training, how many were training now, how many each instructor trained, how many per class, per skill.

Jadwiga and Danuta deferred to Milos, and he shone under her father's spotlight. He went into exquisite detail about the program for the training of a Neuri Knight; about how the training was designed intricately to address the entire instrument of mind, body, and spirit. Jadwiga's arena was the mind; Danuta the spirit and emotional training; and he was in charge of the physical. Her father lifted his eyebrow.

"You're very young for so much responsibility."

"I've been here since I was fourteen," Milos responded. "Vigorously trained, I assure you."

Jadwiga and Daunta laughed lightly.

"I came as a refugee… a runaway. Just as you were at that age, I believe?" Milos said.

Bridget Grace was startled. Her father's history was not unknown. He'd been a tracker of children when he lived in the Mojave Desert after he left Armand in New York City. Stories had been written about him though he eschewed any publicity. But he did not talk about his history. This was known and kept as sacrosanct as were the Neuri texts.

She felt the subtle shift in her father, the almost imperceptible narrowing of his eyes, the setting of his jaw. And with his shift, with the boldness of Milos's remark, the room changed as well. She glanced toward Milos. Had he known what he had done? Was he aware of his overstep? But Milos remained as open and eager as a child, reveling in his position to be addressing the man he so admired. Her father absorbed Milos's remark without comment.

"What exactly is the physical training?" Luke asked, his voice emotionless.

Milos continued, his enthusiasm growing, elaborating on each element: breathing, strength, pain tolerance, endurance, skill excellence, horseman—or woman-ship, weapons mastery, deprivation tolerance.

Her father watched him intensely as he spoke. Luke Stone, of course, knew the regimens. He'd designed them. Going meticulously through the protocols with Jadwiga and Danuta before leaving Bridget Grace there four months ago, he then re-addressed the training comprehensively, re-structuring the methods using the survival techniques he had mastered first to endure a brutal childhood, and then to survive the black magician Armand, and finally from the exquisite tutelage of his Cherokee Shaman Shadow Wolf, Grandfather.

"How did you come here?" he asked when Milos finally came to the end of his intricate explanation.

"I told you, as a…"

"Yes. A refugee," Luke cut him off. "A runaway." He pushed his chair back from the table, his food forgotten. "From what?"

The stillness grew in the room. Bridget Grace's head began to pound.

"My father was Neuri." Milos paused.

He glanced down, as if taking a moment, as if Luke's reticence and the mounting tension had finally broken through. He raised his eyes, looking only at Luke. At once, Bridget Grace felt that spark, that streak of fire pass between them. No one else registered the fire she saw, though the tension was palpable.

"He hid his gifts. As if they shamed him. And then, he forced me to hide mine, beating me when I did not."

Bridget Grace gasped softly. She did not know this about Milos. He had not divulged this about his father.

"It ate him up inside. This denial. Poisoning him from the inside out. And then one day, he was gone. Leaving us with nothing. Leaving me with no help. No guidance. My visions grew worse… violent… unrelenting… apocalyptic… My mother…. my mother thought I was a child of Satan…. But I knew… I knew that was not true… Just as you did… just as you always knew it was not true."

Milos looked at Luke, his eyes now sparking with tears.

Luke sat immobile. "Go on," was all he said.

Milos reached for her hand. Grasping it, she immediately felt his anguish. His grief was overwhelming. The images he relayed poured from his heart into her mind.

"She was going to take me to the priests... have me locked in a cell... forced exorcisms... I couldn't... how could she subject me to such a thing? I ran deep into the woods ...deep into my sanctuary... alone... there... all alone... I was accosted with these... visions... nightmares... pounding down on me... sounds of the earth tearing... fire consuming... I no longer knew what was real... what was imagined... I...I cried out for salvation... and then... then... I saw him."

Still her father remained unmoved. As unbending and unyielding as his name. How could he remain so remote, so cold to a young man pouring his heart out to him, just as he had only hours ago poured his soul into hers, his suffering so shockingly similar to what he was hearing now?

"He was tall, dressed in black, with silver hair shimmering in the sun. He pointed me here."

Soundlessly, her father rose.

Beside her, Milos trembled.

Luke Stone gently took her mother's arm who sat beside him.

"Excuse us, Jadwiga. Danuta," he said, his words as deep and chill as winter.

"Wait... wait." Milos cried out half-rising, his hands waving feebly in front of him. "Please... what did I do? What did I say?"

Her father was chiseled in marble. He turned his ice blue eyes upon her, speaking only to her now in their secret language. "You do not know this man."

Only words. No images. No symbols.

Bridget Grace rose as chill, as coolly as her father had done. And in the language only they spoke, she spoke back to him. "It is you who does not know him."

"Come, Bridget Grace," he spoke aloud, his voice shattering the silence. "Your mother and I will see you home."

Bridget Grace remained standing, her eyes locked onto her father's. "Milos will see me home." Then, in their secret language, once more she spoke. "You do not know him."

She turned away.

She cloaked her mind so that he could not enter.

She took Milos's arm and walked away.

σ σ σ

She had never seen him like this. Wild with rage, yes, so consumed with fire and frenzy, he had spontaneously transmogrified. She had seen him contain his rage so that his center blistered, yet outward he projected calm, tranquility, coolness, control. But this Luke Stone tonight had no fiery center. Nothing lived there but ice and stone.

"He has poisoned me," Milos was saying as he prepared tea in her cottage.

She turned toward him. "What do you mean?"

"He will never allow you to be with me. And he has poisoned the others against me."

"I don't understand."

Milos handed Bridget Grace her tea. "Don't you?"

"No. No! Why are you looking at me as if I should?"

"Because you know more than you are willing to admit—even to yourself. Especially to yourself. You always have."

Bridget Grace rose from the couch carrying her tea, sipping of it deeply as if the drink could warm her heart and clear the fog enveloping her mind. "Stop speaking to me in riddles!"

"That's what *he* does. Speaks to you in riddles, parables, hidden secrets, hidden languages, hidden lies…"

"My father does not lie to me!"

"Bridget Grace your entire childhood was a lie! As was mine. As was his! You have no idea who Luke Stone really is."

She turned to him sharply. "That's exactly what he said about you."

"Of course he did. In secret, yes? In your secret language so no one else could hear."

"Did you hear?"

Milos laughed. "I am no one able to break the codes of Luke Stone. I cannot even understand him when he speaks English aloud." He set his cup down. "But you... you are his creation."

"What are you talking about?"

"Control, which is his specialty."

"I don't understand you."

"Yes you do. He has controlled you all your life. Isn't that the reason you ran from him when you were fifteen?"

"He didn't want me to use the gifts."

"Yes."

"He was afraid for me."

"Or of you?"

"You're scaring me."

"I'm speaking the truth to you. A truth you already know."

She trembled. "I... can't.... I can't... do this now."

"BG. Come here."

She turned to him, her face sprinkled with tears. He held out his arms to her.

"Do you love me?"

"Oh, God, yes," she spoke as she folded into his comforting arms.

He held her as he rocked her. "Then, this is all we need. Our love. Then, we have everything."

"I'm so tired..."

"Rest. Just rest..."

The room wavered, like a photograph fluttering in the wind.

"Come. Lie down upon the couch."

"I feel so dizzy."

"The night, your father has upset you. He won't upset you ever again."

Milos lead her gently to the couch, fixing the pillows beneath her head.

"Rest awhile."

Bridget Grace squinted, reaching her hand toward the doorway to her cottage. "Why is he here?"

You should have listened to me, my darling, he whispered to her mind as he fluttered at the edges of her senses. A tall man with brushed back silver hair. She knew this man. *I tried to warn you about him...*

"There's no one here but you and me, my darling. Rest. I'll go prepare the horses."

"Will we ride?"

"Yes."

"Will we fly?"

"Oh, yes. As high and as wide as you wish to soar."

σ σ σ

When she awoke, she was blissfully rested. Her mind was clear, sharply, piercingly clear. Though it was before dawn—the sky outside her window was shimmering pearlescent grey—her room was filled with light, a brittle, crystal light as if made of glass or ice and the light could easily be shattered. Milos sat beside her on her bed, running his fingers gently through her shorn hair and down across her face. Gently, so gently. He was dressed ready to ride.

"Come. We haven't much time."

She knew instantly what he meant, even before he spoke. With the clarity of her mind, she remembered everything of last night, the horror and disappointment of the dinner, Milos's anguish at the way her father had treated him, her rising furor at the man she had so devoutly believed in, trusted, loved.

She also remembered they were leaving.

They were no longer wanted here.

Her father had rejected Milos, and so, he had rejected her.

There was another who would lead them. Another of Neuri blood.

She knew him. She had met him before.

Her father had rejected this other as well.

After living so long in hidden truths and secrets, her mind was now finally opened.

Luke Stone was not the man he had led her to believe he was.

Today, finally, she would fly.

"Do you know where he is?" Milos asked her when she was dressed and ready to ride.

She shook her head. "I have no contact with him. I cloaked my mind against him."

Milos took her chin in his hand, lifting her eyes to him. "Uncloak it."

Bridget Grace stepped back from him, removing his hand. "I want nothing more to do with him."

"BG... you must take your leave of him. Otherwise, this never ends. Otherwise, he will chase you to the ends of the earth."

She turned away from him, and sighing crossed to the window. The sky was lightening. Soon dawn would arrive. "This is dangerous, you understand. I seek; I will awaken him."

"He no longer holds any power over you. Now that you finally know the truth. He holds no power any longer."

She shook her head.

He went to her, wrapping his arms around her, brushing his lips against her soft cheek.

"I've gotten us this far. We are about to leave the land of the living dead. This land of lies. Come with me and fly free."

She nodded her head against his chest. Then, she closed her eyes.

"Can you see him?"

"No," she whispered. "I see nothing but wisps of clouds and fog."

"Call him to you."

She opened her eyes and walked away from him. "He won't hear me."

"Bridget Grace!" He spoke sharply. "Now! Right now!" She turned toward him, bewildered at the sharpness of his voice; her eyes confused.

He swiftly crossed to her, taking her hands in his. "I'm sorry… I'm so sorry…. we need to move. We need to leave… before…"

"Before what?"

"Oh, my darling… I, too, have been lied to all my life. Lied to and betrayed. I, too, want only one thing. To soar, with you. This place… this place is like a sorceress. Sorcerers and magicians surround us. I fear for your enchantment again."

"And yours?"

"Yes, of course. Mine." He lifted her hand to his lips. "Do you not see the vision of our freedom? You saw it last night."

"I did."

"Do you want it still?"

"I want to soar, Milos. I have always wanted to soar."

"Then come with me unafraid. Bid adieux to what's past. It's the only way. You know that."

Slowly, she nodded her head.

"Call to him," Milos entreated. "In the language he will hear."

Bridget Grace closed her eyes. She focused only on him, on Luke Stone. On her father."

"Do you see him?" Milos whispered, his voice rising, moving in closer to her.

Bridget Grace held up her palm. "Hush. Move back. Give me space. Give me calm. Take patience."

Milos did as she bid him.

"He has cloaked himself with protections from his enemies."

"You are not his enemy."

"Calm. Quiet," she whispered to him.

"He walks. All night long, he walks. He does not sleep. He walks and prays." Her voice dropped so low, he could barely hear her. "He walks by the River Narewka."

"Can you lead us there?"

"Beneath the grassy knoll, he walks the waters of the Narewka River."

σ σ σ

They rode as dawn streaked the sky. They rode as Apolonia and Zygmunt rose into the morning mist. They rode until she saw him, Luke Stone, her father, walking below beside the tranquil waters of the Narewka River.

Seeing him, Bridget Grace felt a hollowness in her heart, a depth of emptiness and despair she had never felt before. Seeing him walk, his long legs wading through the water's edge, his eyes closed, his lips moving softly in silent prayer, her heart grew heavy with sorrow.

Beside her, Milos gave the silent command, and the horses descended to the grassy knoll, the same one where she had sat with her father when he had emptied his soul into hers.

She glanced at Milos. His face shone in the growing morning light, shimmering in the fading mist.... his eyes gleamed…

She turned toward her father.

They sat astride their horses, some seventy-five yards behind her father. He hadn't felt her presence nor her approach. Had she been that successful at cloaking him from her? Had Milos also been able to erect a shield against him? Or had Luke Stone gone so deep within himself, within his prayers, that he'd left himself unprotected even as he had raised shields to protect himself from his enemies?

Bridget Grace glanced back at Milos… he was holding something to his lips… a long thin rod carved from the wood of the forest. At the end was a tip fastened from bright green plastic… her heart pounded… she looked into his eyes…

….but these were no longer the eyes of Milos Drya gazing back at her….these were the black triumphant eyes of Armand Jacobi.

Bridget Grace screamed. She lunged for the rod.

Her screamed echoed throughout the forest.

Luke Stone turned towards her.

Too late. Too late.

Luke Stone, her father, fell to the ground.

Bridget Grace threw her head back and howled.

Apolonia rose.

Together, Neuri and Tarpan flew to their fallen sovereign.

Bridget Stone tore from the saddle and ran to her father, kneeling beside him. Her tears flowed like the waters of the Narewka. She laid her hands upon his chest, closing her eyes and praying the ancient Neuri words of healing. But the lion heart was still.

Milos stood beside her, his face exultant. "That will do no good, you know. The poison is too powerful."

Bridget Grace threw her head back and howled.

The roar echoed through the meadow and the wood, reverberating along the flowing waters. The roar rumbled through her body, filling every chamber, every organ, every cell, elongating the mask of her face, lengthening and widening her jaw, filling her mouth with razor-sharp teeth. Her eyes separated and glowed; her ears pointed, her body covered with thick grey fur black at the tips, beige at her neck and long snout.

Milos froze beside her. Ferociously turning toward him, she howled again, her breath fiery. She rose high upon her steady haunches and slashed, with her mighty unbending claws, she ripped his flesh across his face, across his mouth, across the lips that had held the lethal weapon, down across his shoulders, and across his torso.

Streaks of blood bloomed where she slashed.

Milos, pale and trembling, crumpled to the ground immobile.

Immobile, but not dead.

This time, this time, she did not strike to kill.

This time she had the control.

This time she wanted to take the prisoner alive.

Bridget Grace, The Grey Wolf, streaked to the top of the knoll, and howled again, but this was the wail of distress, a cry so mournful, so urgent, it was at once understood and echoed. The keen sent the birds from the trees, sounding the same refrain, and from across the land from the mole and the hedgehog and the shrew, from the bats and the wolf and the lynx, and from the bison, the elk and the wild boar a cacophony of sound arose; and from her people, the Neuri, all in one unified voice, in one chorus, the wail echoed throughout their land and back to her.

They came. Her sharp ears heard before she saw them. Marching from every corner of their village. They came to carry their hero home.

σ σ σ

Luke lay dying.

They had carried him on a bamboo pallet to the Neuri laboratory. Beth had wanted him there, close to the ancient medicines, and in a space wide enough to accommodate all the People who encircled him, offering up their prayers. It was also where the ancient poisons were kept. Jadwiga and Beth were sure Milos devised the poison with which he struck Luke down from the plants being nurtured inside the lab.

Milos's wounds had been tended to, and he was being closely guarded in one of the few cells the Neuri had in their village. The cells had not been used for decades. For decades, there had been nothing but peace. Now, it was with a great sadness that this system had to be put to use again.

Bridget Grace stood at the head of her father. She laid one hand upon his forehead, and cupped the other around the ear that had been shot with the poison dart.

Her eyes were closed as she whispered over and over the ancient Neuri text she had learned in training.

He was the healer. She had only learned to rejuvenate herself. She prayed now for the power of this great gift, the art he knew so well; she beseeched to be empowered with this gift with which to save her father's life.

She breathed deeply. She pushed all other thoughts from her. She emptied her mind of everything but him.

She invoked her father's name.

In their secret language, one mind to one mind, daughter to the father she loved, the father she had betrayed—she called out.

A shudder shook her.

Darkness surrounded her.

Dampness and cold filled her.

Caverns, wide and deep opened before her... caverns twisting endlessly, diving deeper and deeper beneath the Earth.

A figure beckoned... tall... dressed in black with sleeked back silver hair...NO! She bellowed with every fiber of her being... NO! She rose in defiance and pushed him away from her... but his laughter followed, echoing through the cavern as if there were no escape...

Sounds filtered... rushing liquid sounds... the sound of a river flowing.... the river of his childhood... but something was wrong... the golden summer sun reflected off the river... birds filled the trees with song... but as she walked toward them, they took flight... the sound of a thousand thousand wings clattering surrounded her... they swooped down around her... black birds... cawing... diving... she lifted her arms to scare them away... to scatter them from her.

They flew off blackening the sky... covering the sun... the branches of the leafy tress hung with icicles... the river caked with ice.

As she gazed across the river, she saw her father standing on the distant shore... wearing a robe of pure white... his feet without sandals or shoes... she breathed deeply, opening her mouth to call to him... but she had no voice... he did not hear her... he did not turn to her.

Suddenly, smoke drifted toward her... cherry and the essence of pine... smoke drifting from a boat on the water... She saw a man rowing inside, a small man wearing a grey fedora with a single eagle feather attached to the brim... his dark eyes twinkled in the sun, the smoke from his pipe encircled him... from his boat, he waved to her: *Come in... come in...*

He rowed her across the river. He rowed her to her father.

A cabin deep in the wood. Not Bialowieza. Michigan. Michigan, the woods he so loved so much. Shadow Wolf, who he also called Grandfather, sat in his rocking chair on the porch, smoking his pipe. The aroma of the smoke was intoxicating. His presence was intoxicating.

251 σ Realms of Fantastic Stories Vol. 2

She sat with her father on the wooden steps.

There was no wind, but his robes billowed about him.

"I can't go into battle again," her father spoke.

"Lay your burden down, Luke. It's okay. You've done enough now." Grandfather answered though his lips did not move.

"I can't do this alone." Bridget Grace responded to her father. She reached out her hand. "Walk with me."

σ σ σ

The Diary of Bridget Grace Stone
November 30th

I could not let him out of my sight. Once he was healed. Once he had risen from his deathbed, whole, vigorous, restored.

I wanted to return with him to America. I could not let him go.

He told me my work was here. In the village where he had brought me. In the Bialowieza Forest. Mine and my mother's and my grandmother's.

His was back in America—somewhere in America—chasing, once again, the black magician Armand Jacobi.

Armand had gone deep underground—into those caverns I had seen in my vision. Into the damp, the cold, the dark. Like the monster he was, seeking shelter from the dark, sustenance from the black soil, wrapping the cold about him like a shield.

Danuta, his sister, his twin, said he could stay underground for years, perhaps decades. From what Armand had been able to do with Milos, with me, it was apparent his power had already grown since he had battled my father in the woods of Michigan and my father had bested him only four short months ago.

But it was not just Armand's power—however deep, however vast that was. It was drugs. Milos had been steadily drugging me since I had arrived at Bialowieza, zapping my power, my strength, fogging my mind until I was under his control.

Now we wait. And prepare for his ascension back to the earth.

I live with my betrayal like an open wound upon my heart.

There's more my father needs to show me. So much more lies hidden as deep and twisting as those caverns where Armand now dwells. I accept he will show me in time.

What frightens all of us, my father included, and what mitigates my pain enough to allow me to breathe is that I was not the only one transfixed by Milos. Jadwiga was taken in by him as well, as was my grandmother.

The Neuri are a kind people. The code they live by is love, forgiveness, humanity. It had been so peaceful in the Bialowieza Forest for so many decades. Our guard had dropped. Our training had grown flaccid. Our very code will be our destruction if we forget the other part of who we are as a people. If we forget we are as well Neuri Warriors. Neuri Knights.

The day my mother and father arrived to visit me, I overheard some of their conversation with Jadwiga and Danuta before I burst into Jadwiga's office. I heard my mother say: "Then Armand cannot be Luke's father." And Jadwiga answered: "Not that way."

I knew instantly this was the secret my father was keeping locked so tightly away from me.

The day of our walk along the Narewka, he had poured so much of himself into my mind, my heart. He had showed me Jimmy Stone, the man he had grown up with as his father. A brutal alcoholic and drug-dealer who wanted his son to follow in his footsteps. Who, frightened by his son's visions, dealt with them the only way such a brute knows how to—by beating him, imagining he could beat them out of him. The grandmother I adored, his mother was a mere ghost in that house, beaten into submission, kept from her son by threats that he would only suffer more if she dare interfere.

And he showed me Grandfather, Shadow Wolf, his mentor, his spirit guide, and his defender when he fled the clutches of Armand Jacobi. Shadow Wolf is my father's spirit father, his true father.

My father does not yet know about Armand Jacobi. This much he has told me. And we need to know if the black magician's blood flows in our veins. I need to know before the black magician breaches the surface again.

Until then, Shadow Wolf rowed me across the river; he helped me guide my father back to us.

I walk with him.

And so, so armed, and united under the sovereignty of Luke Stone, on to battle.

Bagel on a Stick

Joshua Rem

Chapter One
Access

8 July 1508N

Queen Jasmine was dead.

Assassinated, in fact. A mere four weeks had elapsed since the beloved Queen of Nyobi's murder, and already her country was beginning to fall apart. In response to the inability of the existing branches of law enforcement to identify a suspect, her husband, King Augustus V, had created a special investigative unit that answered only to him. Their mandate was to track down the assassin and bring him or her to justice by whatever means necessary. It was a noble goal, to be sure, and the announcement of this unit's creation had indeed been met by applause in Nyobi's human capital city of Strelas. The problem, as any student of history knew, was that secret police forces tended to stray from their original mandates over time. Very few people could resist the temptations of the almost absolute power that was bestowed upon them by the words, "by whatever means necessary."

Rufino Endicott did consider himself a student of history. He'd been born and raised in Galensdorf, a proud halfling farming community located in east-central Nyobi near the southernmost edge of the Shibiren mountain range. Education was big in Galensdorf because it was considered a three-foot-tall person's only way to get an edge in an unforgiving world, so Rufino knew all about secret police forces and a whole host of other things like law, political science, philosophy, and business management. He hadn't known how to save himself from getting his impulsive ass turned into a vampire mere days after shaving his beard, getting a mohawk haircut, and then dying it emerald-green, but he was borderline brilliant otherwise.

Vampires didn't grow hair, so to this day, almost three years after his conversion, he was still stuck with the green 'hawk. There were worse things, but he was nevertheless far removed from the walking slab of sex appeal that he used to be. His thick brown beard, in particular, had been so fantastically epic that small birds could have nested in it, and he was almost sorry that they'd never tried. The thought of spending the rest of his life without facial hair was depressing, to say the least, but he had no choice but to make the most of the cards he'd been dealt.

In his case, that meant bluffing, and a lot of it. Vampires were so utterly despised in the world of Ch'ulu that entire branches of militaries had been dedicated to hunting down and exterminating them. Nyobi was one of the many nations with a branch of elite soldiers trained to be undead-hunters, but Rufino had never been all that impressed by them. All they ever seemed to do was patrol in groups of four in their shiny plate armour. Supposedly, much of the training to become an undead-hunter involved cultivating a sense that could detect an undead creature from range, so he knew that the patrols weren't just for show. He didn't know exactly how this undead-sense worked, but he did know that it wasn't working very well, for the hunters had never seemed to notice him despite having had many opportunities to do so over the years.

Obviously, he was just smarter than they were, and nowhere was his superior brainpower more evident than in his choice of residence. The vampires of lore favoured the sort of wooden boxes that could be spotted and identified as coffins from half a mile away, but Rufino was much craftier than that. There was an older human art merchant named Mr. Pemberton who owned and operated a trade cart with a broken board on the underside of its double-layer undercarriage—an opening that was just large enough to accommodate Rufino's tiny bat form. Together, merchant and beastie traversed the countryside in what had become a truly heartwarming symbiotic relationship. True, Mr. Pemberton didn't have the faintest idea that his trade cart had been converted into a mobile coffin by a fiendishly clever vampire, but neither did he realize he had a permanent overnight security guard. Anyone who tried to steal Rufino's coffin was gonna get more than he bargained for.

Mr. Pemberton ran fairly predictable routes, so although the little stowaway had absolutely no say in where his mobile coffin was going, he could usually extrapolate the destination from his host's established patterns. For the next few days, he knew, they weren't going anywhere. They'd just arrived in Meridian—an island city on the south-central coast of Nyobi—which just happened to be the place that Mr. Pemberton called home. After nearly a month on the road, the merchant always took at least three days to remind his wife who he was, which left Rufino with naught to do but to stay out of trouble.

Sadly, that was easier said than done—halflings were to trouble as white shirts were to dirt. *Irresistible.* To make matters worse, now that every law enforcement agency in the country was distracted by the ongoing search for the queen's assassin, opportunities for *trouble* could be found at every street corner. Fortunately, Meridian was a large, industrialized city with a human population of well over a hundred thousand, so there was no shortage of legitimate and semi-legitimate things to do. Rufino didn't need to drink blood tonight because his unnatural thirst had been quenched not two days ago, so perhaps he'd swipe a few gold coins and go play cards. Or perhaps he'd sneak into the theatre. Honestly, he didn't care much for plays, but it was terrific fun trying to ascertain who amongst the audience was actually watching the show and who was just sitting there because going to plays was chic.

Yes, he liked this idea. With a wee smidgen of luck, the play that was being performed tonight would be in some obscure foreign language, because then his game would become much more entertaining: he'd have to pick out the twenty people in the crowd of a thousand who actually understood what was being said. His standard technique for doing so was to look for the people who started clapping first, but that would be most difficult because he'd have one or two seconds, tops, before the chic crowd would hear clapping and join in. Vampires needed to have good reflexes, though, and this seemed as good a way as any to keep them in shape. He started west toward the entertainment district, which was just north of the docks.

σ σ σ

Rufino never made it to his destination. His attention span resembled that of a four-year-old on a coffee high, so the unfortunate truth was that most of his plans didn't go as intended. In this case, he was flittering above Candlestick Road along the eastern periphery of the entertainment district when he spotted something that had definitely not been there when last he'd come this way. It was a small business entitled *Carmen's Artisan Sweets,* and unless his admittedly weak bat-form eyes were in dire need of recalibration, what he was looking at was his holy grail: a bakery.

Though vampires did still possess the stomachs from their previous lives, the only substance from which they gained energy was the blood of others, so eating food for any purpose other than to pass for normal was a complete waste of time. Rufino did not care. He'd been a master chef prior to his vampiric conversion, and like a lot of chefs, he was something of an enthusiast when it came to food. He was particularly fond of cinnamon-and-apple bagels that were fresh from the oven, but *only* if they were fresh from the oven; his unforgiving palette was downright offended by stale leftovers. Unfortunately, standard business hours were greatly prejudiced against those for whom sunlight was fatal, so stale leftovers were about all that was available to poor Rufino.

Not this time. It was one thing to ask a man to drink blood for sustenance, to avoid the sun at all costs, and not to reveal the truth about himself to anyone—Rufino could handle that. This wasn't to say that he *enjoyed* his undead existence, because he didn't, but he was willing and able to do what it took to survive. Living without bagels, on the other hand, was cruel and unusual punishment that was going to come to an end right now. *This far,* he recalled the classic expression of defiance, *no further.*

Camping at the front door until the bakery opened was, of course, completely out of the question. He might have been willing to chance it had the business's entrance faced west, but this one faced south and would thus be exposed to the sun fairly early in the morning. There were plenty of illegitimate ways to enter a building, however, and Rufino was well-practised at most of them—such was life on society's unwanted fringe. The real difficulty, he assumed, wasn't going to be in gaining access but in obtaining his bagels and then finding a way to persuade the shop's proprietor that he was gone when in fact he was not. His bat form was small enough that he couldn't even bully a chickadee, but there nevertheless remained the possibility that he would be discovered hiding in some dark corner of Carmen's bakery. If that happened whilst the sun was still up outside....

Risky business, to be sure, but some risks simply had to be taken.

His first order of business was to obtain some spending money. That would be easy enough—gold coins were aplenty in a city this size, and Rufino had long since figured out where some of the strays could be found. His unofficial bank account in Meridian was the donation pool just outside the temple of Ishiira, one of Ch'ulu's most benevolent gods. Ishiirite priestesses were unwaveringly dedicated to helping the less fortunate, as Ishiira herself had done over a thousand years ago, so denying them of resources was kind of a jackass thing to do. On the other hand, he'd made withdrawals from this donation pool on at least a dozen occasions and had yet to be struck down by lightning, so perhaps the lack of consequences meant Ishiira was cool with his as-needed pilfering. *If anyone could be considered less fortunate,* he reasoned, *it's me.*

Just to be on the safe side, he decided to swipe only what he needed for three bagels—one for each year that he'd gone without. Four gold coins would be plenty; unless, of course, the word "artisan" in the bakery's name was being used as an excuse to double the markup. If so, he'd have to do this over two days, but there were many who would argue against scarfing all three bagels at once in the first place. Under other circumstances, Rufino might even have agreed with those people, but this was no time to be thinking about healthy eating.

After a five-minute flight to the north at maximum velocity, which for him was only about twenty kilometres per hour, Rufino arrived at the temple. Part of becoming an Ishiirite priestess was to swear off luxuries of any kind, and their temples reflected this minimalist attitude. Although the building was constructed of high-quality stone and did possess both a clock and a bell tower, its footprint was no larger than that of a middle-class house. What was inside, he hadn't a clue, for he'd never been inside an Ishiirite temple. Galensdorf was all about the goddess Nireldehir, otherwise known as Mother Earth. This wasn't intended as a slight against the other gods, but farmers were very serious about their crops, and any god who felt like making those bloody crops grow faster and healthier was gonna get a temple built in her honour. It was as simple as that.

Rufino landed behind the building, reverted to his humanoid form, and then tootled around front to where the pool was located. The area was well-lit, both by a torch mounted above the temple's entrance and by a pair of ornate streetlamps on the sidewalk nearby, but this didn't appear to be cause for concern because there wasn't a soul to be seen for a block in either direction. With any luck, things would stay that way for the next minute or two.

Five seconds later, he was seated on the raised stone perimeter of the donation pool, scouring the shallow water for gold coins. Spotting one, he reached in and grabbed it, noticing once again that there was a marked difference in temperature between the cold stone and the warm water. The air temperature was twelve degrees Celsius at the most, yet the water was probably three times that, and there was no obvious explanation for the difference. He wasn't complaining, though, for the warm water was yet another luxury that he'd not enjoyed since prior to his conversion. It was briefly tempting to take a bath right here and right now, but the dreadfulness of that idea was beyond description. In fact, he...

"May I help you?"

That wasn't good. Rufino withdrew his hand from the proverbial cookie jar and looked over his shoulder. A middle-aged human woman, dressed in a simple white robe, stood in the doorway of the temple. Her expression of patient disapproval was a carbon-copy of the ones he used to see on the faces of his parents. It would have been far less awkward if this *had* been his mother, though, for this was no ordinary Ishiirite priestess. The robe was a dead giveaway—this was an Ishiirite *high* priestess, of which there were only three in this country of over two million people. He didn't know how powerful this woman was, but one thing was for certain: if any amongst her kind were capable of detecting undead, she could. "Sorry," he told her, hoping she'd get the message that he didn't want to fight. "I just need some money for food."

In the strictest sense, he'd spoken the truth. Bagels *were* food, sort of, and he *did* need them—not from a nutritional standpoint, of course, but from an emotional one. More to the point, this was probably a very generous woman, so he expected his sob story to resonate with her. He was right. "Oh, you poor thing," she said, sizing him up correctly despite having no accurate information. "Why don't you come by at noon? We host lunch for the needy on a daily basis. The portions are regretfully small for humans, but they'll be perfect for you."

Noon. Yeah, right. He couldn't spin a story about being nocturnal, though, lest she begin to suspect that free food wasn't what he was after. "I'll be at work," he explained, "earning the hospital's next paycheck."

"Are you ill?"

Under no circumstances did he want the priestess to examine him with any form of healing magic, for that would surely betray his big secret. "No, it's my folks," he explained quickly, borrowing the tragic story of what had happened to the parents of his former best friend. "Pop's been ill for a long time and the stress is beginning to kill Mum, too. My income and their retirement savings are both gone, and I honestly can't tell if the hospital is happy to take our money or if they set the prices this high in order to encourage people to die and stop draining resources."

"You don't look that old."

It seemed an innocent enough observation, but he believed it to be a test of the story he was weaving. "I'm twenty-nine," he answered her challenge in the strongest possible way—with the truth, "and my parents are only in their fifties. We don't all reach our life expectancy, I'm afraid. Have you been to my home village of Galensdorf?"

The woman surprised absolutely no one by shaking her head.

"It's a farming community," he explained, "and farming is hard work, especially for people as small as us." This poor-me routine was coming along quite nicely if he did say so himself, and the time now seemed ideal for a small dose of righteous indignation. "It's not very lucrative, either—not nearly enough to pay for your damned hospital bills. Why do you tall people think it's okay to bankrupt a man's entire family just because he got sick?"

"Not all of us do," she replied smoothly as she took a couple of slow steps toward him. "I find the idea of for-profit medicine to be abhorrent, as do all Ishiirites. I trust you've tried healing magic?"

That had been the first thing his friend's parents had tried, but healing magic had several regrettable weaknesses. "Yes," Rufino said as he slumped his shoulders, "but it's melanoma, and your magic is powerless against cancer."

The priestess nodded slowly, and as she did so, he sensed that her suspicions were fading away. "Sadly, that's true," she admitted, "but this humble temple will always do what it can for you and your family. You needn't steal that which we would give you freely."

"I'm sorry," he said, and he genuinely meant it this time. "It's just…"

"It's just that stealing is easier than asking for help?" She took the words straight from his mouth. "Yes, I've heard that on more than one occasion, to which I always reply that the more difficult path is usually the one that's more beneficial to the spirit. Isolating yourself will only harm you in the long run." She stepped up to the pool. "How much did you intend to take?"

Rufino sighed. The advice he was receiving was probably sound for a man in the position he'd described, but it wasn't worth much to a vampire. *Open up to others.*

Hah. My life expectancy would be longer if I pinned my head to an archery target. "Four gold," he replied.

"Only four?"

He wasn't sure if her suspicions were reasserting themselves or of she was simply inviting him to ask for more. "It doesn't cost much to feed a halfling," he reminded her. *Especially one who doesn't have to eat.*

"Nevertheless," the priestess said as she reached into the pool and started fishing around for coins, "giving you four coins would return you to this position of desperation in only a couple of days. I'm going to give you fifteen coins, instead, which I hope will last you a full week." She withdrew her arm from the pool and started counting what she'd collected thus far. "If and when this supply runs out, I sincerely hope you'll consider asking for help instead of returning to the path upon which I found you."

He wished he could tell her the truth—he really did—but he didn't think there was a benevolent soul in the entire world capable of accepting what he really was. Vampirism had been a symbol of evil for a long as it had existed, and although he didn't believe himself to be evil, it seemed an insurmountable task to change a three-thousand-year-old status quo. "I'll do that," he lied, feeling like The Ultimate Dirtbag as he did so. "Before I go, though, I do have one question, if I may."

The high priestess apparently required a few more coins, because she lowered her arm into the pool again before saying, "Of course."

"Why is the water so warm?"

She paused for a moment to turn her head and stare at him. "I mean," he went on a bit sheepishly, "the water just seems to be much warmer than the air, and it's been my experience that there shouldn't be much of a difference. I..."

"The meaning is different for each of us who feel the warmth of the holy water," the priestess told him as she returned her attention to the contents of the pool. "You will find the answer to your question somewhere deep within yourself."

He didn't need to be a halfling to see where this was going. "Was that some cryptic way of telling me I should join up?" he demanded. "That I should dedicate my life to helping people like me?"

"That is for you to say," she replied simply as she dropped the coins into his disbelieving hands. "Not I."

Again, that sounded an awful lot like a subtle religious way of saying "yes." It didn't matter, though, because it was safe to say he wouldn't have been able to cut it in their line of work even without the sun thing. He'd been a fairly generous guy before vampirism had come along—he'd even let the hostess at his *Good Eats* restaurant in Galensdorf keep her job after she misplaced his favourite knife—but to dedicate one's life to helping those who might not be what they seemed to be wasn't really his speed. The priestess didn't know it, but by the law of her land, she'd just committed a felony crime by providing aid to a vampire—such was the risk of being so openly generous. "I'll give it some thought," he said as he stuffed the gold coins into his trouser pockets. "Thank you."

σ σ σ

As soon as the priestess was safely out of sight, Rufino shifted into his bat form and hurried back to the bakery, his mind attempting to decipher the Ishiirite's cryptic words as he flew. What was obvious enough was that not everyone felt the "warmth of the holy water", as she'd put it, which implied that he was blessed in some way. In spite of this evidence, he found it impossible to believe that a horrible undead beastie could be favoured by anyone except

Shinzado, the God of Death. He eventually concluded that it was his *quest* and not his character that had earned him this special attention. *Ishiira likes bagels. There's no other explanation.*

Did that mean she wanted him to share? Would he be expected to leave a complimentary bagel upon an altar somewhere so that the goddess herself might have a snack? Or worse, would she want a whole tray *full* of bagels because only mortals needed to count calories? *Good thing I got some extra money.*

A few moments later, he was fifty feet above the target, evaluating his options for access. As he usually did, he immediately eliminated the front door from consideration—Meridian simply had far too many random pedestrians for him to risk being observed trying to pick a lock in his distinctive humanoid form. *Carmen*'s appeared to have a secondary entrance accessible from the service alley behind this row of buildings, but there were a couple of drunks making out in said alley not sixty feet from the door he wanted, so he wasn't getting in that way either. Not yet, anyway.

Plan-C was to go through the air vents that almost all professional kitchens had. Indeed, there were some vents in the rear of the building, but in a rather depressing stroke of misfortune, someone had actually remembered to close them. Discouraged but far from defeated, Rufino then made his way to the small chimney on the roof of the building and set down beside it. He'd become something of an expert regarding chimneys over the years, if for no other reason than because human children liked to leave milk and cookies out for some mythical gift-giving fat man on the eve of the winter solstice. Cookies weren't cinnamon-and-apple bagels, but beggars couldn't be choosers, so he was quite happy to take them.

It was this experience that prompted his use of echolocation to "see" what he was up against before jumping in. Commercial ovens, he knew, were often connected directly to the chimney so that the bulk of the smoke could be expelled before the kitchen workers choked to death. His sound-based vision was capable of sensing whether the door to the oven or ovens had been left open, but he never got a chance to make that determination, for there was a solid surface within the exhaust pipe that was effectively denying him access. It seemed highly unlikely that the pipe had been permanently sealed off because the air vents wouldn't be able to handle all the smoke by themselves. He could only surmise that this was a retractable barrier meant to close off the exhaust system when it was not in use. *What is this, a maximum-security bakery?*

More likely the barrier had been installed to keep insects and other vermin at bay. The inside surface of the chimney was a rough one, which gave squirrels and bats and probably dozens of other kinds of animals something to hold onto whilst descending into the promised land. Regardless of the barrier's purpose, it was clear that his tiny bat form lacked the strength to slide it out of the way. Frustrated, he flittered around to the front of the building and took a brief look. The storefront panoramic window didn't appear to have any openings, and the door just beside it was possessed of two locks, one of which was about four and a half feet off the ground. He'd need a stool to reach that. *This is nuts,* he fumed in the privacy of his mind. *If rats and mice can find a way into commercial kitchens after-hours, why the devil can't I?*

It was a fair question, for he did honestly believe his prodigious halfling intellect to be more than a match for a bloody rodent. He could always break a window, but doing so would encourage the entrepreneur to search the building whilst the bat-burglar was still there to be found, and that didn't sound like a great idea. Besides, he knew as well as anyone that the profit margin in this sort of business was not an especially large one. The last thing he wanted was to force an unwanted expense upon this Carmen lady. Quite the contrary—he wanted to *encourage* people to open bakeries, and he could only do that by finding ways in that wouldn't cost them any money.

That left the back alley. The inebriated youths were still there, of course, slobbering all over each other like they'd skipped the science class about how many diseases could be transmitted via saliva. They might not notice if he turned himself into a dragon and set a few of the buildings on fire, but he wasn't about to risk his identity and his bagels on a *maybe.* He needed to get rid of them, and he needed to do so in a way that wouldn't get him reported to the vampire-hunters. Sadly, this precluded the possibility of running them off in his small-but-ferocious flight form. He'd have to go down there and persuade them to leave, and he expected that to go about as well as had prohibition.

It was excessively difficult for a beardless midget with green hair to intimidate anyone, so it was clear that he wasn't going to get anywhere with the two humans by threatening them. As he started toward them on foot, he decided that the slightly deranged approach was the best way to go. In theory, his green mohawk would tell them that he was capable of anything. If his words also supported that conclusion, he should be able to persuade the two lovebirds that he was more trouble than he was worth. *Get really excited,* he coached himself as he approached his foes, *and talk nonsense. Weird them out.*

A moment later, it was show time. "You're in my spot!" he accused them from ten feet away.

There was a depressing lack of cloud cover, so there was plenty of moonlight with which to see, and what he saw did not inspire confidence. He noticed the nose-rings first—both the female and the male wore them, as if putting a piece of metal through one's nostrils could somehow be a symbol of partnership to another who'd done the same. The male also had a lip-ring. In Rufino's humble opinion, lip-rings and kissing went together like broccoli and birthday parties, but now was probably not the time to put voice to that particular thought.

You see, he'd been counting on his mohawk to throw them off-stride, but it turned out that his emerald-green hair was pretty tame compared to theirs. Her long hair was both black and purple—striped not unlike a zebra—and *his* black hair was a clash of opposites: shaved completely on the sides but long enough up top to form a thick braid that extended halfway down his back. Both wore dark makeup and both were dressed completely in black. The female wore a leather jacket; the male wore a short-sleeved shirt that was about three sizes too small. Unfortunately, this virtually skin-tight garment did reveal the male to be fairly muscular, so he was probably more than capable of kicking Rufino's ass. The only *good* news was that the humans smelled of cannabis, not alcohol, so they probably weren't spoiling for a fight.

That could change, though. "Whaddya want?" the male demanded in a voice that managed to be both demanding and happy-go-lucky at the same time.

Rufino's beef had already been expressed, but he could forgive the guy for not paying attention to his surroundings whilst engaged in a game of tongue-tag. "You're in my spot!" he repeated excitedly. "They're expecting me!"

The two humans were understandably confused. "Who?" they asked in unison.

The little vampire pointed toward the moon. "They are, but I have to stand right here or they'll…."

"Who?" the male asked again.

Is there a bloody echo in this alley? "The Triumvirate," Rufino admitted with "reluctance" as he made a shushing gesture, "supreme rulers of the moon."

This was a stretch even for his wild imagination. "But you can't tell anyo…"

"*Aliens?!*" the male demanded incredulously.

Rufino smiled to himself. *They'll be outta here shortly.* "Sort of," he lied, "'cuz they're from the moon, not another planet. They…"

"Can we go with you?"

That wasn't the reaction he'd been hoping for. "Say what?"

The young man stood up and encouraged his girlfriend to do the same. "Take us with you," he implored of his new buddy. "We pledge our loyalty to the Triumv… Trium…"

The little vampire released the breath he hadn't realized he'd been holding. "Triumvirate."

"Triumvirate?"

Rufino was about to ask what they actually taught in human schools when it occurred to him that these two specimens probably hadn't seen the inside of a classroom in a while. "A ruling council of three," he explained as his mind scrambled for a way out of this mess. "This one doesn't like strangers, though, so it would probably be best if…"

"A stranger is just a friend you haven't met yet!" the young woman cut him off with enthusiasm.

"Yeah!" the male was quick to agree.

The poor halfling raised a palm to his face and shook his head slowly. Just when he was beginning to think things couldn't get any worse, however, they did—in three simple words from the female. "Isn't he cute?"

Rufino extracted his palm from his face and glowered up at the woman. Where he came from, the word "cute" was recognized as profanity of the worst kind. His people were constantly hearing it whenever they dared venture into tall-person towns. If one wanted to describe a halfling male, adjectives such as "rugged" or "handsome"

271 σ Realms of Fantastic Stories Vol. 2

could be used without offense, and even "dreamboat" was tolerable under the right circumstances. He did daresay that he was a little dreamy, so he could hardly fault a woman for describing him as such. "Cute," on the other hand, was one step removed from a declaration of war against male and female halflings alike. What self-respecting adult wanted to be lumped into the same category as toddlers, puppies, teddy bears, and comic-strip characters?

Before he could put voice to his objection, however, someone beat him to the punch. "Huh?" the human male demanded.

However relaxed that guy had been a moment ago, it was clear that he wasn't now. "Whaddya mean, 'huh?'" the girlfriend insisted. "Isn't that midget-badass look the most adorable thing you've ever seen?"

Adorable. That was even worse than *cute.* Rufino could bite his tongue no longer. "Why not just tie a ribbon around my head and take me home to your folks?" he growled.

Unfortunately, it appeared that the slightly-mind-altered female was taking his sarcastic suggestion seriously. "Yes," she said as she started toward him, "I think that would be... hey!"

The young man had taken his companion by the forearm and was now attempting to lead her away. "Come on," he urged with impatience that was undoubtedly fueled by jealousy, "let's go."

"But I..." the woman argued as she pulled in the opposite direction.

"We need to find some ribbon," the boyfriend suggested quickly.

The young woman saw the logic in that. Rufino was impressed in spite of himself as he watched the two humans leave. For a boy to separate his girl from the competition under the guise of being helpful was tricky enough to begin with, but to do so successfully whilst as high as a kite spoke very well of this one's mental acuity. Oh, sure, he'd have some explaining to do whenever she caught on, but it was far easier to beg forgiveness than it was to compete with Rufino for a woman's attention. Like the most notorious vampires of lore, he simply exuded sex appeal— surely human women just described him as *cute* or *adorable* to avoid making their own men feel inadequate.

Quite admirable, really.

Anyway, now that the potential witnesses were but a painful memory, Rufino hustled back to *Carmen's Artisan Sweets* and started casing the back entrance for vulnerabilities. Again, there weren't any—the door could only be opened from the inside and the two tall, narrow privacy windows flanking the doorway didn't open at all. There were two small rectangular push-out windows above the taller ones, but there was no overlap and thus nothing for Rufino to grab onto with a broomstick. *They're probably locked anyway,* he grumbled in resignation. Never before had he encountered so much difficulty in entering an ordinary business, but the fact that this bakery was apparently under lockdown was strangely symbolic considering how his quest for bagels had gone these past three years. *They're not even trying to hide it anymore,* he growled as he glanced up at the heavens. *They're just messing with me now.*

It was probably still possible for him to sneak in when someone showed up and opened the door, but to do so would take an already sketchy risk/reward ratio and tilt it even further in the wrong direction. Yes, fresh cinnamon-and-apple bagels were the be-all, end-all of culinary indulgences, but they weren't worth dying for. Dejected, the little vampire slowly walked around to the front of the building. Kicking the door and spitting on the welcome mat wouldn't get him into the bakery, of course, but it would make him feel a tiny bit better, and there were precious few ways for a vampire to accomplish this. He could smoke as much cannabis as had those two humans *combined* and it wouldn't do jack to him, nor would alcohol or any of the other standard ways to put a bandage on a bad mood. Not only did the vampiric existence kinda suck, but he was stone-cold sober for the entirety of it, which made it suck even more.

There was the occasional peak, though, in the valley that was his unlife, and he unexpectedly encountered one as he tootled up to Carmen's front door in his humanoid form. There, sandwiched between the door itself and the large panoramic window beside it, was an inconspicuous vertically oriented mail slot that had managed to elude his bat form's eyes. If not for his desire to kick the door in frustration, he would have missed it altogether. *Note to self: don't assume.* Sometimes the front entrance was the best way in, and he'd be a fool not to recognize that. He should have looked it over with his superior set of eyes before writing it off.

What was done was done, though, and he'd once again demonstrated the wisdom of the words, "better lucky than good." Unfortunately, there was nothing for him to land on and the surrounding surfaces were too smooth for him to climb. To make matters worse, this mail slot's cover was of the push-to-open variety, so there was no way for him to prop it open with a stick from out here. He'd have to ram it. Now, he did consider himself quite the expert when it came to precision crashing, but landing on a moving person and barreling through a thin metal door were two completely different things. Not only would this mail slot afford him precious little in the way of clearance, but he'd have to roll onto his side at the last second in order to squeeze through.

A delicate task, to be sure, but pulling it off would mean bagels. That was all the motivation he needed.

A few moments later, after ducking out of sight and metamorphosing into his bat form, Rufino was thirty feet above Candlestick Road and lining up his special delivery. He couldn't see the target from up here, but it was probably still there; and more importantly, there wasn't a soul to be found for as far as he could sense in any direction. With an excitement that a man who was probably about to sustain a mild concussion had no business feeling, he pitched down and began his run.

The approach went perfectly. The mail slot became visible once he closed to within forty feet, which eliminated much of the guesswork. A few minor corrections of his heading, a few flaps of his wings to maintain his forward momentum, and he was on course. In his mind, he could see exactly what he needed to do in order to bulls-eye the target, and it was all so elementary. At fifteen feet, he adjusted his course so that he was pointed toward a spot that was two inches to the left and nine inches above the opening. At eight feet, he rolled to the right and began to drop toward the thin metal door, confident that he was about to score a perfect hit.

Then there was a gust of wind.

It wasn't much, but it was just enough to turn Rufino's moment of triumph into a face-first collision with a rather unyielding panoramic window, resulting in his crumpling to the packed-dirt sidewalk in an inglorious heap of hairy flesh. Fortunately, the kinetic energy generated by his featherweight flight form wasn't enough to do any serious damage to him or to anything else, so he was able to regain his senses a short moment later. Frustrated, he returned his attention to the heavens and gave whomever was watching the best glower he could manage. *What gives?* he complained bitterly. *Warm water, remember? My quest is blessed, so buzz off.*

There was no response. He hadn't really been expecting one, so there was naught to do but to get back into the air and take another run at that mail slot. As he began his second attempt, though, he promised himself that he was going to return to that Ishiirite high priestess and file a formal grievance if he ran into any more nonsense. Ishiira probably wasn't the one who was playing games with him, but she sure wasn't doing much about the joker who was. Surely blessed minions such as he were entitled to a small amount of divine protection. *Just enough to ward off the practical jokes,* he sent a silent plea into the heavens, *that's all I ask.*

It seemed to work, because his second attempt to barrel through the mail slot was successful, and he found himself inside a cardboard box that was obviously Carmen's mail-catcher. Now it was a male-catcher as well, having cushioned his crash-landing quite nicely. With but only the most minor of injuries, Rufino worked his way out of the box and thoroughly assessed his new surroundings. There was a series of transparent display cases to his right and a series of inclined shelves to his left, all of which were empty except for those in the clearly marked day-old section. There was standing room on the other side of the display cases, so that was probably where the money was kept—if there was any money left overnight—but Rufino didn't care about that. Directly ahead, on the far side of the room, was a doorway that could only lead into the business part of the business, where the bagels were created. And the other stuff, too.

Victory was at hand.

Chapter Two
Denied

The storeroom and the kitchen turned out to be one large room. In Rufino's experience, this was unusual, but he wasn't complaining. Quite the contrary, in fact—this one-room design granted him direct line-of-sight to each of Carmen's four ovens from his hiding place at the top of a shelving unit against the west wall, and he *definitely* wanted to watch the creation of his beloved sweets. It could be a long time before he'd have the opportunity and the nerve to do this again.

The baker arrived at approximately 04:00. He was a young adult who was six feet tall with black hair and a strong build—a good-looking dude by human standards, though he was sadly lacking in facial hair. He lit several candles around the room and then began the process of making cookie dough. Rufino was initially somewhat offended that mere cookies were taking priority over *his* bagels, but perhaps he was looking at this the wrong way. *The longer the bagels are put off,* he reasoned, *the fresher they'll be when it's time to buy.*

It wasn't until the baker had several trays of cookies in the first oven that he began the process of making bread dough. Rufino took special interest in this, for he'd inferred from the name of this shop that it didn't do a whole lot of business in plain bread. If not for the loaves he'd seen back on the day-old shelf, he might have assumed this place dealt exclusively in junk food. Since the young man had started off making junk food, however, there seemed a reasonably good chance that Rufino was now looking at his bagels in their infancy. He was right. Not long after he realized what he might be looking at, the baker pulled a baking sheet from the shelf above the second oven, upon which he placed a dozen lumps of the freshly kneaded dough. He then began to sculpt that precious raw material into the shape of rings, which certainly would have caused the little vampire's heart to beat faster were it still capable of beating at all. *There's only one thing missing.*

The missing ingredient wasn't introduced to the first tray of bagels or even to the second, but before the baker started to prepare the third batch of rings, he fetched several juicy green apples from storage and cut them into thin slices with practised hands. He then placed the apple slices into a skillet and added several more ingredients: butter, nutmeg, sugar, salt, *cinnamon!* It was all Rufino could do to keep from squeaking in delight as he observed from afar. *Better make a bunch of those, bro,* he sent silent encouragement toward the baker. *Demand is about to soar.*

The ex-chef continued to supervise for the next four hours, eventually reaching the conclusion that the young human was very competent at his craft. The finished bagels looked absolutely mouth-wateringly delicious, as did just about everything else that had come out of those ovens. *And the smell...mmmm!* Rufino had experienced olfactory orgasm six times since the baking had begun in earnest, and the seventh episode was now steaming his way like a runaway train. Only one hour remained until opening time, but he wasn't sure he was going to make it. He wanted to taste-test everything in this room, starting with one or more of those fabulous bagels that were now sitting unguarded on the counter closest to the merchandising area. It was a darned good thing his bat form was too small to carry anything larger than a small cookie, else he almost certainly would have done something stupid by now.

The woman that he presumed to be Carmen showed up at 08:15. Like the male, she had black hair, was taller than average, and was noticeably good-looking, which raised the possibility that they might be siblings. Regardless, it was obvious from the beginning that she knew her way around the kitchen, for the first thing she did was to mix the ingredients for some more bread dough without consulting the instructions. *A woman after my own heart.*

The conversation between Carmen and the male started out strictly casual, but after a few minutes, things got interesting. "There's a delivery due in ten minutes," she said.

The man nodded. "I'll take care of it."

Rufino liked the sound of that. It was probably just flour, sugar, and maybe yeast, but there was a slim chance that some more cinnamon would be in there too. "After that," she went on, "I see no reason why we can't open a few minutes early today."

The baker smiled. "It's been a good morning. Everything's turned out well so far."

The woman smiled back at him. "Don't sound so surprised. You are quite good at this, you know."

The compliment did nothing to dampen the baker's already good mood. "I know," he agreed, "but still, you know as well as anyone that bread doesn't always rise the way it should. The stuff's been unusually co-operative this morning."

I'll be quite happy to take the credit for that. There was an old saying: a watched loaf never rises. That was obviously false, for Rufino had been staring at them all morning and they'd turned out perfectly. "They look great," she agreed. "The multigrain is on its way?"

The young man nodded. "The first four'll be out of number three in about five minutes. They can cool while I'm downstairs."

"Perfect," Carmen smiled again. "I'll start to set up."

These seem like very nice people, Rufino decided. A moment later, however, he realized he shouldn't be surprised. Of course these were nice people, he reasoned, because *only* nice people would open a bakery where he could find it. Were he not a vampire, he'd be hell-bent on making these people his new best friends, starting with that very attractive young lady. *She owns a bakery—she's a keeper.*

"Before you do," the man interrupted Rufino's train of thought, "would you do me a favour?"

"Of course," Carmen was quick to reply.

He looked around the kitchen and storeroom with an odd expression on his face. "Let me know if you hear lip-smacking?"

"Lip-smacking?"

He nodded. "I've been hearing it all morning."

Oops. Rufino had a sort of subconscious habit of smacking his lips when he was hungry and surrounded by food. Apparently, it happened whilst he was in bat form, too, and now he had a problem. He could evade a casual search with relative ease, but if Carmen and her business partner decided the sound was real and tore the place apart looking for the source, they'd find him. Nice people like these might not want to kill a harmless bat, but they would almost certainly want to put him outside, which would make for a very long day of playing hide-and-seek with the sun. *Happy thoughts, happy thoughts….*

The woman hesitated a moment, and her expression hardened quite noticeably. "And you've checked for intruders?"

The male nodded. "There's no one here, and there are also no signs of forced entry."

Rufino hadn't been aware that the man had been *looking* for signs of forced entry. Either he was making it up in order to impress the girl or his skill set was far more diverse than he'd let on. "There's only one explanation, then," Carmen decided.

"What's that?"

She smiled again. "It's a ghost."

The man snorted. "You mean you didn't have this place checked out for ghosts when you bought it?"

The question was significant in that it confirmed that Carmen was the sole owner of this place. Siblings these two may be, but it was now clear that theirs was an unequal partnership. "Of course I did," Carmen insisted quickly. "This is a new ghost, and it's stuck in our world until it eats cookies one last time."

Ghosts and cookies? Rufino chastised her in silence as he rolled his eyes and shook his head. *Don't be ridiculous.*

"Works for me," the male said with a smile of his own. "Now I have something to blame when a handful of them go missing."

The little eavesdropper liked the sound of that. He'd done so much "quality control" on his own cooking at *Good Eats* that he most assuredly would have been fired if he hadn't been a co-owner. Since it sounded like this young man's shameless snacking was coming straight out of Carmen's bottom line, the establishment of a scapegoat sounded like quite an excellent idea. But then, Rufino would have expected no less from one so sensible as to become a baker. *You may never become rich, my friend,* he told the man, *but the happiness you'll spread will more than make up for it. You are enlightened, man—absolutely enl...*

His train of thought then jumped the rails, for the young man was now engaged in a most peculiar activity. About twenty heavy bags of flour had been tucked into the south corner of this west wall of the storeroom, and he was now moving these bags into the centre of the room. There was seemingly no explanation for this course of action, but what was even more peculiar was that Carmen was aware of what her subordinate was doing and didn't seem to be bothered by it. In fact, she'd taken over the kitchen duties so that the male could do whatever it was that he was doing. Rufino didn't recall hearing them arrange a changing of the guard, though, and the lack of verbal communication implied that they'd done this before. *What's going on?*

In curious fascination, the little vampire watched as the young baker finished moving the bags of flour and then removed the items from the first of the two tall metal shelving units against the west wall. Once those items were all safely on the floor, he grabbed the shelving unit's two closest vertical beams and slid the unit into the space previously occupied by the bags of flour. In Rufino's humble opinion, the storeroom had been laid out quite efficiently and was hardly in need of redecorating— particularly since the next shelving unit in line was the one he just happened to be camped out on. *Good job,* he complimented the man as his anxiety level began to grow. *Looks great. You can stop now.*

The human male wasn't listening. He removed the items from Rufino's shelving unit, which could only mean the little vampire was about to go for a ride. Unfortunately, the surface of the top shelf was exquisitely smooth metal that gave him absolutely nothing to hold onto, and he didn't dare use his wings to maintain his position out of concern that Carmen would turn around and spot him. All he could do was to take up a position on the pulling side and hope he didn't slide off the opposite end.

Rufino did indeed end up going for a rather bumpy ride as the young baker pulled this unit into the space previously occupied by its twin, but he was never in any real danger of going over the edge. Nevertheless, he was not amused. *You know what this place needs?* he stewed in frustration as he tootled over to the north edge of his shelf. *Wood shelving units. Traction is a beautiful thing, and...*

He never got a chance to finish that thought, for the baker was now kneeling in the space where the second shelving unit had stood just a moment ago, running the palm of his right hand along the floor as if searching for something. Maybe the man *hadn't* been clearing space for the delivery, as Rufino had thought. *Did Carmen lose an earring?*

A moment later, the young man used the thumb and index finger of that same hand to grab onto something that Rufino's bat-form eyes couldn't even see, and proceeded to open a two-foot-by-two-foot trapdoor that had been indistinguishable from the floor itself. On the other side of that door was a stepladder leading down into a cellar. It was then that the hairs on the back of Rufino's head began to tingle, and the effect was amplified tenfold when Carmen handed her brother a lit torch for his descent into whatever was down there, as if what was happening was no big deal. Indeed, underground storage wasn't illegal in and of itself, but the fact that the siblings had gone to such lengths to hide the entrance to this cellar told Rufino that whatever was down there was something they didn't want the health inspectors to find.

A part of him could understand and appreciate that. Queen Jasmine had been a bit of a safety buff, which had empowered the health inspectors who worked on her behalf to act like holier-than-thou jackasses. They'd even forced Rufino to wear *beard nets* when he was handling food at *Good Eats*. Beard nets! So what if a tiny amount of beard hair got into someone's corn? And while he was on the subject, so what if he only washed his hands a couple times a day? Dirt and germs were good for the immune system! Trying to avoid illness by sterilizing everything was akin to trying to build muscle by avoiding exertion. *Whatever*. The air was thin up where tall people kept their brains, so perhaps a bit of inconsistent logic was to be expected from them.

Rufino was also getting a bad feeling in the pit of his stomach, though, as he usually did when he found himself in over his head. The sensible course of action, he knew, was to forget he'd seen anything, acquire his bagels as planned, use his culinary background to arrange for a brief tour of the kitchen, and then ask to exit via the rear door. It would suck having to hide behind this building for the rest of the daylight hours, but he was no longer certain he'd be able to remain inside without Carmen's knowledge. People with secrets tended to be a little paranoid, so it stood to reason that she'd be paying close attention to the comings and goings of her customers.

If there was one thing Rufino Endicott had demonstrated over the years, however, it was that he wasn't all that sensible. He knew perfectly well how to stay out of trouble, but he had yet to learn how to *act* on his knowledge of how to stay out of trouble. A part of him desperately needed to know what was in that secret cellar, so instead of taking the easy way out by buying his bagels and then leaving, he decided to stay right where he was. When Carmen closed up for the evening, he'd be free to check out what she and her brother didn't want anyone to find. There was still a chance that their secret was reasonably innocent—perhaps they were simply trying to avoid paying ridiculous tariffs on some imported booze, or something. If so, he could always wait out the night and buy his bagels tomorrow. A lost day was a small price to pay for a clear conscience.

σ σ σ

Carmen had an excellent day of business, and Rufino was more than willing to take the credit for that as well. After waiting out an entire business day, he was so fit to be tied that he could have gone for even a stale leftover or three. Naturally, there weren't any—the bagels, the cookies, the cakes, and even the bloody loaves of bread were completely sold out, and he was convinced it was because the jackass upstairs didn't want him to have anything. *Figures.*

With nothing left to sell, Carmen did a little bit of cleaning and then went home at 17:45. Rufino waited until 18:30 to emerge from hiding. When he finally did, he felt compelled to complete his inspection as quickly as possible. There was, after all, still a chance that one of the siblings would return and catch him red-handed, and that would seriously suck.

Unlike the two vertically gifted humans, the little vampire was incapable of removing the items from the upper shelves, so he decided not to bother clearing the lower shelves either. To do so would be pointless—the fully-loaded shelving units weighed at least two hundred pounds whereas he weighed forty-four pounds soaking wet. It wasn't like he'd be able to pull these stupid things fast enough to overcome the inertia of the items they carried. If not for the traction afforded to him by the rough wood floor, Rufino might not have been able to move the units at all.

It occurred to him right away that he could save himself some work by repositioning only the four bags of flour closest to the first of the two shelving units. This would only permit him to slide the first unit about a foot toward the remaining bags, but a foot of clearance would allow him to rotate the second unit forty-five degrees and then pull it diagonally into the middle of the room. *The same result for about half the work,* he reasoned. *What's not to love?*

Plenty, in fact. The bad news started when one of the bags of flour—which he was forced to drag because they weighed fifty bloody pounds—ran into the business end of a splinter and started leaking all over the floor. Then the second shelving unit, as he was pulling it, got caught in a small hole in that very same booby-trapped floor, resulting in a change of velocity that was just abrupt enough to overcome the inertia of something on one of the upper shelves. Rufino paused to listen as the unseen item fell over, started rolling, and eventually found its way over the edge of the shelf. It was a fancy porcelain cup, of course, or at least it *was* a fancy porcelain cup until it hit the floor and smashed into a dozen pieces. *Oh, come on,* Rufino grumbled toward the heavens once again. *Precariously placed porcelain? Have you run out of original ways to torment me?*

There was no answer, of course, which left Rufino with naught to do but to complete his chaotic reorganization. A minute later—the shelving unit now safely out of the way—he was on his knees searching for the means to open the hidden door. It didn't take him long to realize one of the nails in the floor was too small for the hole it occupied. When he saw that he could remove the nail with ease, he also realized that if he re-inserted the nail at an angle and then pulled straight up, the trapdoor would come along for the ride. The technique worked—with the door now out of the way, he found himself staring at the stepladder that Carmen's brother had used to descend into the cellar. Instead of following in the other's footsteps, however, he simply shifted into his bat form and hopped into the darkness.

As he descended, he emitted a series of rapid clicks. His echolocation told him the cellar was a rectangular layout approximately six hundred square feet in size and a lot longer than it was wide. More important than the square footage, however, was the orientation. The room stretched approximately seventy feet to the south, which—unless he was sorely mistaken—extended beneath the sidewalk in front of the building. It made no sense to rip up a sidewalk during construction and thus inform thousands of random pedestrians that a secret cellar was being built, so it stood to reason that this hidey-hole had been built after the fact. *That would have been as dangerous as hell.* What was it about this place that had made it worth the risk to someone?

Rufino had a possible answer a moment later. Carmen had mentioned earlier that a delivery was due in ten minutes; a few minutes later, after stating in no uncertain terms that he'd take care of the delivery, her brother had rearranged half the storeroom to come down *here*. A delivery person had shown up at the service door half an hour later, but Rufino didn't recall Carmen saying anything about the man being behind schedule. She'd been quite friendly, in fact. *Could the real delivery have taken place down here?*

He didn't see how that was possible, unless.... *Seventy feet sounds about right for this cellar to reach the sewer beneath the street.* He took a whiff to test his theory, and sure enough, the room didn't smell all that great. *Could there be another secret door somewhere along that far wall?*

He knew a good way to find out.

A moment later, Rufino was on the ground two feet in front of the south wall, emitting burst after burst of exploratory clicks as he searched for anything that might be a door-opening mechanism. There was nothing obvious— no levers, no switches, just a torch mount about five feet up the wall. Again, he couldn't reach that without help, so he hopped over to an eighteen-inch-by-eighteen-inch cube at the base of a big pile of indistinguishable crap and pressed one of his wings against it to determine if its material was strong enough to support his halfling weight. He was delighted to discover that it was a wooden crate, so he shifted into his humanoid form, got into position behind his new step-stool, and then shoved it sightlessly over to the south wall. Once he was in position, he climbed onto the crate and felt around for the torch mount.

Upon locating that mount, he tried pushing on it, pulling on it, rotating it left, rotating it right, and even talking to it. Nothing happened. He didn't know what else to try, so he slapped the wall in front of him in frustration and was about to hop off his stool when he heard the faint grinding noise of brick against brick. His eyes were still telling him nothing, of course, so he re-shifted into his bat form and started echolocating again to see if anything had changed. Sure enough, the brick that he'd smacked had depressed into the wall about a quarter-inch and a door-sized portion of the wall itself had swung in ever so slightly. With the sweet taste of success now on the tip of his tongue, he shifted forms again and used his halfling arms to pull the door open further.

As could be expected of a secret brick door, it weighed about a million pounds and also seemed to be self-closing. Rufino abused several of his poor muscles trying to wrestle the thing open. When he eventually succeeded, though, he learned much. The door did indeed lead into the sewer—his nose told him everything he needed to know in that regard. He wanted to know more, however, so he shifted forms again and started to echolocate his new surroundings. His most significant observations were that the secret door opened onto a worker's wooden footpath that was elevated several feet above the bottom of the sewer, and that there was a ladder leading up to a manhole cover a short distance to the west. The sun was still outside waiting to barbeque him, of course, so he didn't dare open the manhole cover right now. It could very well come in handy later, though.

He turned around, for it was high time that he pop open one of these wooden crates and see what all the fuss was about. The crates were all nailed shut, but surely there'd be something upstairs that could help him overcome this minor obstacle. After a few minutes of careful scrounging, he was able to locate a claw hammer behind the customer service counter just beside the display cases. At first, he didn't understand why bakers would need or want to keep a hammer around, but then the explanation hit him like a bolt of lightning: *they need it to open and re-seal the wooden crates downstairs. Duh.*

Now armed with a most excellent tool, he returned to the cellar, randomly selected a box to open, and then dragged it to the base of the ladder at the north end of the room where there was still a smidgen of light. Maybe he should have been able to guess what might be inside a box that was six times longer than it was wide or tall, but he drew a blank as he pried away and was thus unprepared for what he eventually found inside.

Swords.

Longswords, to be more precise. The blades were thirty-nine inches long and two inches wide, but it was immediately obvious that the blades themselves were irrelevant. The cross-guards between a sword's hilt and blade were normally just round, flat, unremarkable pieces of metal, but these ones were octagonal, looking the part of miniature stop signs. To make matters worse, on the other side of the hilt from the cross-guard was the pommel, and the pommels of these weapons were also distinctive in that they were shaped like tiny heater shields instead of spheres or cylinders. This design was known to Rufino and to everyone else who spent any significant time in Meridian. It denoted that the bearer was of the city guard, the branch of law enforcement responsible for monitoring the city gates and keeping the riffraff out of the more exclusive parts of town.

Which left him in something of a pickle. Unless he was sorely mistaken, this wasn't a secret stash for the Meridian City Guard. It now seemed clear that the purpose of this equipment was for someone to *impersonate* the aforementioned group of do-gooders. For what purpose, Rufino couldn't say, but there were any number of possibilities to choose from and none of them were good. *People don't impersonate the authorities in order to serve and protect.* Maybe they wanted to extort money from innocents, or perhaps they intended to lead convoys into ambushes, or something.

The little vampire released a defeated sigh and gazed up through the trapdoor. *So, the two of you are mobsters,* he sent angry thoughts toward Carmen and her evil henchman. *You defile the good name of bakeries everywhere with your sinister misdeeds. You corrupt the noble purpose of chefs and bakers who seek only to spread happiness. This ends here.*

Unfortunately, not only did he have to tell someone about this place, but he had to do so *without* betraying his identity. That'd be delicate work; fortunately, there was one group of uniforms that he could *absolutely* count on to take his flight form seriously.

σ σ σ

As darkness fell, Rufino left the secret brick door propped open by a wood crate and then popped open the manhole cover about two inches—just enough for his bat form to slip through. He then took to the sky and began his deliciously ironic hunt for the hunters. In theory, a group of four lumbering oafs in shiny plate armour should be easy enough to find, but his search was complicated by his desire not to wander more than a few blocks from Candlestick Road. Getting lost whilst trying to lead the authorities back to Carmen's secret stash would be bad form, indeed.

After half an hour, he finally struck paydirt when a group of soldiers appeared on Candlestick Road three blocks west of the bakery. All four were large human men wearing undecorated plate armour with special neck-protectors—the latter of which was only worn by undead-hunters to protect them from vampire bites. Curiously enough, the men weren't wearing their standard T-visor helmets, but Rufino didn't know what this meant, if anything. Due to their lack of headgear, he could see that three of the men appeared to be quite young, whereas the one at the head of their diamond formation appeared to be middle-aged. They weren't marching, per se, but they were nevertheless stepping in perfect unison—perhaps soldiers developed a subconscious sense of rhythm. Regardless, they looked like real professionals, so they'd undoubtedly follow him into the sewers if he could catch their attention.

No one could catch a person's attention like a halfling. It was a gift, really. He landed on the roof of the building nearest to the hunters, shifted into his humanoid form, and then played things real smooth. "Hey, meatheads," he spoke in a loud voice, "there's a vampire on the roof."

He immediately metamorphosed back into his flight form, not wanting to be caught with his pants down if one of the hunters turned out to be a champion wall-climber. He needn't have bothered—as he regained access to his superior bat-form ears, he caught the beginning of a conversation that was now taking place on the sidewalk. "All right, class," one of the hunters said in a conversational tone, "pop quiz: an unidentified voice from a rooftop calls you 'meathead.' What do you do?"

There was a brief pause before one of the others spoke up. "I would ignore it and move on, Sir."

Curiosity compelled Rufino to hop on over to the roof's edge to see what was happening. When the four men came into view, he saw that the middle-aged man was now facing the three younger men from a distance of just under two yards and was speaking to them again. "The mysterious voice also claimed there was a vampire on the roof. Does that not affect your decision, Mr. Ross?"

The middle of the three younger men shook his head. "No, Sir," he said, and the *sir* was as sharp as a guillotine. "My undead-sense tells me there's nothing up there, so I would continue with my duties as if nothing had happened, Sir."

Newbies. Rufino could hardly believe it. *The one time I want a crack squad of elite hunters, I get a bunch of rookies who can't tell there's a vampire fifteen feet away.*

But then why is the instructor also ignoring me? It seemed a decent enough question, at first, but then he remembered the old maxim: *those who can't do, teach.* Rufino had never personally believed that—trying to control a classroom full of hyperactive halfling children was one helluva job—but perhaps there was an element of truth to those words in this case. Perhaps this instructor was no longer able to perform his duties in the field due to the loss of his undead-sense, or whatever, and was now teaching newbies as an alternative to being medically discharged. *Figures.*

"You would allow this insult to go unpunished, then?" the instructor challenged his pupil.

That does it, Rufino decided as he hopped off the roof with his wings outstretched. *One way or another, these guys are coming with me.*

He flittered into position about twenty feet behind the instructor as Mr. Ross met his superior's challenge. "Yes, Sir," he answered crisply and confidently. *The poor guy is gonna cramp up if he stays at attention much longer.* "Childish insults should not distract us from our duties. We're better than that, Sir."

"Uh, Sir," one of the other two greenhorns began.

"In a moment, Corporal," the senior man brushed off the interruption and returned his attention to the first rookie. "Quite right, Mr. Ross," he went on, and there was no mistaking the approval in his voice. "Men: as much discipline as was expected of you in the army, twice that will be expected of you as a hunter. Your professionalism must be…"

"Sir," the second rookie spoke up again, more urgently this time.

The instructor sighed and turned his attention to the second man. "I am speaking, Mr. Eaton," he reproved the other sternly, "and I expect…"

"There's a bat doing loops right behind you, Sir."

Not just loops, actually. Rufino was doing loops, rolls, and anything else he could think of to convince these idiots that he wasn't a real bat. In response to the warning, the instructor whirled and started to go for his sword, but froze in confusion when he got a good look at the flying rodent in question. "Can't be," he declared after a moment, "it's too small."

The little vampire didn't want to hear that, so he started combining loops with rolls, chittering furiously all the while. "That bat is going nuts, Sir," the second trainee spoke up again.

"And is that Morse code?" the remaining novice finally joined the conversation.

No, it wasn't, but that was a terrific idea. Rufino knew only as much Morse code as most people, but a demonstration of his tiny sliver of knowledge would be more than sufficient to prove he wasn't what he appeared to be. "Click click click…" He paused suddenly, for his bat voice was sadly underdeveloped and thus incapable of approximating the more drawn-out sound of the dash in Morse code. As his mind raced, it occurred to him that although his *voice* wasn't up to this particular challenge, he did have at least one other way to produce a distinctive sound. *Lip-smacking. If Carmen's evil brother could hear it from clear across the kitchen and over the sound of four ovens, these guys should have no trouble at all.* "Clickclickclick, smack smack smack, clickclickclick!"

"There!" the third student roared in triumph. "S-O-S!"

"That isn't a bat, Sir," Mr. Eaton said in warning.

No kidding, Rufino snorted to himself as he waited for something to happen. *You're not a corporal, you're a captain—Captain Obvious.*

"Maybe we should follow it, Sir," the third novice suggested, thereby establishing himself as the brains of the group.

The instructor seemed to have lost his voice, so Mr. Eaton spoke up to fill the vacuum. "It could be a trap," he warned.

"If it is," Mr. Ross pointed out as he drew his sword, "it's our responsibility to flush out the rabble."

"Indeed it is, Corporal," the instructor agreed as he found his voice—or perhaps he'd never lost it and had simply been observing the thought processes of his charges, "but keep your weapon sheathed for the moment. We don't want to alarm any civilians until we're certain it's necessary."

Having sensed that a decision had been made, Rufino turned to the east and started flittering for all he was worth. "Now," he heard the older man say behind him, "follow that bat!"

σ σ σ

Rufino had difficulty staying ahead of the four men. Even wearing fifty pounds of heavy plate armour, they were able to match his maximum speed and they weren't even breathing hard by the time they reached *Carmen's. The conditioning of the king's soldiers is incredible.* Fortunately, it would take one helluva diet before any of these men would be able to follow him through the opening he'd left in the manhole, so he was able to squeak into the sewer unmolested. As the bootsteps slowed to a halt just above him, one of the younger men said, "'Course it would be the bloody sewer."

"If you wanted glamour," a voice Rufino recognized as that of the third rookie retorted, "you should have been a noble."

"Hah," the first speaker grumbled sarcastically. "More money than you ever knew existed, rich and beautiful women everywhere you look, delicious food and a…" He paused for a grunt of exertion as he and one of the others lifted the heavy manhole cover out of the way. "…Hot bath every day, and servants to drive you around and do all your laundry. Who the devil would want a life like that when you could traipse around in sewers at night with us?"

"I can't imagine," the instructor cut into the banter. "Paulson: fetch one of those street lamps. Everyone else: weapons."

Rufino heard the sound of swords being drawn, at which point the instructor started down the ladder first. As a former member of the Galensdorfian militia, Rufino did respect this man for being willing to lead by example, but now wasn't the time to stick around for handshakes and pleasantries. He took off toward Carmen's secret door and eventually past it, chittering loudly all the while so as to give his pursuers something to follow. It was only when he was satisfied he was out of visual range that he stopped and turned around to see what was happening with his pursuers.

Three of the hunters were standing in the ankle-high water waiting for the fourth, who was now descending the ladder with the requested street lamp. They had indeed drawn their swords and would be ready to move as soon as Paulson completed his descent. Rufino started clicking again in encouragement. "That way," Mr. Ross said as he correctly identified where the sound was coming from.

"To what end?" Mr. Eaton wanted to know. "I don't see no ambush. Why would someone want a squad of vampire-hunters to think he's a vampire if not to lead them into a bloody ambush?"

"Wait a minute," Mr. Paulson, The Brain, spoke up, "what's this?"

That question was music to Rufino's hairy little ears. With an excitement that almost matched the euphoria of when he'd baked his first bagels, he watched as the extremely promising young vampire-hunter hauled himself up onto the worker's footpath and stepped toward the secret brick door that had inexplicably been propped open for anyone to find. The other three were interested now, too, and gathered at the edge of the footpath as Mr. Paulson pushed the door open and went inside. "Looks like a storeroom," one of the onlookers observed.

"Did the city build any secret stashes down here?" Mr. Ross asked.

"I don't know," the instructor replied thoughtfully, "but it's possible. We'll have to make some inqui…"

"Sir!" Mr. Paulson exclaimed as he emerged from the storeroom. "Check this out!"

As the young soldier handed one of the fake city-guard longswords to his superior, Rufino knew that his work was complete. These guys weren't the idiots that he'd initially believed them to be. There was simply no way they'd fail to recognize the significance of this find. Once again, he was right. "I may not know much about what's supposed to be down here," the older man admitted after a moment, "but I *do* know the city guard doesn't have any secret weapons caches. Eaton! Ross!" he barked to get their attention. "Start opening those crates! Paulson, see if you can find another exit."

"Already done, Sir," Mr. Paulson reported in a voice that sounded quite satisfied. "There's a trapdoor to the surface on the far side of the storeroom. It was left open, too."

"Find out what's up there," the commander ordered.

σ σ σ

The aspiring vampire-hunter accepted his assignment with enthusiasm and was gone for almost two minutes before he returned to report. "It's a bakery, Sir," he said in what sounded like subdued disbelief. "*Carmen's Artisan Sweets. My girlfriend loves this place.*"

"Well, she'd better think about finding a new bakery," the instructor told his star pupil, "because this one's about to go out of business. Ross and Eaton have already found enough weapons and armour in those crates to equip a *dozen* false guardsmen, and there are still a lot of crates left to open."

Mr. Paulson hesitated a moment before saying, "Sir, something's bothering me."

"Yes, Corporal?"

It hadn't sounded like a challenge, merely a question, which allowed the subordinate to speak his mind without trepidation. "Why us, Sir?" he asked. "Why did that little guy come to us about this place instead of going to the guardsmen or the police?"

"He came to us," the sergeant replied softly, "because he knew a squad of undead-hunters would have no choice but to follow an intelligent bat. The guardsmen and the police might have ignored him."

There was a moment's pause. "Do you think it was actually a vampire, Sir?"

Dead silence filled the air for almost twenty seconds before Paulson spoke again. "What do we say in our reports, Sir?" he asked. "The truth?"

The older man shook his head slowly and what seemed like regretfully. "I haven't lied on a report during my entire twenty years in the service, Corporal," he said, "but I'm sorry to say I don't see an alternative in this case. If I go to my superiors and tell them that something that *might* have been a tiny vampire somehow discovered this highly illegal storehouse and then played chicken with a squad of hunters long enough to lead us right to the goods, all four of us will be bounced from the service for spinning tall tales." He paused for a moment to scratch his chin. "I don't want to lose my career over this, so as far as anyone else is concerned, we were on Sergeant Raduloff's Sewer Tour when we noticed a secret door that hadn't been closed properly. There was no unidentified third party, clear?"

The novice nodded. He didn't look too happy about being instructed to file a false report, but perhaps he also realized this was one of those times when truth was far stranger than fiction. "Understood, Sir. I'll tell the others."

Mr. Paulson turned and re-entered the storeroom, leaving Sergeant Raduloff alone on the footpath outside the door. Rufino, sixty yards down the pipe and thus quite invisible, decided to make one last-ditch effort to salvage something from this mess. These guys would undoubtedly be showered in praise for their "discovery", so perhaps he'd be able to take the debt that now existed between them and turn it into something tangible. "I know you're just dying to thank me..." He heard his own words echo three or four times, so he was certain the officer could hear them too. "...So here's your chance. Tomorrow at midnight, bring three fresh—*fresh*—cinnamon-and-apple bagels to the playground in Central Park." He didn't know if the veteran vampire-hunter had any experience as a waiter, but hopefully the man would be able to handle such a straightforward order regardless. "Do that, and we'll call it even. Cool?"

σ σ σ

Not cool, as it turned out. Rufino waited in a tree beside that playground for almost four hours the following evening before he finally resigned himself to the fact that Raduloff wasn't coming. It made perfect sense, of course—the man had any number of possible reasons not to show. Maybe he was on duty elsewhere in town. Maybe he was on his way to the castle in Strelas to be honoured by the king. Maybe he simply couldn't find fresh bagels at midnight, either. In any event, the only true surprise was that no one showed up to try to capture the creature that "might have" been a vampire. *I guess that's gratitude for you.*

Thus, Rufino Endicott was once again denied his prize—this time in the most outrageous way possible. *Mob bakery. Give me a break.* If he didn't know better, he would have sworn he was a mule who was being subjected to the infamous carrot-on-a-stick trick. He could certainly see the scrumptious treat that was dangling in front of his nose, and boy could he ever smell it, but it was just out of reach and he seemed incapable of rectifying the situation no matter how hard he worked. It was briefly tempting to go hunting for another bakery after coming so close to success this time, but that impulse was short-lived. *What would I find in the next bakery?* he asked himself instead. *Explosives? Rebels? Cauliflower?*

He didn't know, but it would surely be ridiculous. He was the whipping boy for at least one of the gods, and gods could come up with all sorts of crazy stuff.

His next impulse was to return to his mobile coffin and wait for Mr. Pemberton to hit the road again, but then it occurred to him that he was forgetting a potentially critical detail. *The warm water in Ishiira's donation pool. Is it still warm? Was it my destiny to help the authorities find that stash? Am I forsaken now?*

Ten minutes later, after returning to the temple and making certain there were no Ishiirite high priestesses skulking around in the shadows, Rufino dipped his hand into the water, expecting it to be the same temperature as every other pool in the city. To his surprise, however, the water was still unusually warm, and the answer to this puzzle was beyond even his robust ability to reason. Was he destined to do something *else* that met with Ishiira's approval? Had the goddess actually found it in herself to judge a vampire for *who* he was instead of *what* he was? Was his undead skin simply having some sort of weird allergic reaction to holy water?

Find out in *The Rufino Factor!*

About Our Authors

About K.C. Sprayberry

Born and raised in Southern California's Los Angeles basin, K.C. Sprayberry spent years traveling the United States and Europe while in the Air Force before settling in northwest Georgia. A new empty nester with her husband of more than twenty years, she spends her days figuring out new ways to torment her characters and coming up with innovative tales from the South and beyond.

She's a multi-genre author who comes up with ideas from the strangest sources. Those who know her best will tell you that nothing is safe or sacred when she is observing real life. In fact, she considers any situation she witnesses as fair game when plotting a new story.

Social Media Links:

Facebook: https://www.facebook.com/K.C.SprayberryAuthor/

Twitter: https://twitter.com/kcsowriter

Blog: http://outofcontrolcharacters.blogspot.com/

Website: www.kcsprayberry.com

Goodreads: http://www.goodreads.com/author/show/5011219.K_C_Sprayberry

Amazon: http://www.amazon.com/-/e/B005DI1YOU

Google +:
https://plus.google.com/u/0/+KcSprayberry/posts

Pinterest: http://pinterest.com/kcsprayberry/boards/

Manic Readers:
http://www.manicreaders.com/KCSprayberry/

AUTHORSdB:
http://authorsdb.com/authors-directory/5230-k-c-sprayberry

Readers Gazette:
http://readersgazette.com/world/rgmembers/2953

Authors Den: http://www.authorsden.com/kcsprayberry

Instagram: https://www.instagram.com/kcspray02/

If you enjoyed this story, check out these other Solstice Publishing books by K.C. Sprayberry:

Protector of the Phoenix

The Evans family has always been the Protector of the Phoenix. The heavy mantle has passed from father to oldest son for hundreds of years—until an accident in the breederies changes everything.

Trank's dreams are of Wizard Camp and teaching about his wonderful world to young wizards and witches around the world. He has plans, none of which include working at the family's legacy. After an accident in two of the breederies, he finds himself with the heavy mantle of Protector shoved on his shoulders, a mere day after his fourteenth birthday.

Not only is he thrust into the drudgery of protecting the Phoenixes, he has to continually fight to prove that he can do the job when the father of his best friend attempts to wrest the position of Protector from the Evans family. Can Trank do what is needed and prevent a reoccurrence of the accident that took so many of his family? Will he succumb to the intense work and quit to escape what he views as something that is making him so unhappy?

http://bookgoodies.com/a/B01IFFLYCE

To Live and Die

Troy Ailel left his farm behind upon his parents' deaths, answering the call for Armsmen to protect the galaxy from an unknown evil. He expected to fight, but not the enemy he got, nor for the cause he sought.

http://bookgoodies.com/a/B0193S7U5W

Darkness Within

There lies in all of us darkness, an evil core which may hinder our decisions. How we deal with that darkness is what defines us as human—or not.

Herm has been the protector of the forest for many years. He now has the duty to choose his successor—and his three candidates all personify the statement he greets them with. A braggart, a self-proclaimed coward, and a woman who seems unable to understand her position. How can Herm select a new protector with such a terrible collection of individuals?

http://bookgoodies.com/a/B01LZY9PL3

About Noelle Myers

Noelle Myers is an author, avid photographer, cook, and baker who lives in the frozen tundra of North Dakota. She writes fantasy, historical inspirational romance, and is branching out into contemporary mystery novels. When she is not working her businesses or writing, she runs a non-profit to help victims of sexual assault and violent crime. Her remaining "spare" time is spent with a fabulous tribe of friends and family having amazing adventures.

Social Media Links:

Facebook: https://www.facebook.com/noellemyersauthor

Twitter: https://twitter.com/NJM_Author @NJM_Author

About Justin Herzog

A native Floridian whose resume includes everything from police officer to personal trainer, Justin Herzog fell in love with books from an early age and turned to writing as a career because anything else would have been unthinkable. He is married and currently lives with his wife in Orlando, Florida. They have one dog. He can be reached at jherzogwriting@gmail.com or http://www.justinherzog.com

Social Media Links:

Facebook: https://www.facebook.com/justin.herzog.7

Website: https://www.justinherzog.com

Goodreads: https://www.goodreads.com/user/show/65045327-justin-herzog

Email: jherzogwriting@gmail.com

If you enjoyed this story, check out these other Solstice Publishing books by Justin Herzog:

First Wave

When it comes to the world of the supernatural, the citizens of Hawaii are luckier than most. The year-round sunshine keeps the vampires at bay and the lack of wild game ensures that no werewolves overstay their welcome. But every culture has its monsters, and on the island of Oahu, it falls to Marcus Aries, a martial arts instructor with the ability to harness his inner spirit, to keep them in check.

When a five-year old child with ties to the Hawaiian drug cartel goes missing, Marcus sets out to bring him home. Unfortunately for him, not everyone wants the child to be found, and the line between ally and enemy soon grows blurry as warring factions collide. Caught in the middle, Marcus finds himself fighting against insurmountable odds, with an innocent life, as well as the future of the entire island, hanging in the balance.

https://bookgoodies.com/a/B073X557CS

That Summer Day

Fun in the sun turns into a nightmare after a murder.

A summer reunion ignites romance.

City vs Country: which one will prevail?

Goldilocks and Baby Bear like you've never seen them before

A promise leaves them wondering about the future.

Summer Solstice on a distant planet provides adventure, romance, and mystery for two, star-crossed lovers.

Can a stranger save her?

The fate of the world lies with a conflicted angel

The longest day of the year. Fun in the sun. Renewing friendships. Continuing traditions. Adventures of all sorts. K.A. Meng, Debbie De Louise, Stephy Smith, Justin Herzog, K.C. Sprayberry, Candace Sams, Margaret Scott, and Alex Pilalis bring you stories to entertain on this very special day.

https://www.createspace.com/7271865

About K.A. Meng

K. A. Meng lives in North Dakota, in the same town she grew up. Her love for the paranormal started at a young age when she saw her first ghost.

Today, she spends her time writing paranormal, mystery, sci fi, fantasy, horror, and everything in between. When life drags her away from it, she hangs out with her son and friends, goes to movies, watches TV, plays board games, walks her dogs, and reads books. She is actively involved in a writing group and wishes to some day visit Disney World.

Social Media Links:

Website: www.kamengauthor.com

Facebook: https://www.facebook.com/KAMengAuthor/

Twitter: https://twitter.com/KAMengAuthor

Google+: https://plus.google.com/u/0/+KAMeng

Blog: http://www.kamengauthor.com/blog

Instagram: https://www.instagram.com/kamengauthor/

Goodreads:
https://www.goodreads.com/user/show/31651336-k-a-meng

If you enjoyed this story, check out these other Solstice Publishing books by K.A. Meng:

Superior Species

Ivory Ames has caught the attention of four gorgeous guys. At Los Roshano University this isn't normal, even when all the upperclassmen have perfect physiques, flawless complexions, and hypnotic looks. That's not even the weirdest part. The town has a strict sunset curfew because of wild animals attacking.

To keep her friends and herself safe, Ivory must figure out the truth behind the town's mysteries before it's too late.

https://bookgoodies.com/a/B01LXDGJM6

Superior Species Book 2 Finding Karen

Ivory Ames has learned the truth about Los Roshano, New Mexico and the university she attends there, but it isn't what she expected. Monsters exist. They've been running the town in secret to fill their ranks. She vows to keep her friends and herself safe from their evil clutches.

As soon as Ivory makes her pledge, her best friend is missing. The race to find Karen Bakke is on before she is killed or worse.

https://bookgoodies.com/a/B072F34WF9

About E.B. Sullivan

E.B. Sullivan, PhD, a Kindle short story bestselling author, is a clinical psychologist who loves writing fictional tales. She draws inspiration from the amazing people she has met and the magnificent places she has visited. Her home, nestled in an enchanting California forest, is an idyllic setting to stir her imagination in penning creative stories, novellas, and novels.

Social Media Links:

Website: http://www.ebsullivan.com

Blog: http://www.ebsullivan.com/blog.html

Facebook: https://www.facebook.com/ebsullivan1

Twitter: http://www.twitter.com/ebsullivan1

Amazon Author Page: viewAuthor.at/EBSullivan

If you enjoyed this story, check out these other Solstice Publishing books by E.B. Sullivan:

Novels

Tarot Haunting

Cassandra's surname, Visconti, traces back to one of the first tarot decks. The Visconti-Sforza tarot cards, created in the fifteenth century and used in parlor games, symbolically convey Judeo-Christian faith teachings. Hundreds of years later, the occult claimed the decks. Although Cassandra feels haunted by a phantom "tarot ghost" to tell the world about tarot's pathway to God, as a Catholic, she feels she should avoid the decks commonly associated with fortunetelling. Hired by a famous TV personality, Jared Ashbel, to research tarot and present her findings on a segment of his *Fact or Truth* series she faces tests to her Christian faith, struggles with her passionate temptation toward playboy Jared, and encounters profound opportunities to discover her true self.

https://bookgoodies.com/a/B071Y39NX5

Between the Vines

In her memoir, Lucia recounts poignant memories of life on a vineyard. She takes her first steps, experiences her first kiss, and learns primary lessons between the vines. Swept away by a passion to transform luscious grapes into superb wines, Lucia embarks on a romantic adventure laced with both tender and harsh realities. Cultivating grapes demands work, devotion, sacrifices, and expertise. Knowledge, timing and luck are necessary to make fine wines. Enlisting Old World philosophies and wisdom Lucia attempts to tackle personal and professional challenges.

https://bookgoodies.com/a/B01CO4611G

Short Stories

Island Homecoming

After years of pursuing a successful career, Anton plagued with guilt, bemoaning regrets, and bereft of faith, returns to the island of his youth. Once on familiar shores, he discovers most of the population has abandoned his homeland. In the process of accepting his island's fate, begging his father for forgiveness, and reconnecting with his past love, Anton faces spiritual challenges.

https://bookgoodies.com/a/B06XZV4HHX

War Kisses

Millie, a middle-aged spinster, witnesses WWII changing everything and everyone. Yet she's surprised when her school board lifts a marriage bar—banning married women from teaching—to alleviate a drastic teachers' shortage. In this new, liberated atmosphere, Millie is attracted to a dashing Air Force General, but fears becoming a victim of, hot, passionate, and fleeting war kisses.

https://bookgoodies.com/a/B06VY3W3SN

Balou Castle

Soon after arriving in Scotland, Cora wonders if the medieval castle she inherited from her mysterious Gran is a gift or a family curse. While renovating the structure, a frightful ghost haunts Cora's dreams and stalks her through gloomy spaces. Nightmares of her vile ex-husband intrude her thoughts. Between harrowing encounters, in order to keep her sanity, Cora savors the time she spends with a charming man who ignites her untapped passions.

https://bookgoodies.com/a/B01M35E1UB

About Leigh Podgorski

Leigh Podgorski is an award winning playwright and screenwriter. Among her favorite projects are a play and documentary on Cahuilla elder Katherine Siva Saubel entitled *We Are Still Here* and the one-act play *Windstorm* for which she interviewed Dr. Elisabeth Kubler Ross. Leigh's novels include *The Women Debrowska* that is loosely based on her own Polish ancestry, *Ouray's Peak* which follows the story of one matriarchal Ute Indian lineage, and the metaphysical mystery series *Stone Quest* that follows visionary Luke Stone and his never-ending battle with the black magician Armand Jacobi. *Stone Quest,* so far, includes *Desert Chimera, Gallows Ascending, and Neuri Shape-Shifter.* Several of her theatrical monologues have been published by Meriwether Publishing, Gerald Lee Ratliff, editor. Her newest release is *Western Song* published by Solstice Publishing. When Leigh isn't writing, she can often been found in the kitchen creating new recipes and making them for family and friends. She also enjoys spending time with her daughter Hannah, husband, Dave, and her two dogs, Beagle Piwo, (Polish for beer—travel story), and Eli.

Social Media Links:

Facebook:
https://www.facebook.com/leighpodgorskiwriter/

Twitter: https://twitter.com/leighpod52?lang=en

LinkedIn: https://www.linkedin.com/in/leigh-podgorski-3682649/

If you enjoyed this story, check out these other Solstice Publishing books by Leigh Podgorski:

Western Song

A timeless love story filled with rich unique characters played out beneath the wide Wyoming sky about a bull riding rancher and his recently deceased best buddy's Thai immigrant mail order bride; as she discovers the true power of freedom, he discovers he's lost his heart.

https://bookgoodies.com/a/B072VR7W5S

About Joshua Rem

Joshua Rem is a professional driver based out of Vancouver, Canada. His true self—the storyteller—only comes out at night, which probably explains why he is so interested in vampires. His fondest wish is that his stories will bring laughter and inspiration to those in need, as they have done for him.

Social Media Links:

Website: www.joshuarem.com

Twitter: https://twitter.com/joshua_rem @joshua_rem

If you enjoyed this story, check out these other Solstice Publishing books by Joshua Rem:

Leap of Faith (The Rufino Factor: Book One)

"Chomp necks and don't get caught: the life of a vampire as Rufino Endicott would have described it before he became one. Six years later, he knows that dodging the angry men with the swords is the easy part of being what he is, and that the paranoid, isolated lifestyle is the real enemy. Oh, he's deluded himself into believing that his life isn't so bad, but that bubble is about to burst.
One night, completely out of nowhere, Rufino develops feelings for one of his potential blood donors. In doing so, he beings to realize just how much his vampirism has cost him, and how much he wants to regain what he's lost. What he doesn't realize is that this woman is not who she seems to be, and that his road to recovery will be a treacherous one."

https://bookgoodies.com/a/B073G6N79G

The Darkest Depths (The Rufino Factor: Book Two)

"Rufino Endicott's attempt to reclaim a part of his lost life hasn't gone well thus far. Betrayed and left for dead by the druid-sorceress, Kiralyn Frostwhisper, the little vampire now finds himself enslaved by the dark magic of an unstable necromancer. To make matters worse, his captor has raised an entire army of zombies for the purpose of assaulting the nearby township of Tundora, home of twenty thousand innocent people.
Rufino is now faced with an awful choice. He can do nothing, which will guarantee his own survival at the cost of his soul, or he can risk almost certain death to try to save

a town full of people who would kill him in a heartbeat simply for being a vampire."

https://bookgoodies.com/a/B01L7QUIVQ

Made in the USA
Columbia, SC
04 September 2017